TRUE
TO THE
GAME

TERI WOODS

TRUE
TO THE
GAME

WARNER BOOKS

NEW YORK   BOSTON

This book is a work of fiction. Names, characters, places, and incidents are the product of the author's imagination or are used fictitiously. Any resemblance to actual events, locales, or persons, living or dead, is coincidental.

This Warner Books edition is published by arrangement with Meow Meow Productions, P. O. Box 866, Havertown, PA 19083.

Book design by Charles A. Sutherland

Warner Books
Hachette Book Group USA
237 Park Avenue
New York, NY 10169

Visit our Web site at www.HachetteBookGroupUSA.com

Printed in the United States of America

First Warner Books Edition: May 2007
10 9 8 7 6 5 4 3 2 1

LCCN: 2007920289
ISBN: 978-0-446-58160-8

This book is dedicated
in loving memory
of my father, Clinton "Brother" Woods,

and to

my mom and my stepdad.
Thank you for being there.
You are always there and
You are always right.

I love you.

Jessica,
you are what life
is all about.
I love you.

Mommy

ACKNOWLEDGMENTS

Meow Meow Productions would like to thank the following for all their past support, time, efforts, concern, and moments shared, which have helped MMP in all its endeavors as an independent publishing house:

Phyllis and Corel the financial institution for MMP, thanks for the dough mom! Leon Blue (how did you do so much for me? You are truly that legendary nigga and that's why I fuck with you. One, nigga, always), Sheena Lester (I try to be nice to people, you just are. Thank you for being so nice to me and for being my editor), Brian Murray, Shirley MacIntosh, my brothers Chucky and Dexter, Ms. Hughes and Radio One (You are a magnificent lady and a true role model. Thank you for helping me), Queen Latifah and the *Queen Latifah Show* (How can I thank you? Thank you!), Robert Morales and Ayanna Byrd, Leah Rose, Mia X (your story is next; you are amazing), Amil (if you need the shirt off my back nigga, Wha? I got you!), Queen Pen, Nelly and Camp QP (for opening up your door and always keeping it real, One), Method Man, Red Man, James Ellis, Shauna Garr (I love you both and even though it's been a battle this last year, I truly and sincerely appreciate your various efforts

on this project. I really do! You two just don't know how much —
with or without the deals—thank you for everything), Tariq and
Uniquest Designs (thank you for everything you do for my Web
site and for me personally, thank you for the past year), Dar-
ryl Miller, Esquire (you understand shit I can't even read; you
are that nigga. Thank you!), Michael Jackson, Esquire, Milli-
gan and Company, Anslem Samuels, Carlito, Tone Boots and
Lamont Henchman, Branson and Eddie (thank you for holdin'
me down Uptown), *Don Diva Magazine*, Tiffany Maughn and
Cavario (fire escape nigga 4th Fl.), the *FEDS Magazine*, Dave
and Antoine (Smokey) Clark and Monique, Niki Turner, the
many individuals locked down and still holding me down and
of course the Streets. You held me down, you helped take True
to a level I wouldn't have been able to by myself. Thank you so
much.

I can't go without saying to the various distributors and many
bookstores and individuals who sold my book published under
my company, MMP, to the people across the country—thank
you for giving my book the chance to be read! It is a pleasure
doing business with you all. Thank you.

TRUE
TO THE
GAME

GAME ANTHEM

As you struggle to hustle, taking gain after loss, don't get discouraged. Just remember who's boss. Handle your business, and always watch your back. Don't sleep on the stick-up boys waiting to attack. As you creep through the streets, the crack fiends holler. They've done any and everything just to give you those dollars. I hope it will last. I hope you make something of it. Time will tell if something good can come from it. But as you count the highs, count the lows too, and whatever you do, forever remain true. What choice do you have? It's in you by nature. Your only fault is . . .

Being a player.

1988

A NIGHT OUT

Harlem, New York. It was the summer of 1988, and it was hot. Too hot. Harlem had to be the hottest place on the planet in the summertime. Exiting the West Riverside Drive on 125th Street, Gena was amazed to see so many people standing outside a nightclub. "Damn, look at that limousine, girl. We need to be with them!" Laughing out loud, she was now suddenly anxious to get uptown.

"We damn sure do," said Sahirah, looking smug. It was amazing; there was nothing like it: 125th was a mini Greek playland in the middle of Harlem. Gena had no understanding. It wasn't like Philly. It was larger, and the niggas looked like Eric B and Rakim, with humongous gold chains and diamond medallions the size of bread plates. If it was meant to represent wealth, that shit did its job. And Gena liked it. She looked at the girls and could not help staring at them. They had no clothes on. They were sexy and revealing, and Gena wanted to be among them, fucking with niggas, getting her life on. New York was the shit. There was no way she could live there, though. It was so fast, too fast. Fast niggas, fast cars, and fast lifestyles. The magnitude was large, as was the amount of men. Even the cars in New York looked different. Gena didn't know if it was the rims or the tires or what was going on. The dashboards were customized, leather MCM and Louis Vuitton seats, not to mention the detailed piping and thousand-dollar sound systems. That shit turned her the fuck on. Everything about New York turned her on, especially the guys. And to think, this was all so normal for them.

Suddenly, Sahirah did an about-face and shouted, "No! Look at that BMW. Is he the man of life or what?" Riding by, there he was with a squad of brothers deep in his Beemer. She couldn't contain herself. Leaning out the window, she called, "Hi!" Turning back to Gena, she grabbed her arm.

"Girl, don't he look good?"

"Sahirah! Bitch, is you crazy? This is Harlem! You just can't wave at these people up here!" Gena tried to pull the top of her friend's body back into the car.

"Oh, shit, Gena. He's pullin' over."

"Yeah, but he's all way on the opposite side of the street."

Against Gena's protests, Sahirah made a U-turn into traffic, causing every moving vehicle to screech to a standstill just so she could meet the guy driving the BMW. She greeted them even as she double-parked just behind the Beemer, waving and calling to the driver.

He stepped out of the car, fine as wine, and walked toward the girls. "What's up?"

"What's up?" Sahirah repeated.

"What's your name?" he asked, walking up on them.

Getting out of the car, she replied, "I'm Sahirah. What's yours?"

"Rasun."

"I see you have Pennsylvania tags. You from Philly?" Sahirah asked.

"Yeah. Tell your girlfriend to get out of the car."

Gena insinuated herself out of the car and chimed, "I'm Gena."

Rasun openly admired what he saw.

"What's up, Gena? I'm Rasun. That's my homey Quadir in the car. Why don't you go over there and talk to him?"

"What does he look like?"

Smiling, he told her, "Go and see."

How convenient, she thought, *Sahirah got the driver, and I got the passenger.* When she reached the other car, she announced, "Hi. I'm Gena. Your friend Rasun told me I should come over here and talk to you."

Quadir studied Gena as though he'd just been introduced to a goddess.

"My name is Quadir."

After another minute, he thought he should say something and stop staring. "So. Do you live in New York?"

"No. I live in Philly. What about you?"

"I live in North Philly."

"Oh. I live out West."

"What are you doing up here?"

Gena thought quickly how to cover her and Sahirah's man-hunting designs on this side of the Lincoln Tunnel. "Well, my aunt is sick, and I just came up here to spend the day with her." *It's just a little white lie*, she told herself. *It can't hurt.* "What about you?"

"Business, had to take care of some business," he told her, thinking about the kilos of cocaine in his trunk. "What's a pretty girl like you doing out here in this big city all alone?"

"I'm not alone." Gena's head was reeling from Quadir's blatant adoration, and every square inch of her body sported a blush. "I'm with my girlfriend, Sahirah."

"Oh," he said, looking at Sahirah as if to say, 'How the hell will she save you?' Shifting back to reality, remembering the kilos of cocaine in the trunk of the Beemer, he said, "We got to go, but I want to see you tomorrow. Will you be in Philly tomorrow?"

"Yes. Wanna switch numbers?"

"Most definitely."

She said good-bye to Quadir and pocketed his number. Even though he wasn't driving, he was nice and he was dark-skinned, and that was definitely a plus. Not to mention the diamond bezel Rolex watch he had on. *Damn*, she thought, *the man is dark as night, but his beard and his moustache was so sexy.* She would definitely be trying to see him tomorrow, which for her was a lifetime away.

Gena and Sahirah partied hard and met many guys that night, but, like a magnet, Quadir kept turning up in her thoughts. Before Gena got on the Turnpike, she went uptown to 145th Street to get a Willie burger. She loved Willie burgers. Nothing could fuck with them in the middle of the night. No lie, like 125th Street, the saga continued; mad money niggas were everywhere.

She got some gas from the station down the street and was ready to make her journey back home. Crossing the George Washington Bridge, she couldn't help but look over at New York City's skyline. New York was the most happening town she knew of. She always hated leaving.

Finally reaching Exit 6 Gena thought, *Home sweet home*. It was about 5:30 AM when they reached Sahirah's mother's house. Gena parked the rental car and looked at her best friend and the slobber and spit dribbling out of her mouth.

"Sahirah, wake up. We're home." She nudged her leg and called her to wake up after she parked the car. Sahirah was out, and Gena knew it would be a struggle to get her back to life. Another few minutes of calling out to her friend and Sahirah finally wiped her mouth and opened her eyes.

"Come on, let's go. I'm tired. You've been sleeping. I haven't."

"Oh, did you see the EPMD guy, Erick?"

"How could I have missed him? He almost hit your simple ass when you jumped in front of his Benz! You really have some serious issues to deal with."

"Don't even try it. You got nerve. You're jealous 'cause I got Kendu's number. Don't be mad. Besides, I saw you talking to what's his name? Quadir. Yeah, him."

Sahirah talked as if Gena had behaved as poorly as she did. "What about this guy? Look at our picture. Now tell me he isn't all that. I could have sucked his dick right out there on 125th Street."

"I just know you could have, and I'm sure you will," stated Gena with more sarcasm as she shook her head.

"And that motherfucker in the Range Rover? If it wasn't for you, I would have really got my young life on."

"I just know you would have."

"Well, what did you think of him?" Sahirah insisted. "Do you think he was cute, or what?"

"Sahirah! Think the fuck of who? I don't know who you are talking about."

Sahirah paid her no mind. Once they were inside the house, Sahirah started counting the telephone numbers, which she had collected over the course of the evening.

"Seven numbers!" she hollered.

Gena couldn't help but to look at her friend in disbelief. "I'm going to sleep."

Gena and Sahirah had been friends since they were five years old. Both grew up down in Richard Allen, the projects niggas wouldn't go to if they wasn't from there. When Sahirah was twelve, her family moved out to West Philly on 54th and Race Street. Even though they didn't go to school together after Sahirah moved, she and Gena always kept in touch.

When Gena turned seventeen, her Uncle Michael got her an apartment on Chancellor Street. He paid all her bills. No one in her family knew. Gena had pleaded with her uncle for years to move her out of the projects. He had really been there for her, and whenever she wanted something, he would help her. He kept her in a rental car and gave her money whenever she asked for it. She was fortunate to have someone in her family who made it and could show her the way. She knew plenty of people her age who had no one they could turn to in time of need.

That was one thing Gena could say for herself. Even though she was raised in the projects, she had family who believed in taking care of the kids. Some people didn't have family like that, and Gena knew it. Some parents didn't give a fuck one way or the other. Do what you gonna do, 'cause you gonna fuck something up anyway. That was the attitude. Half of Gena's friends had parents who said, "Hey, we got a party to go to," and that's where they were, at the party partying. Or if they weren't at the party, they were too busy getting high. Then you had the motherfuckers sitting right there in the house not giving a damn whether the kids were in the house, in the street, hungry or safe. A whole generation sat back, and said, "Fuck it. I'm not gonna raise my kids." Hence, the saga began.

Shit was rough as hell in Philly. That's why Gena liked her

little trips to other cities. Gena and Sahirah had done their share of city hopping, too. Seeing that there was other people out there, not just West Philly or the projects, was positive reinforcement for them. They went to the Harbor in Baltimore and met niggas with boats. They went to D.C., liked the guys but couldn't take the go-go scene. They traveled to Atlanta and met brothers with pets. From Miami to New York, they were there. They constantly received flyers for out-of-town parties in the mail. Life was just one big party. Gena was into the party scene. The same faces, the same places, and the same circles.

When the Junior Mafia began spreading cocaine throughout the city, money was flowing like water from a faucet, and niggas were givin' it up as if it were leaves on trees. Gena's whole entourage of male companions were young, handsome, and very wealthy drug dealers. Hustlers who loved to come on a set and just break a nigga off. It was too good to be true, and don't talk about sex. You were definitely getting broke down for dropping down, wasn't no questions asked. Gena and Sahirah dropped down, way down, for the lifestyle they were living. The only way not to give the sisters their props was if they weren't getting paper. Thoroughbreds of the streets, getting money was what it was all about, and any way you could get it, you was supposed to.

Across town on a little side street, sat a burgundy Cadillac. The driver was eagerly and carefully aware of the sound of the street. He had been sitting in the car for three hours waiting in anticipation. The movement of a tree branch blowing in the wind grasped his attention. He turned back to the gray screen door across the street; *3601*, he thought to himself. Deciding that would be a good number to play, he reached into his shirt pocket and pulled out a small bag of cocaine. He dumped a tiny pile between his thumb and his pointer finger and held his hand up to his nose. After he fed his nostrils, he took his tongue and licked his hand clean. On the seat beside him laid an Uzi semiautomatic. He picked up the gun and took out the clip. Restlessly he threw it back in already knowing it was loaded. The gray screen door flew open and four guys emerged. They hopped into an MPV, never noticing the burgundy Cadillac following them.

The next morning, Gena woke up to the sound of Sahirah's four brothers and sisters acting like they were out of their minds. "What time is it?" she asked as Mrs. Bowden walked by the doorway.

"Oh, good morning, Gena. It's nine thirty, baby. You want some breakfast?"

Hell no, thought Gena. *I want some sleep.* "No, ma'am," she replied. "I have to go. Tell Sahirah to call me." Gena was out of there with the quickness.

On the way to her house, she stopped to get her favorite pancakes. At the intercom, she hollered, "No pork! Do not put pork anywhere near my food. Do you understand? No pork. I don't want to see it."

The poor girl at the window looked as if she had something to say but didn't. Gena gave her the money and waited for her food and change.

A burgundy Cadillac with black tinted windows sped across the parking lot. All of a sudden and out of nowhere, thunderous gunfire jolted Gena out of her reverie and continued to echo through her body. The bullets sent a screeching sound through her body as the gunman met his target aimed for the four guys in the MPV. Gena's mind yelled run, duck down, hide, get the fuck away, settling on none until her survival instincts took her through the natural progression of ducking down and getting her ass out of there. She sped away from the takeout window and tried to exit from the parking lot when the burgundy Cadillac Sedan Deville with gold trim, tinted windows, and spoked rims cut her off. She slammed on the brakes and missed hitting the driver's door panel by inches. For one long moment, she looked right at the driver. He had an Uzi semiautomatic in his left hand and had his right hand on the steering wheel. In that one moment, he looked at her, and their eyes locked. Gena knew him from somewhere, but did not remember from where. Wondering whether she should say hi, she just sat still as a stop sign and stared at him.

Wondering if he should drop her ass too, he pointed the Uzi straight at her head and pulled the trigger. Nothing happened. He tried the shit again. The clip was empty. The thought went through him, *Yeah, dis is her lucky day.* He threw the gun on the floor of the caddy and sped away.

Gena sat there shaken and confused. She'd never had a gun pointed at her before. She just knew her beauty saved her. Little did the simpleton know, she had almost become a statistic. Her heart was pounding like drops of hail on a windowpane. Talking her hands into obedience, she wrapped her shaky fingers about the steering wheel and instructed her right foot to come back to life and ease up on the brake, moving slowly toward the exit. She carefully looked both ways before entering onto Fifty-second Street. She drove in silence, creeping down the street, not even listening to the radio.

She couldn't believe what had just happened, and she kept checking the rearview mirror to see if anyone was behind her. Man, her mind was playing tricks on her. The burgundy Cadillac was so clear in her mind and the license plate tag, Mafia-23, was even clearer.

Reaching her favorite parking spot between the two trees in

front of her door, she noticed Jamal's—her boyfriend—Pathfinder parked down the street. She looked close and couldn't believe it. Jamal was sleeping in his jeep outside her door!

She walked over to the jeep and knocked on the glass window. Jamal jumped out of what looked like a very uncomfortable sleeping position.

"Where the fuck you been?"

Gena just looked at him, as if she didn't know what he was talking about.

"I spent the night over Sahirah's, Jamal."

"Oh, that gold-diggin' bitch with the matching hat and shovel?" Climbing out of the jeep, he continued, "I thought I told you I didn't want you hanging around her!"

"I know what you told me, Jamal, but this is a free country and I can do what I . . ." The words were lost as her body made its way to the pavement with the force of Jamal's backhand. Then he picked her up and began his accusations.

"I know you been with another man, bitch. Ain't no way you was sleeping with Sahirah unless you and Sahirah is fucking each other. Shit, I been out this motherfucker all night, waiting for you!"

The tears had already begun. "I wasn't with nobody."

"You're a motherfucking liar! Why you got to lie?" The question was stressed with another pop upside her head, causing her to spin around and fall into some bushes.

Deciding it was best to remain in contact with the earth, she pleaded with him, "Jamal, I wasn't doin' nothing." She looked up and saw Ms. Gladys looking out her third floor window, watching everything. Rising to face him, she said, "Jamal, I'm sorry. I won't go out with her anymore."

"Where the fuck did you go?"

"I didn't go nowhere." Slap was the sound that could be heard as he hit her again.

"Gena, don't make me kill you out this motherfucker. Where you been? I said where the fuck you been all night long?"

Too scared to say she had gone to a party in Harlem, she just looked at him.

"I'm getting tired of your shit."

"Jamal, I don't want to fight with you. I'm hungry, and I'm tired."

"That's because your trick ass was out in the street all night."

The accusations gathered storm clouds to her eyes. "I'm not no trick, Jamal."

Focusing directly on his right eye, she realized at that moment any feeling she had for him was gone and she was ready to kick him in his nuts and run for safety, as usual. The nigga was crazy; it was in his eyes. If he walked away and she never saw him again, it would make no difference to her.

Jamal had been in her life now for a year and a half. He was possessive, controlling, and basically a nuisance. She'd met him down in North Philly on Twenty-second and Ridge in a pool hall. He was real sweet and nice in the beginning—nothing like now. The day they met was dreary and it had begun to rain. He offered her a ride home. He asked her if she would like to get something to eat. She said yes. Gena didn't miss no free meals.

Next day, he was at her door.

"Hi! What are you doing here?" She was dressed in only a towel and shower cap.

"Get dressed. I'm taking you shopping."

They visited every boutique and shoe store that came to his mind. This all made Gena very happy. *What luck*, she thought. They reached her apartment and, indeed, he was more than welcome to come in. Only way she could get all her bags in the house, anyway. Once she was finished poring over her purchases, hardly remembering buying any of it, and putting everything away, she realized she was happier at that moment than she'd ever been, but didn't know why.

Jamal had rolled a joint, which he referred to as a *spliff* for the two of them and lit it as she collapsed onto the sofa. "I'm so tired. Jamal, why'd you take me shopping and buy all this stuff for me?" She really looked confused about the whole thing; the weed was taking effect. "I mean, you don't even know me."

"That's okay. You're gonna let me get to know you, right?"

"Right." *Anything you say*, she thought, looking totally satisfied at her diminished closet space. She passed the spliff back to Jamal after choking half to death and decided she had enough. For no reason, she jumped up and shut the mini blinds. Jamal realized she'd become paranoid and he became determined that he wouldn't miss his chance before she was too far gone. Through a short tirade, he tried to chill her out and before she even knew what happened, they were on the floor kissing, Jamal pulling at her clothes.

"What are you doing?" She knew she should stop him. "Don't you think we should get to know each other? Don't you think you should wear a condom? We don't really know each other all that well." He silenced her with a kiss and she knew her struggles were in vain; before she knew it, he was inside her.

"Doesn't it feel good?" he whispered. She could only think, *You're fucking a stranger, and you need to get him off of you.* But for fear that he would get mad and take back all he'd bought her, she got in the groove and, before it was all over, he was asking her, "Who's pussy is this?" And she answered, "Yours." After dinner, Jamal dropped her off. For the third time, she looked over her new clothes, then took a bath and slipped into one of her new nightgowns. She no sooner sat down to begin calculating the total of the price tags when the phone rang.

"Hello?"

"What are you doing?"

"Nothing. I just finished taking a bath and I'm wearing the Victoria's Secret nightgown you bought me."

"Gena, I can't sleep."

"Why? What's the matter?"

"Because I can't. I'm coming to get you."

"When? Are you joking me?"

"No. I'm on my way." Before she could protest, Gena heard the dial tone.

Hmm. Can't sleep without me, she mused. *My shot is the bomb.*

In twenty minutes Jamal was ringing her bell. She was dressed, packed, and ready to go. Thereafter, Jamal refused to sleep without her. He wanted her there morning, noon, and night. He took her to school and picked her up. It got to the point where, if she went to the bathroom, he was there, sitting on the edge of the tub. Watching her. My, how things changed. Now, he was beating on her in the middle of Chancellor Street. Gena wiped the tears from her eyes as Jamal got into his jeep, belittling and demeaning her verbally. Looking at her hands, she saw blood from where she fell in the bushes. She noted the neighbors as she walked to the steps of her house, watching them all standing on their porches and peeping out of windows. "Nosey motherfuckers. And didn't nobody help." Inside her apartment, Gena went straight to her mirror. She looked horrible, her face was red, her head was pounding, and she was hungry. Her pale skin, all sore and scratched, throbbed an achy pain and the tears returned. She had to break away from Jamal.

It was like he owned her. She knew it too, but what could she do about it? How could she break away from him? Without him, she had nothing. With him, she was miserable with money. She needed a plan. On the one hand, she knew that if she tried to stop seeing Jamal it might cause her more harm than good. On the other hand, eighteen-year-old Gena wanted to have some fun.

Entering her bedroom and turning on the television, she laid down on her bed. So tired, she was falling asleep when she heard the news bulletin. An anchorwoman was standing at the very restaurant she had just left. Behind her sat a navy blue swiss cheese MPV in the parking lot. Three people had died at the restaurant on Fifty-second Street, one was listed in critical condition. If not for an empty clip, she'd have been one of those statistics.

Gena offered a prayer to God, thanking him for his many blessings.

RECOVERY

Waking from a peaceful sleep, Gena immediately dialed her neighbor's phone.

"Hi, Markita."

"Hey, baby, I heard what happened. You all right?"

"I've felt better."

"I been calling you and calling you all damn day."

"I was sleep. You got anything over there to eat?"

"Girl, please. You know it's the first of the month. You want some dinner?"

"Is it dinnertime?"

"It's 6:30 PM Gena, you slept all day."

Markita brought Gena pork chops smothered in gravy, mashed potatoes, and cabbage.

"Damn, Kita, you know I don't fuck with no swine. Why you bring me this? You might as well brought me a plate of shit."

"I can take that food home, sister. You don't have to eat it."

Gena sat there hungry as hell, looking at the food as if it were something a diseased yak left behind. Her mind was telling her one thing, but her stomach had a more urgent message. After a very short debate, her stomach won, and she ate the potatoes and cabbage after removing the pork from the plate. Markita had to tell her to slow down.

"Gena, I want to talk to you about that man of yours, honey. If it's one thing that I do know, if he beat you up once, he'll do it again. Gena, you don't need no man like that in your life. You are young and pretty and you could do better for yourself."

Gena listened while she finished eating her food. Markita would have to go, 'cause she wasn't about to listen to some shit she already knew. Suddenly, there was a knock at the door.

"Damn, what if that's your loony-tune-ass man?"

Gena headed for the door. "You got my back, right?"

She relaxed when she peeked out the peephole and saw who it was. "What's up?" Gena said, opening the door for her cousin Gary.

"What's up? Damn, what happened to your face?" He shook his head in disbelief already knowing Jamal had hit her again.

She told him the story, waiting to hear Gary say he was gonna go hunt his ass down and fuck him up for her. Instead, he reminded her that he had warned her about him when she first started seeing him. He also reminded her that the boy was large.

Gary didn't know what to do. He wasn't trying to fuck with Jamal like that.

"Man, just stay the fuck away from him." As an afterthought, he asked, "You want me to tell Gah Git?" Gena thought of her grandmother, Gah Git, who raised her since she was four, when her mother died. It was Gary, Gena, Bria, and Brianna who all came up together, all first cousins, all grandchildren. Bria and Brianna were two years younger than she was and Gary was a year older. The years were hard and rough on her grandmother, who had raised four boys and three girls, then at one point had three of her children and their children, a total of twelve, in a three-bedroom project unit. So, she fussed a lot and prayed a lot. But her propensity for sending her grandchildren to the store night and day because she "Gotta Git" this and "Gotta Git" that earned her the nickname "Gotta Git," which progressed naturally into "Gah Git," their grandmother.

"Tell Gah Git? Hell no, don't tell her. Please, whatever you do, don't tell nobody in the family 'cause they'll run right back to Gah Git and tell her."

"Don't worry, Gena. Shit gonna be all right." Handing her a couple hundred dollars before he left, he advised her, "Just stay away from Jamal. You hear me?"

Markita went outside on the porch while Gena listened to her answering machine.

Hollering outside, Gena announced, "He called!"

"Who called?"

"This guy I met last night."

"See, that's why you got your ass kicked."

"Shut up before I don't let you catch this." Since she started fucking around with Jamal, Gena had developed a habit. She'd reached the porch again and began rolling a spliff.

"Okay, but that's still why you got your ass kicked."

The sun went down, but the sky was still orange. Markita and Gena sat out on that porch and smoked the spliff, talking about Jamal and the ass kicking he gave her.

"Was the neighbors looking?"

"Girl, the Vietnamese people were watching. Everybody was rooting for you though, especially when he knocked you into the bushes. Shoot, Tonya said she thought you was gonna kick him and run, like before. Girl, that was some funny shit, the last time y'all was out here." Gena and Markita sat there laughing and telling jokes about Jamal. Meanwhile, everybody who walked by them asked Gena with intense sincerity whether she was all right or okay.

Markita just laughed at her. "I told you all these nosey motherfuckers got out their beds this morning to watch you and tune time out this motherfucker."

Gena went inside to answer the phone.

"Hello?"

"Hello. Is Gena there?"

Not recognizing the voice, she asked, "Who's calling?"

"This is Quadir."

Gena beamed. "This is she."

"Why didn't you call me back? I left a message on your machine."

"I'm sorry. I was just about to. So, what did you do today?"

"I slept all day long. You were the first thing on my mind when I woke up."

"You say the sweetest things. Or do you just say that to all the girls?" she prompted.

"No, baby doll. You're the first girl I woke up thinking about."

Oh, she thought, smiling from ear to ear.

Quadir continued, "So, what's up with you for the night?"

"Nothing. I'm just gonna take a nice, hot bath and climb into bed."

"I thought we were going to Atlantic City." While Gena was trying to come up with an answer, not remembering anything mentioned about A.C. last night, Markita came running into the bedroom like a wildcat with its tail on fire.

"Gena!! Jamal just pulled up!"

"Did you lock the door?"

"Yeah."

Quadir asked her, "Who are you talking to?"

"Oh, my neighbor. She fed me dinner tonight."

"I would have fed you."

"Oh, you're so sweet, but I got to go now."

"I'll see you in a few."

"You don't know where I live."

"Yes, I do. Sahirah is here. We're on our way over there." Then he hung up the phone.

Chickens couldn't have made more feathers fly. Gena looked from the phone to the door. The phone had a dial tone and the doorbell was ringing. "I am not going out there, Markita!"

Her friend's mind searched for solutions. "Hide in the bed or something. I'll answer the door."

She headed for the front door as Gena jumped in the bed and pulled up the covers. "Motherfucker ain't gonna hit me," Markita swore as she picked up the Ginsu knife from the counter on her way.

"Who is it?" Markita stood ready with her trusty Ginsu.

"You know who it is. You seen me pullin' the fuck up when you ran in the house and shut the door."

"Don't be getting smart, okay?"

Ignoring her admonishment, he demanded to know, "Where's Gena?"

"She's sleeping."

"Well, I want to see her."

"She don't want to see you, and you lucky I wasn't home this morning 'cause I'da came outside and kicked your ass, Mr. Big

Man wanna beat on women." Kita was looking out the window at him now.

"Here. Give her these."

Kita looked at the boxes he had in his hands. "Leave them on the porch."

Kita waited a few minutes and when Jamal was gone, she opened the door and picked up the five boxes and took them into the house. In each, Gena found twelve long-stemmed roses, each box containing a different color. Red roses, pink roses, yellow roses, white roses, and white roses with pink edges.

"What the hell this motherfucker buy all these flowers for?"

"I don't know but you can give me some of them flowers, if you don't want them," she said, munching on a cracker.

"You can have them."

"Gena, that nigga done brought all these flowers over here feeling guilty. That's how women beaters are. They always say sorry. Shit, don't mean nothing and neither do these flowers."

"You want them you can have them."

Leaving the roses in their boxes, she walked away from them. Thinking about Quadir, she felt her power return.

"Remember the guy I told you I met in New York? He's coming over."

"For what?"

"To see me, to be with me. What don't you understand?"

"He's gonna see you alright, and if Norman Bates comes back to this motherfucker, you gonna see. Do you understand that?"

"I'm gonna take a shower. Let me know when they get here."

She was nearly finished when she heard the doorbell and quickly stepped out of the shower and into her robe. Patting dry, she looked at her face through the steamed mirror. It wasn't that bad, but it was noticeable. Down the hallway she could hear the sounds of her company in the living room. She hung her towel and walked down the other end of the hallway to her room. Just as she was kneeling over to slip on some panties, Sahirah stormed into her bedroom to let her know Markita went home. "Do you know how to knock?" asked Gena with her arms folded over her naked breasts.

"You act like I haven't seen you naked. You look different though. Your breasts are bigger," Sahirah said, looking at her girlfriend's nakedness.

"Thank you. I've been drinking my milk," she said winking at Sahirah.

Seeing her friend's reflection in the dresser mirror, Sahirah asked, "What's happened to your face?"

"Jamal was outside waiting for me this morning."

"What?" Sahirah listened with her jaw down to her clavicle, beginning with the shootout, Jamal's attack, and the three deaths at the fast food restaurant.

"I knew that motherfucker wasn't right, ever since his ass crashed into a wall on that motorcycle."

"Well, I have had enough of Jamal. The next girl can have him. She turned back to the dresser mirror, inspecting her face. Sahirah knew she meant what she said.

"Oh, I forgot to tell you. Quadir Richards is the man of life."

"Why is Quadir the man of life?"

Smirking, Sahirah served up her gourmet dish. "My cousin use to mess with his sister, Denise. Girl, sit down and let me tell you. G, the boy is paid. The BMW? It's his. He has a Range Rover too. Guess what? He is a millionaire. Can you believe this shit? A real life millionaire drug dealer right here in this house," Sahirah said, plopping on to the bed next to Gena.

Gena was starting to like the sound of this. The hair on her back was standing up straight.

"Guess what else? He is supposed to be seeing some girl named Cherelle that lives up in Germantown, but she wouldn't know what to do with that motherfucker if he came with a booklet."

"He got a bitch? Why'd he lie?" Gena tried to be disinterested.

"No, girl. Are you deaf? He's seeing the girl, he's not claiming her. Rasun said he don't have nobody at home. The bitch is none of that but some change, G. I'm telling you, girl, you are in the house. You could just take over shit and move that bitch right to the curb. You know what I'm saying?" Sahirah was just a-smiling. Sahirah knew Gena. She knew Gena was a con.

She continued. "I'm saying the kid been bugging out all night over you."

"Word?"

"Word. The nigga is definitely trying to see you. Aren't you glad we went to New York? Isn't this shit blue?"

"Yes, so blue." Gena was all smiles.

"Girl, you found the jackpot, mark my words. You know you're taking me shopping for this one, right?"

"You know I got you covered. Tell him to come here for me?" Sahirah left for the living room.

In another moment, Quadir entered Gena's bedroom. The man was fine. He had on a pair of blue jeans with a polo shirt and a brand new pair of sneakers. He had just been to the barbershop. His beard was nice and groomed, and for some strange reason he looked much better than he did last night.

"What's up?" Then he noticed the marks on her face. "What happened?"

She told him the entire story. "I won't be seeing him again."

He was glad to hear that, but wasn't too sure if he should be in the house without Ena, his favorite nine millimeter, which was in the car.

"No one is gonna come in here, are they?"

"No one has keys except for me." She reached up and ran the back of her fingers over his cheek. "I don't even miss him. I'm glad he's gone. I wish I could just get away, you know?"

"I know. I've been wanting to get away myself. You gonna go away with me?"

She looked him straight in the eye. "Mmm huh."

"When can you go?" he asked.

"Whenever you're ready. I can go right now."

"Let's go to A.C. first."

FIRST DATE

Quadir knew exactly where to go. He drove over to Atlantic City. After buying everyone back in Philly a pair of Gucci sneakers, they gambled. Sahirah lost every bit of the $550 Rasun had slowly given her. Gena, on the other hand, was doing mighty well, taking the $1,000 Quadir handed her and winning, winning, winning. She ended up with close to $4,000 by the time the night was over at the blackjack table. Later, they took the escalator up to the third level where there were several restaurants to choose from. Once they were seated, Quadir told Rasun about his little run-in with Jerrell Jackson. Rasun didn't like nothing about the Junior Mafia.

"Quadir, don't mess with him. He wants to be Scarface. Own the fucking world and shit. He's the type will stab you in the back. Don't fuck with him, Qua."

"Ock, that will never happen."

Gena was curious. "Who are you talking about?"

"Man talk," Quadir said. "Nobody you know, anyway."

"I know who you're talking about," said Sahirah.

Rasun jumped in, trying to shut her up. "You don't know nothing."

"Yes, I do. You were talking about Jerrell Jackson."

Gena brightened a little. "Oh, yeah, I heard about him. Isn't he supposed to be the leader of the Junior Mafia, or something?"

"Yes," said Sahirah.

"Really?" Gena turned to Quadir. "How do you know him?"

"What difference does it make? He isn't the mob."

Sahirah wouldn't stop. "He's the leader of the Junior Mafia. It is the mob, okay?"

Rasun spoke up, "Well, how do you know him?"

Sahirah warmed to her gossip. "One night, I was with my girlfriend. She was going out with him a lot. Anyway, he gave us a ride back to her house."

Qua didn't like her no more, and he didn't believe one word she said. The girl might have been telling the truth, but nine chances out of ten, the bitch was lying through her teeth. He threw some money on the table and got up.

"Let's go. Gena, you know how to drive?"

"Yes."

He handed her the valet stub. Gently, she pulled Sahirah over to her and hissed through her teeth, "You talk too much!"

The drive home seemed to take forever. Everyone had fallen asleep and Gena had no one to talk to. She reached over and rubbed Quadir's leg. He opened one eye and squeezed her hand. "You still want to go away?"

Gena wasn't sure she was hearing what he wasn't saying. "Isn't nothing gonna happen to me, is it?"

Warming to her childlike fear, he told her, "Baby doll, I wouldn't let anything happen to you. I'll protect you from all harm," he said, as he winked at her.

Gena pulled up outside Rasun's house and dropped Rasun and Sahirah off. When they were alone in the car, he asked, "What time will you be ready to go tomorrow?"

"Ready? Where we going?"

"I don't know. Let's go to the Bahamas."

"Are you serious?"

"Yes, I am."

Gena just stared at him. She remembered how anxious Jamal was when they first met. Then she wondered should she just leave town with Quadir. What if something happened to her? What if he was just as crazy and deranged as Jamal? She looked into his eyes and didn't have a clue. He could be a rapist, but she already made up her mind. If he wanted to take her to the Bahamas, then she was going.

She turned on to Chancellor Street and pulled up in front of her door. "Five o'clock. I'll be back at five," he said.

"I'll be ready," she said, real serious.

"So, I'll see you later."

"Later." Gena just sat there looking at him. For some strange reason she couldn't get out of the car. Something was holding her. She didn't know what it was until he reached over and put his hand around her neck. He pulled her closer to him and kissed her. At first, he just touched her lips with his, lightly. Then, he opened her mouth with his tongue and gently probed. Confusion and heat filled her like nothing she'd ever felt before. Like magnets, drawn to one another. It was magic.

Our first kiss, Gena thought, in the safety of her apartment. Sahirah was right: Quadir Richards is the man of life.

The next morning, she had much to do! Shopping, hair, nails, packing. And that was only the beginning. The phone pulled her out of a trance.

"Gena, it's Jamal."

"Oh. Hi." Ice crept into her veins.

"You all right?"

"I'm okay. How are you?"

"I don't feel good. I have a sore throat and a fever."

"Have you been to the doctor?" she asked him.

"No, I'm not going to no doctor."

"Well, I hope you feel better."

"Are you gonna come over to take care of me?" She could hear the faint hope in his voice. Thinking to herself, *Hell no, bitch. Die.* With satisfaction, she informed him, "Jamal, I can't. I have to go to the beauty salon and get my hair done."

"Well, what about after you go and get your hair done?"

"After that, I have to go to the mall and pick up a few things, and I have to get my nails done. You know what I think? I think, I'll get my feet done, too. So, I don't think I have time to come over there. I have a very busy day."

Jamal felt like he was getting the brush off, and he didn't like it. Not one bit. Everything he had done for her meant nothing. He could die and it wouldn't mean anything to her. "Well, Gena I can tell when I'm not wanted."

"Jamal, why do you say it like that? I thought we understood that it wasn't working when you beat me up."

"Gena, you always gonna be mines. What do you mean when you say it isn't working?"

Is he brain dead? Gena thought to herself. "Jamal, I can't come and see you. I'm confused. I need some time. I want us to just be friends."

"Fuck you. All you bitches are the same. You ain't shit!" shouted Jamal.

With enough serene confidence to make his brain explode,

she continued, "See, that is the very reason right there, why we are not together."

"Everything is my fault, right? You're the one who wants to be at every party on the East Coast. You're the one who stays out all night with other niggas. Yes, you do. Don't lie, Gena. Tell the truth. For once, be truthful. You and that Sahirah bitch stay out in the street all night chasing behind niggas. I know what you do. You don't fool me."

"Jamal, first of all let me tell you something, okay? I don't chase behind nobody. I get chased. And I am not out in no street all hours of the night, either!"

He cut her off and really let her have it. He accused her of everything under the sun, saying incredibly hurtful things. She found a wellspring of understanding that told her it was because he was hurting. If the things he were saying were true, it would cut her real deep, but what he was saying made her mad. Jamal had lost his mind calling her with a whole bunch of bullshit. She hung the phone up.

That was it, conversation over. And when he called back, she turned off the ringer. She wasn't about to listen to any more of his threats and accusations.

Quadir was down in North Philly collecting the money everyone owed him. He went to the house where Gena had dropped off Sahirah and Rasun. Rasun and Sahirah were in a good sleep when Qua woke them up, knocking at the bedroom door.

"What happened to your hair, Sahirah?" Qua asked her, as she brushed by him going into the bathroom. "Ask your friend!" she spat back at him.

"Nasty little thing, ain't she?"

"Yeah, she's not a happy camper." Ra grinned and gave Sahirah another $300, but she continued to grouse when Qua told her she would have to catch a cab home.

Quadir and Rasun cut through the park in West Philly to see Ms. Shoog. Ms. Shoog was a little elderly lady he did business with. Shoog was something else. Back in her day she ran a speakeasy and a gambling spot. She even ran the numbers game. Shoog had it all. All the men raved about her. She could have had her pick of any of them, but chose none. By the time she was ready to choose, she had so many kids by so many different men and the streets had beat up on her so bad, she was considered not the marrying type. Shoog was a hell of a woman, though. Quadir listened to everything she said. He might not follow her instructions, but he listened.

He knocked at her door. One of Shoog's granddaughters let him in. She had so many grandchildren. There must have been at least fifteen people living in the three-story row home on the narrow one-way street of the 2200 block of Bouvier Street. Entering the kitchen, he placed a bag holding a quarter kilo of cocaine on the table.

"I need you to cook this up for me, Ms. Shoog."

"Fool, you always needing something. The only time you come to see Shoog is when you need something," she said, pointing her finger at him. "I got the family coming over today. I got enough cooking around here to do already." Shoog could cook her ass off. She use to cook and sell platters when she was running her speakeasy, back in the day.

"Those niggas used to pay me to cook their food for them and you gonna pay me to cook this shit for you."

"Don't I always pay you?" Quadir considered, for a moment, this woman he'd come to count on and saw that the once proud and sassy woman had slowed under the burdens she'd carried for so many decades of doing for others.

"Come on, baby, what's the matter?"

"Everything," she said.

"What?" He softly touched her shoulders and sat her at her own table. A barely discernable squeeze and a touch to her cheek brought a sad smile.

"It seems like you just don't be getting too far out here in life, Quadir. You do what you got to do to survive out here; you try your damndest to see that there's some food on the table and clothes for the kids, and it don't get you nowhere. Bad ass motherfuckers around here now don't listen. I done brought mines into the world. These ain't mines. They killing me, Quadir. Sure as there is a God in the sky, these bad ass kids is gonna be the death of me. Eight damn kids that ain't mine and here, look at this."

Ms. Shoog pulled out a paper from her apron pocket and handed it to Quadir, hoping that her scam would work. Ms. Shoog always had a scam.

"What is it?"

"It's a get-the-fuck-out notice. I been paying the mortgage on this house now for twenty-seven years. I only got three more to go then this house is mine. After all this time, you'd think they couldn't do this." Her face began to crumble.

"How much do you need?" said Quadir, locating the total due on the paper. "Oh damn, Shoog you had me worried! That's all you need? I got that for you, baby. Calm down."

"Quadir, stop your lying. You hardly pay me when I cook this shit up for you. So I know your black ass not gonna pay all that!" She looked at Qua as if it were all his fault.

The truth of the matter was that Quadir always paid Shoog whatever she wanted. The price wasn't always the same, but

Shoog got paid. He would even stop by to see how she was doing and not ask her to do nothing for him. The bottom line was everybody wanted something. Everybody had a story. Qua separated the two. He was always gonna look out for her. It was the right thing to do. "Cook my shit up, Shoog," he said as he went outside. He came back in and handed her a bag of money. Shoog snickered on the inside but on the outside showed a look of gratefulness Quadir had never seen.

"There. That will save your house."

Shoog couldn't believe it. It worked. It was as if the Lord blessed somebody else and they passed it on to her.

She could barely whisper her thanks. "That's gonna be more than enough, Quadir."

Qua was glad to bring hope to someone who deserved it. "Here, get yourself something and get something for the kids." He pulled out a wad of money from his pocket, peeling back a couple hundred-dollar bills. Qua had money all over him.

"I don't mean to fuss at you, baby," she said, changing everything up. "You're the only one that understands. Oh, Qua, I wish that damn John-John had turned out like you," she said, now standing up and reaching for an empty mayonnaise jar, going about the business she was in.

She took the cocaine and mixed it with baking soda. She poured the combination in the mayonnaise jar and added the right amount of water, cooking batches at a time. Shoog knew what she was doing too.

Gena got dressed and called a cab, going straight to LeChevue Beauty Salon in South Philly.

"Hi, Gena," said one of the girls who worked there. Everyone knew her.

She saw Beverly, her stylist. "What's up, Bev?"

"Yo, G," Bev smiled, "Where you been?"

"Nowhere, trying to get my life on."

"Guess whose pregnant by Rik?" Beverly asked.

"Who?"

"I'm not gonna tell you. I know how you run your mouth."

"Who? I won't tell."

"Veronica."

"He been fucking with her?" Gena said, turning her face all up.

"Girl, she said she told him she was pregnant and Mr. Rik ain't called her back since."

"What?" Gena couldn't believe it.

"I'm telling you, shit is crazy."

Beverly finished the girl who was in the chair and took Gena over to the bowl, talking about everybody under the sun. Gena told her how she had been up at the fast-food place when the three guys died. She didn't say nothing about the guy driving the caddy. Nothing said in a beauty salon is sacred. Everybody knows your business as it is. Gena didn't tell no secrets, but she stayed to gossip.

"Well, you know I don't fuck with Jamal no more."

"Why?"

"It just wasn't working, Bev. I care about him, but I can't see myself being with him."

"Well damn, you don't seem too sad about it!"

"I'm not. It's for the best."

"Girl, I don't believe you're letting your Jamal go. He treated you real good."

"Money can't buy love."

"Hell, it can buy mine," said Bev.

"Mine too!" said the girl sitting under the bowl beside Gena.

"Shit, he didn't try to take nothing back, did he?" Beverly asked.

"No, but if he wants his shit back he can have it," said Gena.

"I wouldn't give him nothing back," said Bev.

"Neither would I, honey. Keep your shit. Don't give that nigga back a damn thing," said the girl sitting under the next bowl.

Gena and Beverly just stared at the girl for a few seconds and when Beverly finished washing Gena's hair, they went to her station.

Gena couldn't wait to let go the good shit. "I met this guy though," she said.

"Who?" asked Bev.

"His name is Quadir."

"Quadir? Quadir from North with the BMW?" asked Bev.

"Yeah, you know him?"

"Yeah, he supposed to be fucking with Dawn's sister Cherelle."

"He give her anything?" asked Gena.

"I don't think so. He probably got her a pair of sneakers and shit, but he ain't throw that shit to her like Jamal threw it to you, 'cause if he did, she would be in here running her mouth about it."

"What she look like?" Gena wanted to know.

"She don't look like nothing. She your average light-skinned bitch," said Bev, admiring Gena's chocolate skin tone.

"She don't look better than me, do she?" Gena asked.

"Hell no. Girl, Quadir ain't no joke. The boy is large as hell. Jamal ain't never seen no money compared to that motherfucker. Girl, Quadir's middle name is stock and you would want to invest," said Bev.

"Guess what?"

"What?"

"I met him Wednesday in New York. Last night we went to Atlantic City and today he's taking me to the Bahamas."

Beverly put the curling iron down. "Bitch, lies."

"No, I'm dead serious. So Cherelle can forget about him 'cause I'm getting ready to put my thing down."

"I guess he just playing Cherelle."

"I guess so," said Gena.

"Damn, she act like she really in love with him, too," said Bev.

"She'll get over it. That's the way love goes," said Gena, with extreme confidence.

"So, you just dropped Jamal when you started fucking with Qua?"

"No, I met Quadir after me and Jamal had broke up."

"Here," said Beverly, handing her the hand mirror so she could see the back of her hair. Gena got a pump with a long strand of hair hanging down the side of her face.

"So, when are you leaving?"

"In a couple of hours. I have to go shopping, buy some luggage and I have to get my nails done."

"I know you're happy," said Bev.

"I am. It's something about him," she said.

"Yeah. The man is rich," said Bev.

"No, it's not that. It's the way he looks at me, and the way he talks to me, you know, like we're on the same vibe. It seems like he's always been there, watching me." Gena sat there with a gleam in her eyes talking about the man, while Beverly wished it was her.

"I gotta go, Bev. I got to meet Sahirah. We're going shopping."

Gena got bathing suits, fashion accessories, short sets, summer dresses, and luggage.

Then the girls went to Nice New Nail Salon on Lancaster Avenue. Pam was booked, but acted like Gena had an appointment and squeezed her in. Sahirah and Gena sat in the nail salon talking about Quadir and how nice he was, especially since Jamal was so mean.

"I'll be glad when someone comes along for me," Sahirah said.

"Sahirah, you got to settle down with somebody. That's what you got to do. I know they a pain in the ass, but it's like a job. Besides, niggas sweat you half to death when you got a man. You stay single too long, then niggas gonna think that there's something wrong with you. Everybody gonna do their thing, you dig me? It's all about respect. I would have been the lowest bitch on the planet if I had taken them guys up on their propositions, but since I didn't, I showed loyalty to Jamal when I was with him. Girl, all them niggas think I'm a saint. You got to prove that you are woman enough to be true to your man. That's all you got to do. You're not going to get no respect dealing with a brother on that "wham bam, thank you, here you go ma'am" tip. You need to know that the brother got your best interest at heart. Money don't mean he care. You can't run tricks on the big boys. Tricks are for kids. So, you just chill. Slow down, baby. You moving kinda fast, that's all."

Sahirah just sat there looking at her friend, knowing what she was saying was true, but she was having fun and just couldn't see herself with no one man.

Gena finished getting the last coat of paint on her fingernails. "Oh, guess what!"

"What?"

"Guess who the fuck is pregnant by Rik?"

"Who?"

"Veronica."

"That slut. He went up in her ass raw? What's he on? Rik better check himself. I'm saying, though, don't he fuck with some girl named Lita?"

"You know, I think he does."

"It probably ain't his," said Sahirah. "She probably don't know who the father is. The bitch is nothing but a whore." Sahirah bristled with righteousness.

"You don't like the girl 'cause of Troy."

"I don't like the bitch 'cause she always up in your man's face. Watch, I bet the bitch will be fucking Jamal in a minute."

Gena sat on the side of the wall until her nails dried, talking to Sahirah. The girls were like sisters. Sahirah really didn't want Gena to go, but she couldn't tell her not to. Gena would be all right; Sahirah knew that. She was gonna miss her friend.

"How long you guys gonna be there?"

"A week or two."

"Send me a postcard?"

"I'll do better than that. I'll bring you back something," smiled Gena.

Sahirah helped her get outside with her bags. A cab pulled over and an Israeli gentleman stepped out the car to help Gena with her bags. Being as though Sahirah had lost her money in Atlantic City, Gena slipped three hundred dollars in the palm of her hand. Sahirah took Gena around her head and gave her a hug. The girls kissed cheeks and let each other go.

"All right, I'm out. I'll see you when I get back."

Sahirah waved good-bye and went back into the nail salon as the cab pulled away from the curb.

THE GETAWAY

Ms. Shoog was finally finished cooking the cocaine. She was letting it cool now so it could harden. "Didn't it come back good?" She was smiling at her success, revealing her missing teeth.

"Yeah, Shoog. You doing it," he said.

"Motherfuckers tell you I don't know what I'm doing, you tell 'em they is a lie, you hear me?"

"Yeah, Shoog. I hear you," said Qua. He grabbed two large plastic bags and put the rocks in them. "All right, Shoog. I'm out."

She walked him to the door and talked him into his car.

Rasun looked in the bag. "Shit looks like Shoog didn't beat you this time."

"She beat me for a couple thousand to save her house," Quadir said knowingly. Turning back to Ra, he asked him, "Now, you sure you can handle this?"

"Man, give me the bag," Ra said snatching the bag out of Qua's lap. "I know what to do with it. I'm gonna cap this shit up tonight and be ready tomorrow."

Quadir had some reservations about Rasun's ambition. "I want you to watch out for Jerrell and those sucker ass niggas, you hear me?"

"Man, what's the matter with you? That girl got you nervous. You don't have to check me, baby," said Ra.

"I'm not nervous. I just want you to watch yourself."

"It's Gena. She got you all fucked up in the head, nigga. I know she do," said Ra.

"You don't know nothing."

"Watch, by the time you get back that girl gonna be wearing your pockets."

"Man, get the fuck out of here," said Qua.

"But I'm saying, as fine as she is, she could wear my pockets too, boss," said Ra.

"She is all that. Isn't she?"

"Sis definitely got it going on."

Ra got out the car with his bag, compliments of Shoog's superb cooking abilities. "Later," he said.

"Later," Qua said, pulling off. He drove straight to his hideout and took all the money he'd collected earlier out of the trunk. Once he was in the apartment, he went straight to the closet door and unlocked it, exposing a huge safe where he had been keeping his money for years. He turned the knob, entering his combination. *Click.* Qua opened the door. His money was safe and sound. The safe took up every inch of space in the closet, standing taller than himself. He had old school money in the motherfucker. He took the money out the bag and threw it in the safe, locking it back up.

He then packed two suitcases. He made sure his credit cards were in his wallet. He had everything together: his clothes, his money, everything he could think of. He paced around the room, walking back and forth, making sure there was nothing he had forgotten to do. He went back over to the closet and made double sure the safe was locked, then grabbed his luggage and stepped.

Gena was sitting on the porch when she saw Quadir's BMW turning onto her block. Her heart started pounding and an inner thought of how she looked to him entered her mind. He pulled up in front of the door, as Gena waved to him.

"You ready to go?"

"I'm ready," she said.

Rasun delivered Gena and Quadir at the airport, happy to be in charge and happy to have his BMW. Their flight, though somewhat turbulent, landed without a hitch.

"Damn, my ears are still ringing," she noted, annoyed. "How long will it last?"

"Who knows? For me, I wake up in the middle of the night with my ears ringing, so I can't tell you."

"Oh my God," she said. "I thought we were going to die. The plane was rocking and shaking. I thought something was going to happen."

"It was enough to make me buy a boat and sail the fuck home," he said like he meant it.

After three and a half hours on the plane Gena understood how he felt. The only difference between them was that Gena liked to fly. She had always wanted to travel by air.

"Look at those trees! Will those kind of trees grow in Philly?"

Not a hundred and one questions, he thought to himself. "I don't know, baby, but they grow in California."

"Have you ever been here before?" she asked.

"Yeah. Twice before." Looking around, he said, "We gotta get a cab." They located their baggage and Qua spotted the taxi stand.

Entering the first available ride, he told the driver, "The Valiant Hotel on Paradise Island, please." The driver was very nice, making lots of conversation, but didn't seem to know where he was going.

Qua nudged Gena, whispering, "I swear I just saw the same damn building. Twice."

"Maybe you're having a déjà vu, from when you were here before twice," she said with an attitude.

"Gena, baby, I'm telling you. He don't know where he's going," whispered Quadir.

The driver seemed to have been through this type of distrustful whispering before. "Me doe know, but me fine de way. Me know what to do," he said pulling out his map.

"Damn, he don't know where he's at."

"Qua, why don't you give him directions; you been here before."

Quadir paid her no mind. "Man, how you don't know where you're at?" he asked.

"Me no from here, mon. Me from Jamaica, mon. Me a Yardley."

"Oh, Lord," said Gena, collapsing into giggles.

"Well, don't you see nothing that looks familiar?" asked Qua. "Gena, stop that laughing."

"Dot's de bridge, mon," he said, pointing far away.

"Okay, that's the bridge," grumbled Qua. "What about the bridge?"

"De bridge takes you to Paradise Island, star. Relax, star. Me fine de way."

Gena glanced over at Qua, who was shaking his head in frustration. "We are going to get there, Qua," she said.

"I don't know how, baby. With lost Rasta here behind the wheel, we might not make it," he said. They looked out of their respective car windows, trying to quell their misgivings.

It wasn't Philly. It wasn't anything like Philly. There were no skyscrapers, and no city streets. No graffiti and no broken-down row homes. It was beautiful. It was nature at its finest. Gena was so glad she was there.

Finally, they reached the bridge. The view was breathtaking, the sun glinted off the yachts, liners, and small fishing boats, some moving, some idling, all completing the canvas. Quadir paid the driver, as a bellboy approached to assist Rasta with the baggage.

"All right, Rasta, man, you learn where you're going, okay? I'm gonna tip you 'cause I know shit is rough for a brother, but the next time you give me a ride, man," he continued, handing the Jamaican a one-hundred dollar bill, "I don't want to ride in circles, okay?"

"Yah, me know," the Rasta said. Qua kept saying "Me know, me know," as the bellboy took the luggage inside the hotel. Gena was so glad to be there, pointing at this and at that. The scenery was too tropical. There were Bahamian musicians playing island music and there was a bar. Sliding glass patio doors across the expansive lobby led to the swimming pool. Beyond the pool was nothing but white sand and clear crystal blue water that you thought existed only in commercials.

Gena looked through the patio doors. It was a party. People were dancing and clapping and there was a man singing on a platform, which was lit by poles of fire set at each corner. Gena had no energy to join the party after all that shopping, hair-doing and flying. She was tired.

Qua walked over to her. "Do you want your own room?"

She didn't know what to say and tried to hide her surprise. She had planned on sleeping with him. As a matter of fact, she expected him to want her with him and his suggestion left her, well, stupefied. But, she recovered. "I hadn't really thought about it."

"Well, how about adjoining rooms? That way if you want privacy to shower or change, you will have it, and if you need me I will be right there 'cause our rooms will connect."

"Okay," she said, smiling up at him. That smile and those eyes made Qua melt. He had to have her. When he finished signing for the rooms, he found Gena outside.

"You ready?"

Was she ready? Oh, was she ready. "Sure," she said, as demurely as a sister who got picked up in Harlem and had the shit kicked out of her the morning she got home could be. Quadir had two keys in his hands, "Which room do you want?" he asked, holding out the keys in his hands.

"Room 808," she said, as the bellboy led them to their rooms. He opened their doors for them and carried their things inside each of the rooms. He had nothing to say, but he did manage a smile and thank you when Qua handed him a twenty-dollar bill. "Why do you give money away like that?"

"Because he needs it," said Quadir, walking over to the balcony. They had a great view and hadn't even reserved the room in advance. Gena looked out the balcony with him for a few minutes, but she was so tired all she wanted to do was lie down.

Qua, on the other hand, was thinking about nothing but a spliff. He had carried the weed right through customs in a vitamin container in his suitcase. Shit was great. Qua sat on his balcony and looked at the water. This was what it was all about. This was living. Quadir wanted to travel the whole world. He had been in Philly all his life, the streets all his life. That wasn't no kind of life. He could base his home in Philly and he could always deal with the streets, but he didn't want to be out there like that all his life. It wasn't the way. He knew there was something better for him.

Gena laid on the bed, silently watching Quadir as she thought about her grandmother who had raised her since she was four, when her mother died. Her mother . . . she never thought about her. No one spoke of her mother. Gena never knew why. All she knew was that when she was little her father went to prison and her mother died. She didn't even remember her mother, not one memory. It didn't seem that bad to her that her mother was dead, and the fact that she never had a mother didn't seem to bother her. She loved her mother for bringing her into the world. She loved her for sharing her beauty with her and for her hands, her soft and gentle hands. But at sixty-two, Gah Git had patience and a lot of wisdom. She definitely had taken care of her grandbaby Gena. Gah Git took care of all her grand-babies. She told them stories about where they came from, she taught them all right from wrong, and she made them all go to Sunday school when they was little. She was a miraculous, God-fearing woman, and very strong. Gena loved her grandmother; she was the only mother she knew.

Quadir walked into her room. He had just taken a shower. "Will you put this on my back?" he asked, handing her the lotion. "We can go look around the island tomorrow, if you want to."

"Okay, I want to."

After she lotioned him down, she went into the bathroom,

showered and changed into a baby blue satin pajama set. Then she laid down beside him.

"You want to go swimming tomorrow?"

"Whatever you want to do," Quadir said, reaching over her and turning off the light. He laid back down and pulled her close to him. His strength could be felt as he consumed her in his arms, holding her close to him. Gena could feel his breath and hear his heartbeat as she laid next to him. He was divine; she couldn't believe it. He felt so warm and his hold on her was so relaxing and so comforting. She felt safe.

Gena laid next to Quadir thinking of all she had done and all the places she had been, all the men, every single last twenty-nine of them. Could she say they just got in the bed and held her? They might have fed her, bought her something, laid her body down, and gave her a couple dollars, but none of them simply held her.

They slept in until the afternoon. When they finally crawled out of bed, Quadir went into his room to change while Gena got herself together. By the time Quadir came back into the room, Gena looked like the girl he met in New York, not what he woke up to.

Downstairs was sunny and bright. People were in the pool and the musicians were still playing the island music. The bar was open and people were ordering drinks already. Gena grabbed a pamphlet at the information booth at the front desk.

"Oh, look! A boat ride! Can we go?"

"Whatever you want," Quadir said, winking at her.

After they had breakfast in the hotel restaurant, they went and toured the island. Qua wanted to see the nude beach and, of course, the casino. There was lots of water and lots of shops.

That basically summed it up for the island, so they went across the bridge into Nassau. There was a man selling conch shells.

"Qua, look," she said.

Gena said that at everything she saw. They rented mopeds and rode around the island all day and finally took a road that led into town. It was full of merchants who had everything you could think of, from jewelry to clothes. Quadir saw a dress hanging on a mannequin in a store window. "Gena, you would look good in that," he said.

"Do you think so?" she asked.

"I really do."

He walked into the shop and told the saleslady he wanted the dress in the window.

Blatantly, the woman stood aloof and distinctly replied, "That dress is eight thousand four hundred and ninety dollars." She did an about face and waited for his reply.

"I don't believe I asked you for the price of the dress. I want the dress that is in the window. Do you not work here?" he asked politely.

"Yes, of course," she replied.

"Well, if I'm getting ready to spend eight thousand on a dress, wouldn't you wanna get ta steppin' and wrap that shit in a box, 'cause I'm getting real tired of the small talk." Quadir looked around and studied the store. The people were appalled by the rude display of behavior and the saleslady couldn't bring herself to move. Meanwhile, another saleslady had attracted Gena to the shoes. "Qua, I have to have these. They would go perfect with that dress. Can I get them, please?" He got her everything she wanted. Gena was getting used to spending other people's money, and she did it very well, too. After dragging him around the island like a rag doll and making him carry all but two of the bags, Qua was tired, hungry, and ready to go back to the hotel for a restaurant meal and a nap. They got a cab and went back across the bridge to the Valiant Hotel. "Let's order a movie and eat in," Qua said. He felt like lying down. Once they got upstairs, he took Gena's things in her room and went into his. He wanted to figure out how much money he had spent. He wasn't spending no money tomorrow. *Gena gonna take her trick ass down on the beach and call it a day,* he thought to himself, just as Gena opened the door to his room. Quadir had stacks of money lying beneath him on the floor. Quickly he bent down and brushed it under the bed.

"Are you busy?" she asked, trying desperately to see what was on the other side.

"Yeah, I'll be out there in a minute," he said, pushing her out the door and closing it behind her. He picked up the phone and called Rasun.

"As-Salaamu Alaikum."

"Alaikum As-Salaam? I miss you, man. When you coming home?" Rasun was glad to hear from his hero.

"I just got here. So, what's going on? Everything safe?"

"Yeah, shit is tight. I'm gonna meet the boy Rock tomorrow and everything else has been running real smooth. Marlon Hawkins wants you to call him. I told him you was down in South Philly."

"What else been going on?"

"Nothing. Stop worrying."

"Alright, I'm out. As-Salaamu Alaikum."

"Alaikum As-Salaam."

GOTTEN AND GONE

Back in Philly, the summer heat had driven everyone outside onto the sidewalks, porches, corners, and streets. There were open fire hydrants with bursts of water spraying children. Even elderly people were outside trying to keep cool.

As usual, Rasun was pretending to be Mac Daddy in Quadir's BMW. He drove to Gena's house, figuring he would surprise Sahirah with dinner and a movie. When Sahirah came to the door, she had this stupid "I can't believe you're here without calling first" look on her face.

"What's up?" Rasun asked.

"Nothing, I was just getting ready to go out with a friend of mine," she said.

"Out? Where you going?"

"Dinner and a movie," Sahirah said as Rasun's smile faded. She looked down at him as she stood on Gena's porch steps. For a moment she remembered the night before last. It had been less than a week since she slept with him and she was already disinterested. Besides, him and Quadir were nothing but whores.

Sahirah was infuriated at the thought of what was going on and was waiting for Gena's telephone call.

"Why does Quadir have Gena over in some Bahamas somewhere with Cherelle? I heard that bitch is suppose to be waiting for him to get there. How is he playing my girlfriend? Answer that."

"Well, I don't know nothing. I don't have nothing to do with it, and I don't know what your talking about," Ra said, ready to go now. "Being as though you got company and all, I'll push up on you some other time," he said.

"Mmm hmm, later," she replied as she turned her back to him and closed the door.

Rasun walked over to the BMW trying to figure where he knew the burgundy Mercedes-Benz that was parked in front of the door. He knew Sahirah had some nigga up in Gena's house. He felt bad 'cause he really liked her. As much as he felt like shouting, *Fuck you, bitch,* he just kept it inside, knowing that she just didn't feel the same. *Fuck it,* he finally said to himself as he turned the sound system up. *There's nine women to every one man out here,* he continued thinking.

Rasun drove back down to North Philly. "What's up?" he said as he pulled up on the corner of Twenty-fifth Street.

"Nothing, man. What's up?" asked Reds.

"You got the money?"

"Yeah," Reds said, pulling a knot of paper out his pocket, handing it to Rasun. "I'm almost out."

"What you got left?" Rasun asked.

"Maybe twenty," Reds said, spotting some girls walking across the street. "Hey, you in the red shorts! Can I talk to you for a minute, baby? Damn, you got it going on," he hollered loud enough for them to hear. The girls looked his way and walked toward him smiling and snickering among themselves.

"Yo, I'll be right back," Ra shouted to Reds, who wasn't paying him any mind with all that ass surrounding him. Actually, he didn't even hear him.

Ra drove off in the Beemer, headed back to his mother's house, and got some more caps for Reds. When he got back, Kenny, Reds, and the whole crew were out on the Av.

"What's up?" Ra asked.

"Rich Green is what's up," Reds answered.

"Man, fuck Rich Green. I will lay that nigga down. He don't want none of this," said Ra tapping a nine that was by his waist side.

"Okay, we'll see what happens when the motherfucker comes through sprayin'. Let's see what you do then," Pookey said knowing that something bad was going to happen.

Paying him no mind, Rasun looked around and asked everybody, "What's on for tonight?"

"I don't know. Wanna go to Chances?" Reds asked.

Ra heard him, but he didn't answer. He was thinking about Sahirah. He wished he was out with her, not getting ready to go to Chances with Reds.

"Yeah, we can do that," said Ra.

"I want to go," Kenny said.

"Me too," said Pookey.

"I'm going," Dontae added.

"How are all of you gonna go?" asked Ra. "Everybody can't go. Somebody has to stay out here and hold down the fort. Kenny, you and Pookey stay out here. Where's Wiz?"

"He went to take his moms a platter," Dontae said.

"Why the fuck do I got to stay out here?" Kenny demanded to know.

"Because, man, you gots to stay the fuck out here. That's why," Reds told him.

"Man, fuck you," said Kenny.

Ra didn't like this bickering. "Yo, why you drawin', Kenny? Man, you know why you got to stay out here."

"Why?"

"Because, man, you can keep track of shit. I know that if you're out here, shit will be cool." Ra had been learning from his mentor. It's what Quadir would have said, assuaging the boy, stroking his ego. Unfortunately, Kenny wasn't trying to hear the shit. He wanted to go to the party too.

"Where's the gat?" Kenny wanted to know, looking at Reds.

"Man, I got it."

"Well, give it up," Kenny said.

"What you need the gun for?" Reds asked.

"Man, what you need it for? You're going to a party, right?"

Reds didn't want to give up the gun. "What the fuck you need it for?"

"Man, y'all leaving me out here with Dontae and Pookey man, no offense, no defense," Kenny acknowledged, looking at them. "So, you gonna have to give the gat up."

"Ock, give Kenny the motherfucking nine, will you?" Rasun huffed, having no understanding why they was always fighting over the guns.

"That's right." Kenny had an ally in Ra. "What am I supposed to do if sucker ass Rich Green comes back around here?"

But Reds wasn't satisfied. "Why I got to give him Ena? This is Quadir's. Why don't you give him yours, Rasun?" He stood tall waiting for Ra's response.

"We can stop by my moms and get Homicide; just let Kenny hold the gun. Damn," huffed Rasun, getting agitated. "You gonna be with me, you don't need a gun."

"Man, fuck that. I needs mines."

"We all need our own guns," said Pookey.

"Well, take that shit up with Quadir when he comes back," Ra said, knowing Qua wasn't giving them no guns like that. Mentally, they couldn't handle a gun. Putting a gun in their hands with their intellect was mayhem and mass confusion, and Quadir knew it and wasn't taking any chances on bucks fucking up his game. Finally, after bickering and debating, Reds gave it up. He and Ra got in the BMW. "We'll be right back," said Rasun as he sped down the Av.

As they drove away, Reds gave Rasun a lecture, which included one hundred and one reasons why he should have never given Kenny the gun. "Man, Kenny will kill somebody with that gun," said Reds.

"He isn't gonna kill nobody."

"You know how he is. I don't know why you want to put a body on the gun like that. The gun was clean, the gun was Quadir's," reminded Reds.

"He ain't gonna kill nobody."

"Well, if Rich Green comes back around that motherfucker, shit is on," said Reds.

Chances was packed. People were everywhere. "Mercy me, the freaks do come out at night. They is everywhere," said Reds admiring all the skimpy outfits and the outlines of what was underneath. "Look what her ass got on. Damn, baby, might as well have worn nothing, just come outside naked, dammit," he hollered across the street to some half naked girls.

"Man, leave them ho's the fuck alone and don't call them over here to us," said Rasun.

"No problem. I'm getting ready to go over there as soon as I roll this spliff."

"Man, I wouldn't want to fuck with none of them girls, man," said Ra.

"You might not want to fuck with them, but you will fuck them, so shut the fuck up," said Reds, laughing at his best friend. Ra knew Reds was right. They both got out the car. Everybody was out that night. All Quadir's people were there, who had individually reached the hundred kilo mark. Rik's boys were on the set, but Rik wasn't with them. The brothers were out. They dealt strictly with Amin, who no one ever saw much of. The boy Rick, who put Jerrell Jackson and the boy Blair on their feet, was in the house with a bottle of Dom in his right hand, and some girl's titty in his left. She didn't mind, 'cause she was half drunk too.

Quadir, Rik, Amin, Blair, Forty, and Winston were all making millions of money in the drug game. Everyone else was down with one of them. Even though the Mafia controlled the majority, it did not affect them from getting paper. It made them targets for being so large. The funny thing about it, though, was that everyone knew one another. Everyone knew who was down with one another. Females might not have known all the players, and for the most part, they didn't, but the brothers did.

Rasun saw Jerrell's Jaguar parked outside. He was probably inside trying to figure out who had more money than him. That seemed to be his main concern in life, having the most drug money. All of Gena's girlfriends were out. Finally Rasun saw Sahirah who was with Winston. *That's whose burgundy Mercedes-Benz that is.* The thought went through his heart like an arrow.

Trying to get past it, he decided to mess with Reds. "Yo, Reds, there goes your girl," said Ra, looking at Veronica across the street.

"Man, I can't stand that girl. She really tried to play me, and for the phone bill at that."

Veronica stopped and talked to Sahirah's old boyfriend Troy. Troy, who use to be Sahirah's man, was now seeing Val who was Jamal's girlfriend before Gena. Val was there; she had a baby by Jamal. Val loved Jamal, but not enough to be faithful, though.

One day Jamal was downtown and there was a brother in his '98 leaning to the side, riding his car with his woman, like he was the owner of both. Jamal, being the psychopath he is, kicked both their asses and put them both out of his car. When the cops came, they didn't do anything. As a matter of fact, Val was all beat up and the other guy needed stitches. But the officers called it a domestic dispute, no bones broken, no harm done. They cleared the scene, and Jamal wouldn't speak to Val anymore even though Val was five months pregnant. Sis wasn't sure whose baby it was, so she followed her heart. Her heart didn't have nothing to do with it when that baby was born the spitting image of Jamal. Jamal loved his son. He truly did, but Val played him for another man and there was no way his pride would allow him to take her back.

"Is everybody out here tonight or what?" Reds asked.

"Most definitely," Ra said.

The majority of the brothers who were out had a woman at home. The funny thing about it was that even though you might be with a guy and really call him your man, you knew in the back of your mind that he wasn't your man. He was his own man first and then anybody's man for the moment. That was the bottom line. The brothers were socially acceptable whoremongers inheriting the earth.

Gena's girlfriends all knew this, but it didn't make a difference. As long as they were spending money, nothing really made a difference. Nothing else mattered.

Inside the club, everyone was really partying. No one in the club was standing still, except the thick ass bouncers. Ra paid one of them fifty dollars to let him in with his nine. You figure how many brothers had their guns on them, and how many guys paid the bouncers fifty dollars. The bouncers got paid.

Everyone was partying and having a good time. Rasun was standing near a table with Rock and his peoples.

"Yo, get with me tomorrow, same place, same time. I'll see you brothers on the outside," Rock said, ready to make his exit. "All right," they said shaking his hand good-bye.

"Yo, you ready to go?" Ra asked.

"Waitin' on you," said Reds as they both headed for the door.

Reds and Ra walked across the street to the car.

"Yo, hold up," Reds told Ra, as he saw a prospective one-night stand. He walked down the street in the opposite direction of the car over to a group of girls.

Ra spotted Winston sitting in his car, but Sahirah wasn't with him. *Where was she,* he wondered as he looked through the crowd of faces. Finally, he spotted her across the street standing in front of the club.

"What's up?" he asked, walking up on her.

"Hi. What are you doing here?" she asked.

He wanted to tell her that he took her personal, that he felt something for her and wanted to be with her, just her, if just for a minute or for longer than that. He wanted her time.

"So, you waiting on Winston or what?" Ra asked as they both looked across the street. Winston was sitting in his car talking to a group of girls that had flocked around his 300 CE. Sahirah knew the girls. She couldn't stand them. Neither could Gena.

"Yeah. How'd you know that?" she asked.

"His car was sitting outside Gena's door earlier so I figured it out, it wasn't too difficult," he said, shrugging his shoulders, as if it really weren't.

"Oh."

"I'm getting ready to go. You want to ride with me?" he asked, praying inside that she would say yes. Sahirah didn't know what to do. What if Winston left her for one of those girls he was talking to?

"You need to come with me, Sahirah. Don't you know about the guys you hang around? Do you understand you need to be careful out here?"

It was really crowded outside the club. Cars were riding back and forth, up and down the street. People were standing all around as if they had no place to go, while other people were walking around not really going anywhere.

"You really think I should go with you?"

"You should know what you should do Sahirah, but if you need me to tell you then, okay, you need to go with me. Look at him with those girls. That's disrespectful to you, and you know it. How you gonna let him play you like that? I would never disrespect you like that. You should have been stepped off," Ra said.

Ignoring his concern for her, she didn't want to let status slip away. Being the one Winston and his Mercedes-Benz went home with would confer royalty on her, and she wanted to be Queen

Sahirah. "He's not playing me. Why don't you mind your own business?" she spat at him.

"Fuck this, I'm out," said Ra, walking away from her, hoping that she would come after him. No sooner had Ra walked away, when Winston's shiny burgundy Mercedes-Benz 300 CE circled from the lot and headed Sahirah's way. Sahirah thought for a minute about Rasun. Perhaps she should go with him, just to play with Winston's mind. Instead, when Winston pulled up, Sahirah got in.

"Who were you talking to?" she asked.

"Just some girls from South Philly. They were trying to get me to give them a ride home." He made to reassure her with a pat on her thigh, but she knew he was lying because those girls were from down the bottom, not South Philly. At that moment when he lied to her she really wished she had went with Rasun.

"Why do you have to lie to me? I know every whore in the city, and they live nowhere near South Philly. They live down the bottom. I can't believe you got to lie. That means you are trying to hide something. What, you fuck with one of them or something?" Sahirah had a serious "tell me the deal" look on her face.

Winston continued driving his car as he turned his radio louder, paying no attention to Sahirah. The only thing in his mind was whether he should just throw her a couple of dollars now or fuck her first and then throw her a couple of dollars. Either way, he was getting rid of Sahirah and quick.

A Cadillac eased up to the light beside him. The two cars were side by side waiting for the light to change, when the Cadillac's tinted window rolled down. A guy in the passenger seat called out to Winston. Sahirah finally quieted herself since she had gotten in the car and she and Winston looked his way. For a split second Sahirah recognized Ran, and as she opened her mouth to say hello, he opened fire on Winston. The bullets came crashing through the steel, one hitting Winston in the shoulder. His body slumped forward on the steering wheel. The Cadillac sped away as shattered glass continued to fall to the ground.

Sahirah ducked down and started screaming. "Oh my God! Winston!" Looking at him, slumped over the steering wheel, moaning, she knew he'd been shot, but at the same moment, couldn't believe it. She felt funny, kind of dizzy and light-headed, *prob'ly just from being scared,* she thought.

He remained conscious and could see her, all hunched down, and wondered if his mouth still worked. "You okay?" He asked, but was more focused on the bullet that ripped through him.

He slowly pulled himself from the steering wheel and lifted Sahirah back up into a sitting position. Her hand passed in front of her eyes on the way back up, and she saw that it was covered with blood. She felt her face and looked down at her lap. Putting her hand to her chest, she could feel the ripples of blood-drenched flesh as Winston realized she'd taken a hit too.

"Omigod, Sahirah! You been shot!"

Sahirah heard him from very far away; there was a more inter-esting channel to watch inside her head just now. Everything was flashing in front of her. People and places that she had forgotten had come to life. All the moments in time replayed themselves as fast-moving images popped in her head. *Oh, there goes me, and Gena, on the swings.* "Hi, Gena." And Mama. "Mama, I don't want no barrettes. I want ribbons. Ribbons is prettier." Her eyes had closed and Winston felt panic. "Sahirah! Sahirah! Talk to me!"

She tried to look up at him, whispering, "Help me, Win-ston, it's burning. Please, somebody help me." She worried that Winston's image was fading but another, more important, occurrence flowed into her vision. So beautiful, just like Reverend Beaumont said. God was right there, shining in all his glory, waiting to receive her. He was the only one who knew she was on her way. And he'd come all the way to Broad Street, just for his Sahirah.

"Sahirah!" Winston screamed, trying to stop the flow of blood that poured from her body. "Sahirah! Come on, baby! Don't die!" But Sahirah was already gone.

HANDLE YOUR BUSINESS

From the time they left the club, Rasun's jaw was still set in the mad position. "You see Sahirah sweating all over Winston? I'm saying, I really like that girl, but she don't want to act right."

Reds's observation was astute. "Fuck the bitch."

Rasun put on his "women ain't shit" act. "Man, that is what I wanted to do, but fuck it, I'm not sweating no female."

"I know that's right."

Ra pulled up on the block Kenny's house was on. "Damn, what the fuck happened out here?"

"Some serious shit by the looks of it," Reds answered.

Ra parked the car, and they both got out and walked up the block to where the police cars were angled to block traffic. A paramedic's van was drawing attention as it made its way through the crowded, one-way street.

Ra and Reds stood on the block and watched with the rest of the neighborhood. It was unbelievable. The chaos and mayhem surrounding Kenny's house was some real major shit. The police were every where. Ra and Reds watched as the police escorted Kenny from the house and into the back of a nearby paddy wagon. His hands were cuffed behind his back and he was calm.

"Damn, what the fuck did he do?" Reds asked, watching the paramedics push a covered body on a stretcher into the back of the ambulance.

A distraught young girl was headed their way and Reds stopped her for a moment. "What happened?"

"Kenny killed his father," she said.

Ra went cold. Grasping the girl's arm, frightening her with his grip, he could only get out one word. "What?"

Trying to back off, she told him, "He shot him about six or seven times, they said."

"I told you not to give Kenny's ass no gun. The motherfucker done killed his pops," said Reds.

Rasun came to himself and let the girl go with an apology in his eyes. Adjusting himself to chase the chill, his quick mind speculated. "What are we going to do?"

Reds really didn't know what the next move should be, but he tried to think. Reds and Rasun just sat there on a neighbor's porch steps trying to put everything into perspective.

Ra was thinking of Qua's reaction. "Man, we should've never gone out. That's what Qua is going to say. We should have stayed out on the Av."

"I know," Reds said.

"I didn't think he would kill his pops, though."

"What are we gonna do?"

"What is there for us to do?"

"We can go get the money," said Reds.

"Motherfucker, is you crazy? Five-0 all up in the house, man."

Ra could see only danger in the suggestion. "I'm not going in the house with Ola running around gathering evidence and shit."

"Well, I know where Kenny keeps everything. I'm going to get the money," Reds said, walking down the sidewalk to the front door. When the cops stopped him, he acted like he belonged. "That's my aunt; let me by." He started shouting and Ms. Parks heard the commotion. She told the police to let him pass by. She had fresh tears in her eyes, streams of water down her cheeks, and a look of hurt in her face.

Once inside, he asked her what had happened.

"I don't know. It happened so fast. Kenny and his dad were cursing and arguing about him drinking and what not. I thought it was going to be okay 'cause Kenny went up to his room and when he came back downstairs, he kissed me on my cheek and said he was going out." Tears tracked the lines in her face, but Reds knew they were not for the dead man.

"Who was drinking?"

She looked at Reds as if to wonder where that stupid question came from. "His father." Wiping tears, she continued, "Anyway, when Kenny went to go outside his father told him he couldn't go nowhere and then they started arguing again. Then, Kenny's dad hit him and . . ." She just sat there. "And Kenny shot him," she said, still not believing it. She had lost a husband to a son and now, possibly, a son to the system. She looked so tired, not from the drama her home had been exposed to, but tired of getting whooped on. She had taken many a beating in her day from Kenny's father and it truly showed.

Reds asked Ms. Parks if he could use the bathroom. "Go ahead, baby," she said. Reds went straight to Kenny's room, opening the closet door and locating the shoebox. He grabbed it and checked the contents. The money and the caps were there, just like always. Kenny must have put the caps back after he shot his dad. Reds quickly grabbed the shit and put it in his pants pocket. *Kenny fucked up,* he thought. *He shouldn't have killed his pops.* He heaved a great sigh and went back downstairs.

"Ms. Parks, I got to go, but I'll be back to check on you."

"Okay." She was crying again.

"Don't worry, Ms. Parks. Everything will be all right. Qua will get him out of jail."

"I sure hope Quadir gets my son out of jail. Oh Lord, Jesus, please don't let them put my son in jail."

Reds could hear Ms. Parks praying to herself as he walked out on the porch and passed all the police officers. He went straight to Rasun and handed him the money and the pack of caps.

"What happened?" Ra asked, stuffing his pockets.

"Man, the shit is fucked up. Ms. Parks said Kenny and his pops was fighting and arguing and Kenny's dad told him he couldn't go outside and when Kenny tried to leave the house, his pops hit him and that's when Kenny killed him."

Rasun stood there looking at his friend. He was trying to understand what Kenny had been thinking. He knew Kenny was an abused child. He knew Kenny had it hard because his pops was a drunk, but he never thought it was that bad for Kenny, that Kenny had to take the man's life.

"Ra, listen to me. You should've seen the house, blood was everywhere. Ms. Parks was all beat the fuck up and shit. It was chaotic. Kenny really killed his pops in that motherfucker," said Reds as he stood there shaking his head in disbelief.

Rasun's head went up, eyes working back and forth. "Ms. Parks was all beat up?"

"Man, you know Mr. Parks beat her ass every night he got home."

"Damn, Kenny's dad on some bullshit, 'cause he wouldn't been hitting the fuck on me," said Ra.

"If you was a visitor in that motherfucker, you would get your ass kicked just like everybody else. That's why I never went inside there when Mr. Parks was home."

"We got to tell Qua."

"I know. He's not gonna like this," Reds observed. "What you think he's gonna do."

"Pay his bail, get him out of jail." Ra was thinking how this kind of news could ruin Quadir's vacation and decided it would be best not to burden Quadir until he knew what the bail was.

The next morning, Rasun woke up around 11:30. He sent his little brother to the corner store to get a newspaper. He wanted to read about Kenny.

"Reds, you sleep?" he asked, eventually waking up Reds. Reds was sleeping comfortably in Ra's little brother's bed.

Poor Rafik, they treated him so rough. When they came in last night Reds put him right on the floor, didn't even give him his pillow or a blanket.

Rafik walked in the bedroom door and surprised his brother with a rolled up newspaper in the face. "Nigga, I'm gonna kick your little ass."

"I'm a kick your ass," said Rafik, slamming the bedroom door.

As Ra scoured the newspaper, Reds observed, "Man, your little brother is bad. If he was my little brother, I would fuck him up." Pausing he then asked, "Is Kenny in there?"

"Wait a minute." Rasun quickly turned the pages. As he smelled an unpleasant odor, he looked at his friend. "Reds, why you fart in this motherfucker?"

He stopped turning pages and uttered, "Oh, shit."

"What?" Reds asked, laying in the bed, trying to figure out why he woke up with a limp dick. Rasun sat there reading the newspaper article, not believing it.

"What?" he asked again, smelling his hands.

"You're not gonna believe it." Ra was in a state of disbelief.

Reds picked the gun up off the floor and pointed it at Rasun. "Man, what does the motherfucker say?"

"Winston was shot and Sahirah is dead." Rasun dropped the newspaper, forgetting Kenny, and ignoring the fact that Reds pulled the gun on him like he always did. Reds promised his dick he'd get back to it.

"What? The boy Winston? Who woulda figured that simple motherfucker would take a hit and live?" said Reds shaking his head reaching for the newspaper Rasun had dropped. He picked it up and started reading the article out loud.

Nineteen-year-old Sahirah Bowden was pronounced dead on arrival at Temple University Hospital this morning at approximately 3:47 AM. Bowden suffered a fatal gunshot wound to the chest area from a semiautomatic weapon. Bowden was a passenger in a vehicle being operated by Winston Trimber, age twenty-six. Trimber suffered a gunshot wound to the left rotator cuff. Police believe Trimber was giving Bowden a ride home from a nightclub when the incident occurred. There are no suspects and no witnesses.

"What the fuck is a rotator cuff?" asked Reds.

"It's your shoulder," Ra answered in a soft voice.

Reds thought to himself for a minute and decided he wanted to know all the parts of the body. "I'm going back to school."

"You need to, if you don't know what a rotator cuff is."

"Fuck you," said Reds.

Ra couldn't contain his frustration. "Damn, Sahirah would be alive if she had come with us. I tried to tell her to come on. I tried to tell her. You know I did, right?"

"Man, I know you tried to get her to go with you, 'cause you liked the girl, and you wanted to fuck her. But she had a choice. Sahirah made the wrong one. It's not your fault. That's the only way I see it. She fucked up. She made the wrong choice, and it cost her, for real. She dissed you, so how could it be your fault?"

"Now Kenny is different," Reds continued, "Because I told you not to put no gun in the boy's hand. Shit, I was worried he was still upset about that girl. I thought the motherfucker was gonna shoot my ass, and you up there telling me to hand the nigga a gun, knowing I fucked his young jawn."

"Kenny wouldn't shoot you."

"You don't know how Kenny is when he thinks you're not his friend. You don't count no more to him. That's Kenny, man."

"Kenny is not my fault," Ra argued. "I gave him the gat 'cause he was gonna be out there without us," Ra said.

"What are you talking about?" They hadn't seen Rasun's mother walk in.

"Nothing, mom."

"What's a gat and who'd you give one to?" she asked frowning her eyebrows.

"Mom, it's nothing mom, really."

"I hope you didn't give Kenny no gun. He killed his father, you know," she said.

"I know," he admitted.

"That's why you sent your brother to the corner store to get that newspaper. I told you Rafik is only nine; he is not allowed outside by himself, and you keep sending him out there. You better start thinking, Rasun, about what you're doing. You too, Reds," she said.

"Yes ma'am," Reds said.

"You boys need jobs. You're gonna get a job, Rasun."

"I don't want no job. Mom, please don't make me work for the white man," said Rasun begging his mother not to pressure him.

"Dammit, a paycheck is a paycheck. You don't want to work for a white man, then work for a black man, but you're gonna get a job, Rasun."

She was righteous. Wasn't nobody in her house gonna lay around collecting dirty money, taking chances with her baby son, Rafik. "You too, Reds. I want both of you to get jobs."

All Reds needed was a hat in his hand. "Yes ma'am. I been looking for a job, Ms. Clair."

"That's good, Reds, but when you gonna get one?"

"I don't know. I don't think nobody is gonna give me a chance."

Rasun couldn't get over Reds, kicking it to his mom.

"Well, Reds, you got to keep trying," she advised. "And take him with you."

"Mom, I been working with Quadir. He's letting me help fix up his apartment building, so I can get my winter clothes."

"Well, I know Quadir is a good person. I know his mother, but you don't need to be giving people no gats or whatever you said. Shit, I don't even know what you're talking about, but I know it don't sound right."

Ms. Clair was finally at the bedroom door, closing it behind her, leaving Rasun and Reds looking stupefied.

"Oh, and Rasun," she said opening the door back up, "your

father said don't think about leaving this house without cleaning up this bedroom," she said, closing the door again.

"Don't kill your pops, man, let's just clean up the room," joked Reds.

"Man, my moms be bugging. She been on me about getting a job for the longest."

"Man, I don't know why you don't go to college or something. Look at you, moms and pops still together. You got a nice crib. Your moms talks to you real nice. Your pops does shit for you. You never been in no trouble. You never stole 'cause your dad always gave you money. He use to give me money, too," Reds said, thinking back to when they were little and life was easy. "I'm saying, if I had all the advantages you had, I wouldn't be out here hustling."

"Man, shut the fuck up with your bullshit. See me after you get a high school diploma. I'll be done with college by then," Rasun said.

"You know what? Fuck you and your attitude. All I'm saying is I wish I could have grown up with you 'cause you got a real nice family. I really dig your moms," said Reds.

Ra thought about what he had, and what Reds never had, which was a mother or a father. Reds was a foster child at the age of five up until his aunt adopted him when he was twelve. "Man, I'm fucked up. You're right, 'cause it's my fault about Kenny and Sahirah."

"No, it's not. I didn't mean it. I really didn't. You gave Kenny the gun because Kenny needed the gun out there on the Av. He wasn't suppose to shoot nobody with the gun, just protect himself. If his pops hadn't beat on him all his life, he wouldn't have killed him. Nothing is your fault, especially Sahirah."

Ra appreciated Reds's effort, but it didn't make Ra feel any better. "Read about Kenny," he said, handing Reds the paper.

"Okay, it says: Twenty-year-old Kenny Davis Jr. shot and killed his father, Kenny Davis Sr. with a nine-millimeter semi-automatic weapon last night. Mr. Davis Sr. was pronounced dead in his home at approximately 1:30 AM. He suffered seven gunshot wounds to the chest. Mrs. Julia Davis called the police while the argument was in progress. When police arrived, it was too late. The argument between the father and son had already ended in a fatal shooting," said Reds, shaking his head in disbelief.

"Kenny snapped," added Ra, shaking his head, too.

"Yo, they got a picture of Kenny, looking crazy as hell. Look at this shit." Reds handed the picture to Rasun. Rasun didn't like what he saw and handed the newspaper back to him. Kenny didn't look right.

Silence filled the room as Rasun and Reds stared at blank empty space, neither saying a word. For a moment Rasun remembered Sahirah. She was so pretty, with her dimples and soft brown eyes that glared an innocence Rasun felt the night they were together.

Reds sat next to Ra and took in Kenny killing his pops. He knew Kenny was in the zone when he did it. He knew how Kenny got when he drank syrup. He knew Kenny was wishing that he was home, getting ready to meet up with the rest of the crew, hang out and kick it with the ladies, just be free instead of in a cell. Pookey said Kenny had drank two ounces of yella and was trippin'. He felt bad for him because when he slept off his high and woke up to the reality of what he had done, that shit was going to hurt.

The silence was too much to handle and Reds had to break it. "You can't control God's setup. Only God knows why he called for Sahirah and Kenny's dad. Haven't you been to a funeral?" Reds finally blurted out.

"Yeah."

"Well, the preacher says that God has reasons for everything. I don't have the answers to why, but I do know that we got business to take care of. Come on."

Slim Sammy, a neighborhood piper, had just finished wiping down the BMW, when Ra and Reds went outside. "Did anybody ask you to fuck with the car?" Ra said, snapping on the older man.

"Chill," said Reds. Every day Slim Sammy would wipe down the cars. Now Ra was mad at him. Reds knew he was upset and told Slim Sam not to pay him no mind. He gave him five dollars and told him to step off. They got in the car and put the brick in the back seat. Reds put his Geto Boys tape in the stereo and sped down the street.

Rasun took the park to cut through the north side to West Philly. He made a left on Lancaster Avenue and traveled down the Av. "Yo, there goes Rock."

"Where at?" said Reds, looking all around for his gold Mercedes-Benz, but couldn't see it.

"Don't you see him? He's right over there," Ra said, pointing at the car.

"Oh, I see him now."

Rasun and Reds sat waiting for the light to change when a black four-door Volvo drove into the bank's parking lot and pulled up to Rock's Benz. Reds and Rasun watched in astonishment as the driver pulled out a Uzi. The gunshots came from out of nowhere as bullets flew everywhere. Anyone within earshot felt a surge of fear and panic. All movement on Lancaster Avenue froze, except for mothers, who never froze when their kids were in danger. Quickly grabbing their babies and ducking behind cars, the gunfire ceased. The only thing left to be heard was the sound of screeching tires making their exit.

Rasun and Reds sat at the light watching everything. Their eyes widened, and both felt so bad for Rock. They didn't know him like that, but he was Quadir's people, which meant he was family. Just looking on, the Volvo pulled up out of nowhere and out of nowhere was nothing but gunfire. In the blink of an eye, the Volvo sped away.

"Damn," exclaimed Reds, "Rock never even had a chance to see it coming!"

Everything happened so fast. Before they even knew it, the Volvo was gone and Rock was left slumped in his Mercedes-Benz with two bullet wounds to the head and four to the chest.

"What are we going to do?" said Ra. He was still sitting at the light. Feeling as if the bullets had just ripped through the metal of the BMW, and into his own flesh, he looked around making sure the drama had ended.

"Let's get the money he had for the brick," Reds said thinking about the thirty grand that would go to the police if they didn't take it.

"Huh?"

"Man, don't sleep!" Reds could hear the sirens all around. Cops would be there with the quickness because it was a bank. "Come on! Pull up next to the Benz." People had begun to crowd around the car, staring in awe at Rock's brains, spilling from his skull.

Ra pulled right up alongside the car, his eyes flicking back and forth at the speed of light as he glanced over trying to get a glimpse of Rock's dead body. Reds jumped out of the car and dashed over to the Benz. The sirens were getting louder and

closer as he opened the door. He knew the people were looking at him. He reached under the front seats and felt a familiar
shape; Rock's gun. He pulled the gun out, stuffing it in his jacket
pocket, frightening an elderly woman half to death at the sight
of that jumbo-sized, stainless steel nine-millimeter. He felt nothing under the driver's seat. *Where's the money?* He got out and
walked around to the passenger side of the car and opened the
door. Reaching under the seat, he smelled success. Bam! There it
was: a plastic bag filled with money. "Hello," he said, grabbing
it. Once outside the car again, he had to get rid of all the people.
"All y'all back the fuck up. Step off, old man. You can't save him;
why you standing there?" He slammed the door and ran back
over to the BMW.

"Flee this motherfucker, Ra."

Ra was out before Reds could close the door. He pulled out of
the lot and turned right on red. Bam, there was Ola, sirens blaring, red and blue flashing lights, on their way to the scene of the
crime. Something about those vehicles that just fucked a brother
up. Reds and Ra sat still as all hell, while the police went speeding by them. "Yes, that's what I'm saying," said Reds, thanking
God the cops didn't stop them. Ra drove on, passing more police
cars rushing to get to the murder scene.

"Yo, roll like an ordinary citizen," said Reds, taking off his
baseball cap.

"I don't believe this shit. Every day someone is getting killed,"
said Ra.

"Did you see him?" said Reds.

"No, I couldn't see shit. Was he alive?"

"Hell no. He was dead. D-e-a-d. Dead like Fred."

"Wait till Quadir finds out," said Ra, knowing the vacation
was over.

"Yeah, we got to call him now."

"I know. I was going to call him after I took care of Rock, to let him know everything was all right."

"Well, shit ain't all right, man. I have never been that close to a body before. I mean, his eyes were open and he was staring at me when I took his money out the glove compartment. And guess what else? He belched. Real loud too." Rasun sat looking at his friend.

"Yo, Ock, this lifestyle ain't healthy for a brother," Reds continued.

Reds was looking in the bag at Rock's money, when he noticed his arm. "I got blood on me," he said, in a low pitch voice like a girl.

"How you do that?" said Rasun looking at him.

"I don't know. I must've brushed up against something in the car."

"Was blood all in the car?"

"Man, Rock's brains were all over the car. I'm telling you, the whole side of the boy's head was gone," said Reds as he looked in the plastic bag at all the money. "I just want you to know, I'm not taking no more money off of dead people or out of their cars or out of their houses, or nothing. It should be a commandment not to take shit from dead people," said Reds.

"It is. It's called Thou Shalt Not Steal," said Rasun, looking at his troubled friend.

"Man, I'm saying the boy was looking at me. I think he seen me taking his money. I think he might have still been among the living. If you could have seen the way his dead beady eyeballs looked at me," he said, trying to shake it off.

"I got to call Quadir as soon as we get back to the spot.

"Yo, what we gonna do with this money?"

Rasun and Reds took a long look at each other, both feeling the same.

"The boy Rock died with a tab and owed Quadir. But, Quadir gonna mark it off as a loss because he dead. We didn't fuck up the rest of the money. Quadir got ninety thousand dollars waiting for him when he gets back, and he only been gone three days. He don't have to know nothing about this," said Reds. He wasn't sure if Ra was feeling him, but he really wanted some of that money. He knew the only way keeping some of it, and not having to worry was if Rasun agreed with him, and never told Quadir.

Ra stole a glance at Reds, and realized the man needed a cheering section.

"We could come up with this money," said Ra.

"That's what I'm saying, me and you, baby," said Reds grasping Ra's hand.

Ra took his time driving back to North Philly. He went to the apartment. Reds grabbed the bags out the car and both of them went inside. Ra went right to the phone, picked up the receiver and called Quadir at the number he'd left. Reds opened up the bag of money, stuffing some in his pocket, as Ra concentrated on phoning Qua.

The hotel operator connected the call to his room. As the phone began to ring, Rasun thought of what to tell him first. He knew Gena would be upset to hear about her roady and figured he wouldn't tell Quadir about Sahirah until he came home. Qua would be real upset about Rock and even more distraught to hear about Kenny's arrest.

Ra let the phone ring about six times when he hung up and called back again. The hotel operator answered and again connected him to the room. Again, the phone just rang and rang.

"Damn, where this nigga at?" he said, slamming down the phone.

STICKIN' AND MOVIN'

Quadir admired himself in an oval-shaped mirror hanging on the wall. The island was doing him good. For the first time in a long time his ulcers weren't bothering him and he slept with his gun on the nightstand instead of under the pillow. His face had no blemishes and the island sun gave his skin tone a chocolaty-bronze glow. He zipped up his pants and buckled his belt.

"Where you think you're going now?" asked Cherelle, as she stood there in the middle of the hotel room floor with her hands on her hips, butt naked and angry.

Quadir looked at her, wondering why she was even there. Why did he bring her along? She could have stayed back in Philly. The only reason she was there was in case things didn't work out with Gena.

"Where's your plane ticket?" he asked.

"Why? It's on the counter."

Quadir studied her and realized that the girl couldn't hold him, let alone handle him. She didn't have the mentality level. He had been messing with her for three months now and was bored with her. She continuously annoyed him. She was unlady-like to the fullest extent and had no class. The more time he spent around Cherelle, the more he wanted to be with Gena, who, on the other hand, went with the flow with a smile and without a hassle. Plus, with Gena, there was no offering wanting something in return, and Quadir appreciated that.

Looking at her reflection in the mirror, as she continued to yell, he knew he was about to step off from her, permanently. *Why did I bring her?* he kept asking himself. He couldn't find one reason to fuck with her, and while she stood there making an embarrassing scene, he was silently thinking of making his exit. He stood face to face with Cherelle trying to figure out what she was talking about.

Quadir dug into his pocket and pulled out a knot of hundreds, peeling her off ten of them.

"Is that for me?" She jumped right up and held out her hand. He threw it on the bed and whispered in her ear, "Don't go nowhere; I'll be right back." With that, he was gone. Feeling comfortable that she could get back to Philly, he left with no intentions of returning to her.

Back at the hotel Gena was in, Quadir headed upstairs on the elevator. He knew he was late. They had dinner reservations at seven thirty and he still had to get dressed. He went in his room, showered and changed, knocked at the adjoining door to Gena's room and made his entrance. Gena wrenched her eyes from the mirror to inspect him as he opened the door to her room.

"You look so handsome," she said, taking in his Armani Raiment. *Hmm. Linen,* she thought. *Hmm. Eggshell. Hmm, it brings out his . . . dick.*

"You look good too, baby doll," he said, nearing her to give her a hug. "You really look good." His hands traveled the outline of her figure, letting Gena know her power over him. Smiling ear to ear, she whispered, "You ready?"

"I was born ready."

Gena grabbed her purse and looked in the mirror at her face one last time. He said he would take her on the cruise ship that sailed out to sea for dinner, and he kept his word. Quadir pulled a knot out his pocket, and put it back in.

"Come on," he said, closing the door. They didn't hear the phone ring as they walked down the hall to the elevator.

The night was a dream, and she just knew they belonged on the cover of a magazine. Numerous candles softly glowed, bringing a romantic vibe to the ship. They sat together, enjoying live entertainment while waiting for dinner to be served.

Quadir reached under the table and put his hand on Gena's leg, prompting her to turn to him. Starring at her he realized for the first time just how beautiful Gena was. Her skin had a coppery glow from bathing in the sun all day. And her eyes were a tranquil light brown. He thought of how he was feeling as he moved his hand up her thigh. He was so damn princely, so inviting. How could she stop him?

When his hand got to where it was aiming, his intent was to ever so gently touch what would have been her panties. Just to see if they were lace. She blushed purple.

"You . . . You're . . . Where's your . . ."

She tried not to let him notice how hard she was breathing, but she couldn't do anything about her eyelids, which were now at half mast with lust. "Oh. I forgot to put some on."

"So," he said, realizing he could have lent her his own breath, which was coming in short pants. "Do you always forget?" He moved his chair a little closer and continued playing. Gena was looking around, hoping that the tablecloth would hide their game from the rest of the patrons. Well, okay, the waiters, too.

"Qua, where are your table manners?" He paid her no mind. "Qua, stop," she pleaded, wet, but wanting to be proper. Of course he paid her no mind and continued until the waiter served dinner. After dinner, some of the other patrons started ballroom dancing. However, neither could see themselves joining in.

Quadir took her by the hand and led her to the deck of the ship. "Come on, let's look at the water." They could see their ship heading into the dock, the night lights brilliantly reflected off of the water. It was breathtaking. The island was beautiful, as were the people. It felt good to be away from Philadelphia. For Gena to be where she was, and to be in the company she was in, was like a dream come true. "I can't believe we are here," she said, squeezing his hand.

"I can't believe I haven't had to answer my pager; no one has been bugging me. I can sleep. My mind hasn't played one trick on me since I been here," he said looking out to sea.

"Is it that bad, Qua?"

"You have no idea what it's like, having people run up to you, asking for money, all day long."

Gena didn't say anything that would have reflected her jealousy, that he probably did give his money freely. "I'm going back inside." As she walked back into the dining room area, Quadir turned to look out at the water. *Women,* he thought. *Bitches, young girls, even old heads, they were all the fuck the same. Confusing as all hell.* Pushing himself from the rail, he followed her back to the dining room.

They walked through the dining area and up a flight of stairs where the other passengers were waiting to depart from the ship. Feet back on the ground, they took a cab back to the island.

The Bahamian musicians were playing on. The hotel lobby was bright and the patio doors that led to the beach gave them a glimpse of people dancing and partying to the sound of the island music. The pool was lit with torches of varying sizes. There were people in the pool, sitting by the pool, dancing by the pool, and running around the pool. It was a rowdy bunch, too; a little too rowdy for Qua, which prompted him to lead her toward the beach.

Gena and Quadir sat on the sand smoking a spliff as they watched the ripples of water bouncing off the moonlight. Each ripple formed a tiny wave before crashing on the shore.

"Thanks for taking me on that ship tonight," she said.

"It was nice, wasn't it?"

"Yes."

"I wanted to throw you on that table and fuck the shit out of you," he said, smiling this boyish but devilish smile.

"I know that," said Gena. "I could tell when your hand was under the table," she said with one eyebrow in the air.

"I wasn't doin' nothin' to you. If I was, it would feel like this." He moved gently, but swiftly, under the front of her dress and eagerly directed his hand to the place he wanted, tickling her silken leg on the way, and his fingers found the split of silky, moistened flesh surrounded by velvet.

"Qua, what are you doing?" Gena asked, looking around to see if any people were close enough to see.

"I'm doing exactly what you want me to do," he said, very politely.

"Qua, stop," she whined.

"You don't really want me to do that," he said stopping for a second before he kissed her, his tongue caressing every corner of her mouth, from her top lip to her bottom. Qua kissed her in the mouth like he had never kissed anyone. He took his other hand and held her behind her neck. He was holding her so tight that she couldn't back away. All she could do was submit to him.

"Come on," he said, pulling her up.

"Where are we going?" she asked, realizing that she had dropped her joint in the sand. Quadir led her closer to the water. "Qua, where are we going? Swimming?"

"Gena, I don't want to swim." He looked so serious. And he was.

He took her to a secluded spot off a wooded area near the water.

"I need you, Gena," he said pulling her closer to him.

Gena pushed back. "Quadir, Sahirah told me all about you. I know you have an entourage of women and everyone is supposed to be trying to see you, or don't you know?"

His hands were memorizing her body, his eyes piercing through to the real Gena.

"I don't want them. I've wanted you ever since the day you were with Jamal on his motorcycle. You had your leather riding gear on. I saw you get off the bike and take your helmet off your head. You were so beautiful. I never forgot your face. I have searched for you. Everywhere I went I looked, hoping to see you. Every time I saw Jamal, my heart would start racing until I realized you weren't with him." He was embracing her now, holding on like she might disappear. "Do you understand? When I finally found you in Harlem, there was no way I wanted to let you go. Only business got in the way. Do you understand?"

Gena had heard every word he had spoken, and she believed him. At that moment Gena melted against him with a passion that flowed through their bodies like the clouds flowed through the skies. He unhooked her dress and guided her down to the soft, white island sand and positioned himself on top of her. He kissed her mouth, her ears, her neck, her nipples, enjoying the shudder she didn't expect to feel. Opening her legs, he gently slid his tongue along her inner thigh, back and forth, over here and over there. Every moment was sheer ecstasy.

Is that Barry White I hear, she thought. "Quadir."

He had found the tiny node that makes a woman a woman and proceeded to lick and suck on her like she was a Tootsie Pop. Gena lay there, gasping, squeezing the pristine white island sand through her hands as an unknown feeling went through her body. *I thought only I knew about that place. I thought it was a secret. I thought men didn't know. I thought* . . . Suddenly, thinking wasn't important anymore. Bucking and moaning, she could only steer herself to that place, that feeling, that could release her from all earthly worries and send her straight into the arms of bliss, where the world disappears for one glorious moment and the soul separates from the body.

"Aahh! Oh, Qua!" Her final thrust left her shimmering, every nerve placated, unable to move. For the first time in her eighteen years of existence, a man brought her the rapture she thought she could only give herself. From this moment, sex would no longer be a one-sided pastime, with Gena expecting only affection and gifts. This was more than she had ever felt before.

Qua knew what it was time for. With his large, gentle, firm hands, he moved her under his body until she was face to face with him.

"Qua, put it in me," she said, feeling possessed by the devil. She had never wanted a dick inside her so bad before in her life. Jamal never made her feel like this. He only worked for his own pleasure. Jamal could only fuck a woman; this was lovemaking. Qua was the man of life.

"Quadir," she moaned as she felt him fitting inside her, stroking her intensely. His dick was so big, she felt as if she had no space left, she was completely full. Each pull of the slow rhythm introduced her to a new thrill, unexpected, and with it a surprise. She was completely relaxed and so into it. Her only purpose was to give her body to him, all of her. She was completely relaxed, and with every stroke and every movement, she breathed with him, wanting more and more.

Quadir wrapped her legs in front of his arms, spreading Gena's body completely apart, lifting her from the smooth white sand while his hardness caressed all the little places that made up her being. She reached up and clamped her hand against his shoulder at arm's length, sliding herself up and down, pulling in breath on the way up, sighing it out on the way down, while he made the gargantuan effort not to discharge a drop while he watched her succumb to his passion.

She commanded him, suddenly, not to move, while her body spasmed. He waited, for a moment, his teeth bared in fierce control, until she breathed again and squeezed him with muscles she didn't know were that useful.

Qua breathed out and began to move, his movements becoming more urgent. She found her passion mounting again as she watched his need overwhelm him. His arms snaked under her shoulders then under her buttocks, lifting her as his beautiful black body moved in and out of her, faster and faster, the veins in his neck bulging in his effort to go where he'd just taken her. The sounds from his throat became louder, louder still, until she felt his pent-up fluid rumble through his body, working its way through his shaft into her waiting recesses. His body spasmed, and he spoke her name.

"Gena."

She'd never known so much passion and power. It was the moment in time women never forget.

Quadir rested his body on hers, not moving. His breathing and pounding heartbeat told her he was still among the living.

In another moment, he was kissing her, tiny, loving kisses over her eyes, her chin, her temple and, between each kiss, meeting her eyes with his.

"Baby, don't speak. Just don't move," he said, nestling his head between her arm and her breast. Gena was exactly what he dreamed. He knew she would be. He knew. His daydreaming was over. He had the real thing now. All the time he'd spent with other girls, picturing that girl he'd seen on the motorcycle with Jamal, was nothing compared with this.

And it had been worth the wait. He finally got up and helped Gena put on her clothes before he got dressed.

"Do you think anyone saw us?" Her eyes were darting about, worrying about who'd seen her or worse: Who'd heard her! Her hair was all over the place and she had that happy *I got some* smile on her face.

"I don't know but if they did see us, I know they wanted to join in," Qua said as he grabbed her tiny waist and gave her a hug. "That was the best pussy I have ever had in my life," he said, combing her hair down. The brothers definitely did agree that all pussy was not the same.

They reached the lobby and Qua wanted to check for messages. For the first time since they had been there, the hotel lobby was empty. *So the Bahamian musicians did sleep,* thought Gena. That was how late it was. There were no musicians, no tourists, no children running about, just silence, as the hotel staff was getting ready for another day. "What time is it?" Gena asked.

"Five twenty-three, baby," said Qua looking at his diamond bezel Rolex.

"I like your watch," said Gena, looking at all the diamonds sparkling from the lobby's track lights.

"You do? I'll get you one," he said, shuffling through the messages. "Rasun has called four times and Reds has called once."

"Call them back when we get in the room."

"I will, I will," he said, rubbing on her ass, lifting up her dress, and playing with her all over again.

Suddenly, she thrust her entire body against him, pierced him to the wall and whispered in his ear, "I want to make you happy." He wanted her to suck his dick.

As the elevator stopped at their floor. Gena couldn't wait to get inside her room. Quadir couldn't wait to get off the elevator either; he had to get to a phone.

HOME

Once they were inside the suite, Qua tried to call Rasun. He had no success; the phone rang and rang.

"He's probably sleeping," Gena said. Quadir sat there with the receiver to his ear, waiting ever so patiently for someone to answer the phone. "Baby, hang up the phone and call him in the morning."

He finally took her advice, but couldn't get it off his mind. "Don't you think he must have really wanted something, if he called four times?"

"Yes, and I'm sure he will call you in the morning if it's really that important." She sounded convincing, but Quadir had a feeling that something wasn't right. He ended up trying again, but there was still no answer.

Gena, back in her room, was undressing for a shower, making sure Quadir was aware of it as she moved around him naked.

"Can I take a shower with you?"

Smirking at her success in getting his mind off the phone call, she told him, "You can do what ever you want."

They had less than five hours of sleep; it was 10:30 AM and the sound of the phone awoke Gena.

"Hello?"

"What's up, Gena? It's Ra, where's Quadir?" the voice said.

Half sleep she called out for Quadir, passing him the phone. "It's Rasun."

The minute Quadir heard the name Rasun, he woke right up when she handed him the receiver.

Finding an upright position, he mumbled to Rasun as he awoke from his sleep. "What happened?" Gena listened to Quadir's end of the conversation feeling something was wrong by the tone in his voice.

"Kenny did what?" Quadir asked. Pausing, he replied, "With my nine. Why mines? Why you give him mine?" Gena steadily nudged Qua, wanting to know what he was talking about. He was gathering all the facts as quickly as he could.

"Rock's dead?" questioned Qua. Gena heard the name and knew exactly who Quadir was talking about. It was such a small world. The same people Gena knew were the same people Quadir knew.

"He got shot in the head? What about the money?" asked Quadir, waiting to hear that it was fucked up too.

"We got the money and the yayo," said Rasun.

"Yo, what are you two, Tony and Manny up in this motherfucker? Find out what Kenny's bail is and stay by the phone. I'm coming home." He replaced the receiver and turned to Gena. "Baby, come on, we got to get home. Someone killed a friend of mine."

"Who?" asked Gena, knowing the vacation was over.

"I don't know who," he said, shaking his head as if he really didn't know. "Guess what? My young boy killed his pops last night."

"Who?" said Gena.

"Remember Kenny? He was in the backseat of the BMW the night we met."

"Yeah."

"Well, him. His pops was always beating on him and his mom. I guess he just snapped."

Gena got dressed and called the airport, switching reservations for an earlier flight. She was unable to get first class and prayed they wouldn't be seated in the rear of the plane next to the engine.

The bellboy collected all of their luggage and took it downstairs. The same cabbie who given them a tour of the island, as he found his way, was there to pick them up. He placed the luggage in the trunk of his cab and opened the door so that Quadir and Gena could get in the backseat.

"You know where you're going, boss?" Quadir asked him as he shook his hand.

"Where you go?" Rasta Man asked.

"The airport."

"Oh, the airport, me can find it."

Quadir pulled Gena over to him and whispered, "We're gonna miss the flight." He asked the cabbie, "Do you know where the airport is?"

"Of course, me know. Me can fine it, mon. Me just look right here for a minute."

Gena couldn't believe the same driver who found his way from the airport was trying to find his way back there. "He is looking at a map. We'll never get there. I might as well drive."

"Might as well."

"What if we don't make the flight?" she said.

"We have to make the flight."

Finally, they reached the airport. Quadir paid the cabbie and gave him another nice tip. The cabbie got their bags out of the car and sat them on the sidewalk so they could be checked in.

"Take care, mon, of yourself and your lovely lady. May de spirit of de Lord be blessed upon you both; mercy shall follow you all de days of your life." He shook Gena's hand and then Quadir's, adding, "Another place and time, sir." Then he walked back to the cab.

"God, is he spiritual, or what?" said Gena, feeling a little chill. For some reason that Jamaican taxi driver who rode them around in circles when they first arrived in Nassau and rode them around on their way out seemed to touch them both in a way that neither of them understood.

Once they were safely on board the airplane, Qua started chewing his gum and stuffing cotton in his ears just like the last time. "Quadir, you look crazy," Gena said as she glanced toward him. "Everything is going to be all right. Here, give me your hand." She placed it between her legs. "See? You'll be fine."

It's good, but it's not gonna save me, thought Quadir as he closed his eyes and started praying.

Gena sat back and looked out the tiny window. She could no longer see the clouds. It was wonderful to be above the clouds, physically and spiritually. She was on a natural high thinking about Quadir. He gave her such inspiration. He wasn't like other guys. He had an aura about him that made you want to get close to him. Like the night she met him and wanted to touch his face. There was something regal about him she could not say no to. So far removed from Jamal. It was different, as if she had no resistance to the man at all. And the way he took her last night and put his thing down. Lordy, Gena was just fucked up and happy about the whole situation.

She looked over at Quadir. *Do you like me?* she wondered as she stared at his eyelids, which complemented his completely relaxed face. After a few minutes of thinking to herself about last night and where the two of them now stood, Gena found herself asking the stewardess for a piece of paper.

"Thank you."

"Sure thing," she said, looking at Quadir's hand stuffed between Gena's legs.

Gena covered very nicely, telling her, "His hand was cold," as she picked up his limp wrist. "It's warm now," she added, putting Quadir's hand back on his lap. The stewardess smiled and went on about her merry way as Gena rummaged in her bag for a pen. She wanted to write a poem for him. She sat there for more than an hour thinking about last night. It was over her head. How could she express it? All the times she had thought she was having sex was a waste of time. Nothing was like last night.

When he awoke from his cat nap, she handed him the piece of paper. Quadir took the poem and turned on his overhead light, reading silently:

The Dream

My eyes are closed, but I see you so clear
I stare in your eyes and the world disappears
Leaving us together, so no one can see
Your body moves closer so you're next to me
Your fingers unbutton and take off my clothes
Your hands moving all over from my head to my toes
Without delay, you start to play

Your brown and warm fingers will find their own way
It's feeling so good and when I touch you back
You're long and you're hard and it makes me wet.
I kiss your chest in a rapture sublime
As your fingers play music in three quarter time
We're caught in a rapture without a doubt
You push my head lower I open my mouth
Hours pass by, you pick up my face
And the look in your eyes states so simply your case
This pussy is yours and you're gonna take it
If I had said no, you know you would've raped it
You flip it and turn it and throw it around
Until you have me face down on the ground
You've found your position, ass up in the air
You get behind me and force it in there
Pushing whatever is stopping your stroke
You fuck me for hours like you're going for broke
You've totally flipped and you're out of control
You're love is insane and I am your goal
You're ready to nut, not a minute too soon
I hear the alarm and I'm back in my room
I open my eyes and I hear the door shut
I thought I was dreaming, but we really did fuck.

Quadir just looked at her; he couldn't believe her little poem had made his dick hard. "Come here," he said pulling her face close enough to kiss her. He folded up the paper and put it in his pocket. The stewardess walked by and Quadir asked her how much longer the flight would be. He was so glad. He wanted it to be over. He wanted to be home. Because of so many cancellations, they were able to get a flight straight to Philadelphia. "I had the best time of my life, Quadir," she said looking into his eyes.

"I did too. I wish we was still there."

"I know! Remember when you fell off the Jet Ski and almost killed us?" she said, laughing at him.

"Yeah, and remember that wave that snuck up behind you and tumbled your ass to shore?" He was laughing as hard now as she was.

"It was really the best. Especially, you know, last night," she said.

"Yeah, it was all that."

"It was so blue."

"So blue?" he said, looking puzzled.

"Yeah, you know, the opposite of having the blues is so blue." She paused for a moment thinking about the time she spent with him, then added, "I wish we didn't have to go home."

He took her hand and squeezed. "But we have to, G. We have to go home."

THE DROP OFF

For the rest of the flight, they talked about past relationships. Quadir confessed to seeing Cherelle, but basically explained why the relationship was over. He was twenty-five, no kids, graduated from college with a bachelor's in psychology, grew up in a fucked up part of North Philly, and was poor until his pops started running street numbers and robbing banks. His dad opened up a little store, and from there he bought a few properties and basically paid his bills on time and established a solid line of credit.

Quadir was a lot like his father. He just wanted to get paid and be legit one day. Quadir grew up without seeing a real Christmas. He had seen plenty of hard times. But his family made sure he got his education. Quadir heard the same speech over and over again. "You gonna go to school, you hear me? You gonna go and you gonna learn. You know why? Just because the white man don't want you too."

Over and over, that was all Quadir heard. If black people didn't go to school, they would always be left behind. That's how it all started. His father told him the black children picked cotton and worked the fields while the white children went to school. "Niggas didn't know shit, and they don't know shit today because they was brainwashed four hundred years ago son. Remember that," his father would go on and on.

But what his dad had preached to him all those years made him a very positive individual. The substance Quadir was filled with set him aside from other brothers who were out there, especially those who hadn't even finished high school.

Quadir was an intellectual. He had made it through illegal means, through the drug game. After college and supposedly studying to be a dentist, he often wondered how he got caught up in the game. He never wanted this for himself. He had no idea that he would turn out to be one of the largest drug dealers in the city, but once he got into the game, there was no turning back. This was not his destination. He was only supposed to pay for school and become a dentist. Hard times hit at home, pops was getting old with no retirement fund. The streets were calling and Quadir answered. Hard times led him to this life, and even with the money, times were still hard, with all the death, drug wars, and jealousy. It was a vicious game and a vicious circle to be caught in.

The money came so easy, and his lifestyle became so large. To stop, even with the money he had saved, would not afford him the extravagant lifestyle he was accustomed to. The more money he made, the more consequences he faced. For every action, there is a reaction. He never stopped to look at those consequences, just as the people who used drugs never thought about the consequences of what they were doing.

Quadir was relieved when their flight landed. Rasun was at the airport waiting for him by the baggage area. They all exited the airport and went straight to the car. Rasun and Quadir were busy talking about all of the events that took place while he was out of town. Gena just wanted to get back to her house and make sure everything was still there.

She knew her neighborhood and she knew the people in her neighborhood. Most of them were no good—people gone bad. Crackheads, bugging for a hit of crack, belittling themselves. Most were penny ante thieves or just fiends doing literally anything to get high. Then you had your neighborhood drug pushers, or other lunatics with forties in one hand and guns in the other, trying to be men. The rest were either the elderly or the harmless, and they made up a very small percentage.

Qua interrupted her thoughts. "Gena, I'm gonna drop you off?" She really didn't want to be dropped off. She just wanted to drop her things off and stay with him. There was a big difference. When they pulled up on her block, everything looked the same. Trash was all over the place. The Vietnamese people were on the corner barbecuing on the sidewalk as usual. Little kids were playing in the street and everyone was sitting on their porches being nosey and talking about everyone they could. Quadir and Gena got out the car. Rasun got her luggage from out of the trunk then hopped into the front seat, tilting the chair backward as he played with the CD player. Quadir walked her up the porch, to her door.

"When are you coming back?" asked Gena, knowing that she should've just played like it didn't make a difference.

"I don't know. I got a lot to catch up on. I'll call you later on though."

A feeling of frustration suddenly covered Gena like a blanket. "What does that mean, you'll call later?" she asked, unlocking her door.

"It means I'll call later. If I can stop back over here tonight, I will. If I can't, I'll see you tomorrow. Gena, I really don't think you understand what is going on. I got shit to take care of. You can understand that, right?"

"I can understand that, Quadir. It's just that I want to be with you."

"Baby, we will be together. Let me go so I can take care of some things," he said. Gena just looked at him as if she couldn't believe he was leaving her. As she opened the door, he pulled her close to him and kissed her, lasting only a few seconds, feeling like an eternity. As Quadir let her go, he winked at her and smiled.

"I'll call you later."

"Bye," she waved. And he was gone.

Gena listened to her answering machine while she started to unpack her bags. Bria, Sabrina, Shay, Kim, Bridgette, Sheila, Mrs. Bowden, Gah Git, Gary, Tracey, Landa, Barry, Brian, Rome, a bill collector, and, of course, Jamal had all called. Jamal, however, had called at least fifteen times. Gena called Ms. Bowden. Her message seemed urgent. At first she couldn't believe what she was hearing. Her heart stopped and tears welled up in her eyes. Gena sat on the bed in a state of disbelief only finding its truth in Ms. Bowden's voice. Why, how, when, and where popped into Gena's mind. Ms. Bowden calmly told Gena the story as it had been told to her by the police.

"I don't know what I'm gonna do without that child here," Ms. Bowden said, sounding heartbroken. Gena couldn't help but feel sorrow. She was so hurt. She couldn't speak. Ms. Bowden, choking back her grief, told Gena of the events she knew surrounding Sahirah's death and the funeral, which was in three days.

Gena hung up the phone and sat in complete silence as tears

fell down her cheeks, reminiscing about the years she and Sahirah spent together. From playing with Barbie dolls and getting sprayed by fire hydrants, graduating from high school, to double dating and sharing their experiences with each other. They had always been best friends. For the rest of the evening and until Gena fell asleep, she thought of Sahirah, wishing she could tell her about Quadir. She wanted to call her so bad, but she wouldn't be there. The only things that would be there were priceless memories.

The days to follow were rough. Gena didn't eat, nor did she sleep. Not only was she in mourning for her best friend, but also in mourning for Quadir. She hadn't heard from him since he dropped her off at home. Now, it seemed as if he'd disappeared. *He said he'd call,* she kept telling herself. It was a horrible feeling of anticipation. *Maybe I should call him.* She had no idea where she put his number the night she had met him in New York. Reminiscing about the fabulous time she had had in the Bahamas only made it worse. The phone rang and she ran to answer, just knowing it was Quadir. But the voice on the other end would say only, "Where you been?"

"Who is this?" she asked.

"Oh! Now you don't know my voice."

Suddenly she did know the voice. It was Jamal. Figures he'd be calling. Damn, she wanted Quadir. Gena was so disappointed that she couldn't hold the simplest of conversations.

"Jamal, what is it? Why are you calling my house this late?"

"Oh, it's like that, now?"

"Yeah. It's like that."

"You're a fucking trip. You ain't shit. You lucky I don't come over there and kick your ass."

Her slow simmer erupted, her mouth so tight in anger she

could barely speak. "I do not have time for you. You are beneath me," she told him, as she hung up the phone. A few seconds later, it rang again.

"What?"

"Well, damn, bitch. Fuck you, too!" he said, as Gena hung up on him again.

When it rang a third time, she said, "Hello," one more time, praying it wasn't Jamal.

"Yo, what up?" said the girl on the other line.

"Hi, Kim. What's up?"

"Nothing, chilling. What's up with you?"

"Nothing. I just got back from the Bahamas."

"You hear about Sahirah and Winston in that shootout?" Kim asked.

"Yeah, and I'm real fucked up about it."

"I know you are, as tight as y'all was," Kim said.

"Her family is real hurt about it."

"Who was you in the Bahamas with? Jamal?"

"No, I went with Quadir. You know him?"

"Quadir from down North Philly?" asked Kim. "I know him. Everybody knows him. I heard he got all the young girls strung."

"What do you mean?"

"What I said. Quadir ain't nothing but a whore. But he's good for a couple dollars though."

"He is?" asked Gena, not seeing her baby boo like that at all.

"Seriously though, the nigga is no joke. Everybody's trying to see him."

"Who?"

"Everybody! Everybody is trying to see him. What part of the breakdown don't you understand?"

At that moment Gena's heart sank. No wonder his ass hadn't called back. After pausing, Kim continued on, "So, what . . . you done kicked Jamal to the curb now that you're fucking with Quadir?"

Gena didn't know where she was coming from. "It's just not going to work out. Shit is over. I can't explain it."

"Did you have a good time in the Bahamas?"

"It was so blue," Gena said, completely changing her tone of voice.

"How'd you get there?"

"We flew over." Gena was loving it.

"I want to go away."

"So, who are you messing with?" asked Gena, figuring she was gonna say Jamal.

"Who aren't I messing with?" asked Kim right back, laughing at the question. "Shit, the man I want is nowhere to be found."

"Well, maybe you'll find him."

"I doubt it. The ones you want are never the ones who want you."

"So true," said Gena, thinking of Quadir.

"I just don't understand why you and Jamal didn't work out."

"Well damn, why is you trying to?"

"I'm saying, Gena, Jamal gave you the world. He did everything. Shit, all those women Quadir got, I would have stayed right there with Jamal."

"All what women?" Gena felt her heart sinking and it was sinking fast.

"All the women he got. The man is a millionaire. Qua's shit is blue."

Gena felt as if she had to defend herself. "Well, he took me to the Bahamas."

"You in there. I'm not saying you're not. All I'm saying is that a nigga like Quadir will be in the Bahamas next week with somebody else. At least with Jamal, you had a motherfucker who came home every night and gave you whatever you wanted. You must not want a brother who's gonna treat you right," said Kim.

Gena had just about enough of the Jamal cheering section. Kim had fucked up her night with the bullshit about Quadir. *Why am I telling this bitch my business,* thought Gena. It wasn't like her and Kim rolled on a regular. Usually she would call about a party or the 411. It was time to check her. "Damn, you got the motherfucker on the three-way? You act like he's the man. If you want him, go be the fuck with him, but don't try to tell me how to run mines."

Kim had heard what she was waiting for. "Gena, you don't have to be getting smart."

"Bitch, you called my house with this bullshit. My best friend has been killed. Just leave me alone, Kim. I got to go."

Kim wasn't trying to start nothing, being as though Gena wasn't the one to have to fight over a man. She just wanted to know what was up with Jamal. Kim tried to cover up the shit as best she could. "You going to the funeral?"

"Yeah, I'll be there."

"Gena, look, I hope shit goes the way you want it between you and Quadir, and I'm sorry about Sahirah, okay?"

"I can't tell. Instead of calling me with some concern, you calling me about Jamal."

"Look, I got to go. There's someone at my door."

"Mmm hmm," Gena said, happy to slam the phone down, hoping Jamal kicked her ass too.

The next day, it was afternoon by the time Gena awoke. Sahirah's funeral was at sundown. The entire day was ruined from the time it began, greeted by mother nature's gift. *Why must it be this way?* It was her best friend's funeral and she had nothing to wear. Quadir still hadn't called. *What could be worse?* It had been three long drenching days without hearing from him, and Gena was a mess thinking the inevitable. *He played me. He was only after one thing, and now that he got it, he's gone.*

The ringing of the phone could be heard in every room of the apartment and Gena picked up the nearest receiver. Because she expected trouble, she addressed it: "Jamal, don't you call this motherfucker no more!" Slamming down the phone made her feel even better. Jamal didn't get a chance to say nothing. The phone rang again. "What?"

"What you fronting for? Some nigga in the house?" he asked.

"Jamal, leave me the fuck alone. I don't feel like you today!"

"Damn! I just called to see if you wanted to use the Cadillac to go to Sahirah's funeral or if you wanted me to go with you," said Jamal.

"Jamal, please. You couldn't stand Sahirah. How are you going to go to her funeral?"

"Why is there so much negativity with you? You don't sound happy," said Jamal.

"I would be if you would leave me the fuck alone."

"See, every time you try to be nice to people they just don't appreciate it," Jamal said.

"You're missing the point. I hope she haunts your black ass."

"Haunt shit," Jamal said. "What, you trying to root me now?"

"Good-bye," Gena said, hanging up the phone, leaving Jamal convinced she had done something to him.

Immediately, she called her grandmother. Gah Git had a house full of grandchildren and was attempting to brush Gena off the phone when Gena told her about Sahirah. Gah Git was sorry to hear about her friend. She knew the streets wasn't no place to be. She raised six children in the streets. Now, she was trying to raise her grandchildren out of the streets.

Gah Git was really sorry to hear Gena was going to her best friend's funeral.

"Don't wear nothing bright like yellow or orange and don't wear nothing too short."

"I won't. I'm so nervous about this funeral," said Gena.

"Well, baby, the good Lord has reasons for everything. Wasn't no one more closer to her than you. Maybe God is trying to tell you something. Gena, you know these things. You live to die," said Gah Git.

Gena stared at her phone. "What?"

"I said you live to die. When you're born into this world, the only thing you're promised is that one day you are going to die, so you're supposed to do the best you can. You're never coming back once you're gone. If you're good, then your soul will rest in peace. If you raise hell like you do half the time, well then, you're gonna have problems."

"Gah Git, stop!"

"Stop nothing. But, I'm glad you're home, baby."

"Me, too, but Gah Git, it was so beautiful there. I could've stayed there forever."

"Well, at least he didn't kill your ass and hide you in some bushes."

"Gah Git."

"Well, what do you call it when you meet a man one day and is off on some fancy getaway to the Bahamas? Did you sleep with him?"

"I got to go," said Gena, getting ready to hang up the phone.

"Have you heard from him since you been back?"

Gena didn't want to answer that question. If she told the truth, Gah Git would disapprove. Then she would preach the same, long, drawn out sermon about being a lady, not a whore. She even had some old Ray Charles song 'bout every time she went in a nightclub, the whole band knew her name, which she used as a metaphor.

"Yes, I've heard from him." Gena felt her heart sink as she lied to her grandmother. "Gah Git, I have to go."

"Well, don't get mad with me. You comin' down later? I'm cooking, so you might as well come and get some dinner. Besides, I want to see you for running off like that."

"Gah Git, I am grown. I can run where I want to run," said Gena.

"Baby, you can't never run from home. Believe that."

"I am not a baby," said Gena.

"Yes, you are; you're my baby. So just run your ass over here after that funeral and get some dinner and stop being so fussy."

Gena hung up the phone and went over to her dresser. She felt twisted inside, confused about Quadir, depressed and saddened about Sahirah, and mad that Jamal would not stop calling her. She pulled out a knot of money from her dresser drawer. She had won $1,800 in the Bahamas and Qua threw her money here and there but she never spent it all. She just told him that she did. "It's gone," she would say with a serious blank look on her face. *Why hasn't he called?* She thought to herself, searching her dresser drawers for his phone number. She looked in all the places she thought she might have put it. Hell, it had been more than a week and with all the weed she had smoked since then, figuring out where she put his number was highly unlikely. "Damn, where could it be?" She searched around the room, to no avail. She took a shower and got dressed. Still searching for Quadir's number she rummaged through the kitchen. She wanted to call him so bad, she didn't know what to do. *Why hasn't he called? Maybe he isn't going to call,* she thought to herself. *Maybe Gah Git was right, maybe I shouldn't have gone to the Bahamas with him. Maybe Kim was right; maybe I should have stayed with Jamal. Not!*

BACK TO BUSINESS

Quadir rolled over from his sleeping position, brought himself to an upright stance, and planted his feet on the floor. He looked around his bedroom. The new burgundy carpet he just had laid set it off. Everything was new and very contemporary. Turning on the sixty-inch screen TV, he turned to videos. As he landed on the channel he threw the remote on the bed and promptly picked up his weed tray.

Things were really starting to happen for Quadir. He was getting money and a lot of it. He had a squad of youngsters who covered the street corners, had old heads who backed him, and he went through 150 kilos of cocaine, if not more, every week. One month he went through 1,200 kilos, that was the best month. Not only were things really going good; he had women. He had more women than any man he knew. He had so many women, you would think he was the only man on earth. They would do anything he wanted. Anything. He lived his life in the fast lane; fast women, fast money, fast cars, and the beeper always needed fresh batteries. Things were falling into place.

Another year and Quadir would be straight. "Just one more year," he thought to himself. He laid there with his boxer shorts on, holding his crotch with one hand, smoking with the other.

Picking up his watch from the nightstand, he noted it was 12:30 in the afternoon. "I really slept in," he thought to himself, walking into the living room. Another wide-screen TV sat catty-cornered against a far wall; a round, aquamarine colored sectional leather sofa, a large glass circle-shaped table, and custom-made peach colored carpet with an aquamarine border going around the wall was his latest interior designs. There was a dining room, but Qua made that into the playroom where he put a pool table and, though he never imbibed, a fully stocked marble bar, all beautifully set off by bi-leveled mirrored walls and Hollywood ceilings. Qua was a man of good taste, and he kept his apartment immaculate.

It wasn't the only apartment he had either. Quadir had a room at his mom's house, another house where he let Rasun stay, and yet another apartment, far from the city, where he could discreetly take his female companions. But no one knew about it. Not even Rasun. He never allowed anyone to know about this place. It was the only place he felt he could relax, the only place he got any good sleep. The old heads had left no stone unturned when it came to Quadir knowing what was out there. The larger Qua became, the more to himself he became. He trusted no one and knew that everyone was out to get him or a piece of him. It was really fucked up, and he learned to be extra careful.

Rock wasn't careful. His funeral was today. Qua could not believe that it was the Junior Mafia who took the boy out, just couldn't believe it. Didn't want to believe it. Quadir knew that killing Rock meant they wanted a war; he also knew that, by no means, should the boy's death go unavenged.

Easing onto his leather sofa, he played back all the conversations he had gathered from the streets. He knew that Rock's death was nothing more than the Junior Mafia sending him a message, indirectly. Rik knew what he was talking about when he said the Junior Mafia was trying to weaken him. Rock was flipping keys getting G's and since Quadir supplied him as well as a handful of others, Quadir was vulnerable through the people underneath him. He had to be certain of everyone he dealt with. The worse nightmare was getting snitched on. All he needed was an indictment behind someone else's bullshit. He didn't want to deal with that no more than his peoples getting killed for buying coke from him instead of the Junior Mafia. He thought about Rock's funeral. He would not be there. He had been asked to be a pallbearer, but demurred. Qua wasn't really sure why he wasn't going. He really felt bad about Rock dying, but going to the funeral wouldn't make much of a difference. Rock was gone, and Quadir would remember him the way he was.

Besides, the ho's be clocking a nigga at a funeral. It's fucked up to say, but it's true. Yeah, they might shed a tear or two, but they're hoping to get a number and meet up with a nigga later. On top of that, the feds would be there taking their pictures and videotaping.

Qua dialed a number from his pager and carried his portable phone into the bathroom while he showered. Dressed, he made himself a turkey and cheese sandwich, then returned to the couch and waited for the phone to ring.

"Hello," he said, answering the phone on the first ring. "Nothing . . . taking it easy, man," he said. The man on the other end controlled the conversation the same way Quadir did with his people. "Next week? Same place? I'll be there."

He then dialed Rasun at his mom's house and told him to meet up with him on the Av. later.

Then he dialed Amar. "As-Salaamu Alaikum," said Amar, answering the phone.

"Alaikum As-Salaam," Quadir replied. "You just the brother I wanted to talk to."

"What's going on, player?"

"Nothing, man. Getting ready to go to this funeral," said Amar.

"You going to the funeral?" asked Qua, thinking of Rock.

"Man, I got two funerals to go to. This girl I used to fuck with and Rock's," said Amar. Quadir realized he was talking about Sahirah. She sure did get around. He thought about asking Amar whether he knew Gena, but decided against it.

"You going to Rock's funeral?" asked Amar.

"No, you know I don't go to funerals."

"I must be there. I'm a pallbearer," said Amar.

"What?" said Qua, thinking about his own refusal of the offer. Quadir let a moment go by. "So, what's happening otherwise?"

"I'm ready to see you. I want to go to Fifteenth Street," said Amar.

"You on a 100th?" asked Qua.

"Yeah, I'm there."

"One hour," said Qua.

"Everything the same?"

"You know it."

"As-Salaamu Alaikum," said Amar.

"Alaikum As-Salaam," said Quadir, hanging up the phone.

Three minutes later he was out the door. He got in a 1987 Cutlass Oldsmobile and went straight to the 4-U-Self Storage, Inc. Inside his compartment was some furniture and a safe. Just like the one in his apartment, only this one contained 523 kilos of cocaine. He grabbed fifteen bricks and put them in a duffle bag. He then placed another one in a shopping bag, which he was going to take to Ms. Shoog's house.

He jumped back in the car and drove to a supermarket, parking at the rear of the lot, then rolled a spliff and set the CD player. He sat patiently, as if waiting for someone in the store to finish their shopping until, finally, Amar pulled into the parking lot. He parked next to Qua. Both got out and shook hands as brothers do.

"What's up, man?" said Amar.

"You looking good, player," answered Qua.

"Yeah, man, you know me. I got to be right for my man."

Quadir and Amar talked for a few minutes. Amar assured Quadir that there was $100,000 in the trunk of the squatter. Quadir in return assured Amar that there was fifteen kilos of cocaine in the duffle bag on the backseat.

Quadir watched Amar get in the Oldsmobile while he got in the squatter Amar had been driving. He dropped the money off at his apartment and put it in the safe. He then headed down North Philly to see Ms. Shoog. Qua pulled onto the narrow one-way street and parked in front of Shoog's house. He grabbed the bag out of the backseat. The moment he opened the car door, he could hear Ms. Shoog hollering down the street.

"And don't come back in this motherfucker until you learn how to act."

She was cursing some man out for the entire block to hear. "You dumbass motherfucker, you. I don't know why I even let you in here. You not fit to be in no house!"

"Who was that?" he asked her, walking up the sidewalk to her door.

"Some nigga my granddaughter brought in here," Shoog replied. "His ass damn sure look like what the cat drug in, don't make no sense. He gonna stand up there and tell me to go to hell. He lucky I didn't break his goddamn neck," she said taking a breath.

"Come on, get your ass back in the house. Titties hanging out and shit. How you playin', Shoog? See, you got all the neighbors looking. Come on," said Qua, walking her back in the house.

Kids was all over the place and as soon as they seen Quadir they ran over to him to get a dollar. The house was always junky, but today it seemed as if there was an abundance of junkiness, cluttering up any space the house may have once had. You could easily tell that too many people were occupying the three-bedroom row home. *Where do all these motherfuckers sleep?* Qua thought to himself, looking all around.

"Shoog, why the house so hot?" asked Qua.

"All these lazy ass niggas in here. Shit, you can hardly breath in this motherfucker. I wish they would come and get they kids and take them the hell on somewhere and buy my fan that them heathens done broke today. They got my blood pressure up so high, Lord, I'm surprised I haven't dropped dead."

She took the bag out of his hand and broke up the coke. "There's no way in a cat's ass you gonna get me in this hot ass kitchen cooking all this shit today. I'll cook some but I'm not cooking it all. You hear me, Quadir?"

"Yeah, I hear you."

As he sat next to the kitchen window talking to Shoog, he felt a cool breeze kissing his face. He talked to Ms. Shoog about everything. She had her ways, but she wasn't nobody's fool; most old people weren't. They had been here long enough to know how not to play the fool. Shoog was full of wisdom. It was one thing to hear her; it was another to listen.

When she was done Quadir handed her five hundred dollars and stepped. "When you gonna get my fan?" she asked.

"Tomorrow."

"Nigga, you know you is a lie. Besides, I'm going to get me an air conditioner, right now."

"You better before your ass drops dead in that motherfucker," hollered Quadir.

He got in Amar's squatter after Shoog cursed him out and headed down to the Av. Everybody was out. It was the crew. Qua was happy to see his bucks out there. He shook hands with everybody and got right in the middle of the conversations with them and started kicking it. "Yo, look at that girl," Pookey said, pointing his finger. On the opposite side of the street, approximately twenty feet from where they stood, a girl had pulled her pants down, exposing herself. She slightly bent her knees and started peeing in broad daylight between two parked cars.

"She really don't give a fuck," said Ra.

"She got to be high," said Reds.

"I told ya'll pipers were inheriting the earth," said Pookey.

Wiz spotted three girls walking down the opposite side of the street. "Hey, baby in the blue," he called out.

"Why are you messing with them girls?" said Pookey, turning his face up.

"Yo, I like fat girls too, don't get that shit twisted. I'm not one to discriminate. Skinny, fat, tall, short, light, dark, it don't make a difference, man," said Wiz.

The girls walked over to Wiz and engaged him in conversation. The rest of them looked at the girls real mean with a "dont even think about it" expression on their faces.

"I got a boyfriend," said the girl in blue.

"So, I got a girlfriend," said Wiz.

"Well, why are you trying to talk to me?"

"Because. Can't we be friends?" said Wiz.

"No, I dont think so," said the girl as if she had checked Wiz out and was completely turned off.

"Well, fuck you, then."

"Man, leave them girls alone. Excuse him," said Qua, as the girls walked by him.

"Fuck you, too," the girl said, walking away.

"Only if you promise to diet."

At that, everyone, even Quadir, had to laugh.

Quadir walked over to his jeep, which Ra had parked up the block. Rasun followed right behind him. They decided that Reds and Wiz would go back up the way and help cap the package. Quadir handed him the keys to Amar's squatter and left.

Across town in West Philly, Sahirah Bowden was being laid to rest. Outside, it looked like a car show. On the inside, Gena saw the girlfriends she and Sahirah traveled with. It wasn't packed, but it wasn't empty either. A lot of brothers were there. Bridgette said she had seen brothers come through for the viewing. It was really nice that everyone came to say good-bye to Sahirah and even though they didn't stay through the funeral, they did come out to pay their last respects.

She was so young and looked so pretty in a soft pink cashmere sweater with a matching skirt. Gena couldn't see her shoes because there were flowers covering the bottom half of the casket.

The preacher's bellowing voice echoed over the body of her friend that lay peacefully beneath his pulpit, the congregation agreeing with him readily. Ms. Bowden had lost control. The funeral nurse rocked her throughout the sermon.

Gena sat with her head hanging low, feeling the loss of her best friend like an empty pit at the bottom of her spirit. Who would she laugh with? Who would she share with? Who would be her friend? As the preacher preached, a tear fell for every word he spoke. Why did the words *beloved friend* make her fill up even more? What about Mr. and Mrs. Bowden? They lost a child! How they gonna deal with that?

She glanced up and looked around the church. There was a huge crucifix suspended behind the ornate wall where the preacher was standing. Large blocks of stained-glass windows allowed the last bit of sunlight to shine through as the service proceeded. The faces of the people sitting in row after row of the beautiful gothic church were just as tormented and distraught as the next.

"Dear God," she prayed, "take my friend Sahirah in your arms. Love her, protect her, give her peace." Gena surveyed those gathered to bid farewell to the young, beautiful girl they all knew, stopping at a familiar face.

All prayers and reasoning power flew from her perspective. She couldn't believe it. *Sacrilege!* He was sitting there two rows in front of her on the right side of the church. He even had the gall to acknowledge that he saw her. *Oh my God,* she thought, feeling that it was appropriate to express the Lord's name. The first word that actually came to her mind would surely be unseemly in this church setting.

Jamal was there, sitting with Kim. Kim who, just the night before last, had preached to Gena about how she should not break up with him. *That bitch,* Gena thought to herself. She felt a little funny inside seeing Jamal with Kim. That miserable man.

She couldn't believe how he had called and offered to bring her, then had the nerve to show up with Kim. She saw right through him. Jealous that Jamal was there with someone else was one thing; the aching betrayal that was setting in made her furious. *Don't nobody need to lie to me. Why didn't she say she was interested in Jamal? Why didn't he say, well, maybe I'll see you there, anyway or maybe I'll bring Kim?* He wasn't paying any respects; he was there to hurt Gena. She faced the altar and concentrated on her friend.

The service lasted more than an hour. Sahirah would be buried the following morning at ten. After today, Gena didn't know if she could take anymore. She had shed all the tears she wanted to and put the memories of Sahirah inside her heart, where they would be forever cherished. Her only consolation was that Gena knew she had a friend in Sahirah, and she hoped and prayed to one day see her friend again. The firm belief that Sahirah would always be with her, plus the memories they shared together, is what helped Gena get through the service.

As the congregation made its way down the aisle and outside the church, Gena just sat still and waited for Jamal and Kim to leave the building. She wanted to watch them leave together to be sure they were together. As they walked down the aisle Jamal was a few steps behind Kim, all smiles. *What the fuck is he smiling about?* Gena thought to herself, as they stopped at her pew.

"Hi, Gena," Kim said.

Gena coldly acknowledged them both, silently rolling her eyes at them.

"Didn't take you long, Jamal."

"What do you care for? Don't you want Quadir?" he asked.

"I don't want him; I am his," said Gena, her eyes glaring at Kim as if she could rip the bitch apart. "I'm through with him.

He's all yours," she spat at her, before staring Jamal down, waiting for him to say one single word out his pathetic sorry face. "If you'll excuse me, I have better things to do," she said.

All of Jamal's feelings were crushed. He couldn't believe it. She really wasn't that upset he was with Kim. His plan failed. At that moment he got the picture that it was really over. "Fucking bitch," he rasped.

"Jamal, you're in a church," said Kim.

"God understands. He made all of you, didn't he?" Jamal asked, looking at Kim, waiting for her to say he was right.

"Come on, Jamal," she said, leading him out of the church.

Outside, Gena saw all her girlfriends. Girls from the beauty salons, girls who worked at the mall, girls she hung out with in the park, girls who were close to both her and Sahirah.

"Yo, G. What's up?" said Bridgette.

"Guess what? Jamal is here with Kim."

Bridgette took the bait. "You should have known. I never trusted that motherfucker. Bitch ain't nothing but a whore. And she don't be bullshittin' when it comes to your man, neither."

"I didn't know the bitch rolled like that," said Gena, knowing that Bridgette was just as slimy as Kim.

"Please, she fucked Adrienne's man and then called her on the phone and told her. She said she felt bad about it and, as a friend, she had to tell Adrienne about her man. Now, you know the bitch is crazy 'cause the day she ring my phone with some shit about my man is gonna be the day she get her ass kicked."

"I'm not fighting over no Jamal," said Gena even though she wanted to.

Bridgette glanced across the street. "Look. Isn't that Quadir?"

Gena's heart raced, her mind scrambled and her eyes darted. "Where? I don't see him." Quadir was in his black Range Rover with the black tinted windows, which Gena had never seen. So, she turned her back, not wanting to be seen, trying to see something she didn't.

"Yo, the kid is so large it's ridiculous," said Bridgette.

Andrea walked over to where Gena and Bridgette were standing. "Yo, what's up? I'm so sorry about Sahirah," she said, giving Gena a hug.

Gena returned her embrace. "I know, I'm really torn up about it."

"Yo, I wonder what he's doing out here," said Bridgette.

"Who?" Andrea wanted to know.

"That kid Quadir, from down North Philly," said Bridgette.

"Oh God. Is he out here? Where? Girl, the motherfucker is a millionaire," said Andrea pulling out a pocket mirror. You would have thought she had a winning Lotto ticket in the palm of her hand. Gena just stood there feeling two disappointments, one after the other. She felt so fucked up inside. What if he was there to see another girl? What could be worse, besides her girlfriends standing there getting their panties wet over a Range Rover?

Qua pulled the jeep over and parked. Gena just stood there with her back turned from him, knowing his every move from the channel zero news reporters.

"He's walking over here," said Bridgette.

"The Lord is truly among us," said Andrea, looking at the sky happy to be near the church.

Gena was so nervous, she wanted to turn around so bad to see exactly where he was. He stepped from behind, put his hands up to her eyes and bent into her ear.

"Guess who," he said.

"I hope it's who I want it to be," she said pushing back against him.

"Who do you want it to be?" he asked, with his hands still covering her eyes.

"I want it to be Quadir."

Andrea and Bridgette just looked at each other in disbelief. Gena wanted to pull him over to the side and tell him how much she missed him, kiss him a thousand times, ask him why he hadn't called, but instead she carried on real cool and casual with the conversation. "I thought you didn't come near funerals," she said after he let her go.

"I don't, but I knew you would be here." Gena just stood there looking him up and down as if she had a serious attitude about something.

"Come here," he said, as he snatched her arm and pulled her over to the side. "What's your problem?"

"Nothing."

"Yes, it is. You want to tell me about it?"

"Okay. For starters you acted like you didn't want to see me anymore when you dropped me off. You never called, and you left like it wasn't nothing to you. Then I come home to find that my best friend had been murdered. You have no idea how I've been feeling. I thought we had something, but I don't know where you're coming from. I thought I did, but I was wrong."

"You got the pager number," he said, cutting her off. "Why didn't you call me?"

"Because I couldn't find it. Besides, you said you were coming back."

"Baby, I was taking care of my business, that's all. If I was fucked up and broke, you wouldn't want to talk to me."

"That is not true. I would too," she said.

"No, you wouldn't. Don't no woman want no broke-ass man."

This was true, Gena thought to herself as she cracked a smile. "Money isn't supposed to matter."

"Yeah, well, tell that to those miners standing over there," said Qua, using his head to point at Gena's girlfriends. Gena started laughing. "Yo, I couldn't stop thinking about you. I missed you," he said.

"I missed you too." Gena went to grab him, but he grabbed her and pulled her close so he could kiss her.

The anchorwomen down the street acted like they were on CNN's payroll. The news bulletin read: Gena got it going on. Don't you wish it could be you! And they wanted more news. Bridgette started walking over to them and Quadir let Gena go. Gena saw Jamal turning the corner and speeding away as if the police were after him, looking right at her.

"Hi, Quadir," Bridgette said, in an *I'm cheap—you can fuck me* voice.

"Hi," he said looking at her. "Do I know you from somewhere?"

"No, I don't think so," said Kim's twin.

"Do you know Black?" Gena asked, putting an end to the madness.

"Yeah, that's my man. That's where I know you from, Black. Where's he at?" Qua said.

"Oh, he's downtown," said Bridgette, gritting her teeth at Gena.

"Well, tell him to get at me."

"I will." Turning to Gena, she asked her if she needed a ride home.

"No, I'm okay." She turned to Quadir, "I'm okay, right?"

"You're better than okay. You're with me now. Come on."

"Where are we going?" she asked as he led her to his jeep.

"Anywhere you want to go, within city limits," he replied opening the door for her.

"I got something for you," she said.

"What is it?" he asked. Gena scrambled through her MCM bag, and pulled out a folded piece of paper and handed it to him. Quadir unfolded the paper and began reading:

Come Back

Where did you come from?
Where did you go? Will you come back?
Or don't you know? Or will you get scared and
keep running away? Forgetting feelings
that won't go away?

You can't shake it, or fake it, these feelings inside.
If you'd just stop running, I'd be by your side.

Forever your lady, forever my man,
For the rest of my life, or until the world's end
I'll love you, you'll see that you can't hide
And these feelings are memories
of moments lost in time

The sooner you realize, the better I'll be,
And my love will always be here, for you, from me,
G.

"Come here," he said. Pulling her next to him, their lips touched as he kissed her deeply. Gena just sat there smiling. She thrived off mad affection.

"Did you see Bridgette? Isn't she a trip? She had no idea that I was seeing you. No one did, except for Sahirah, and then I talked to Kim."

Quadir just sat there, blocking Gena out for a moment. He thought of the bright side of Sahirah's untimely death. Ra told him that Sahirah knew about Cherelle being in the Bahamas with him. He knew Sahirah was waiting to tell Gena. *They should remember Sahirah as big mouth,* he thought to himself as he tuned Gena back in.

"Bridgette is really a trip. She just had to come over there and try to get in your face."

"I dug her. I knew that I knew her from somewhere," said Qua.

"You know her from Black, or you might know her from the boy Rich Green."

Rich Green, Qua thought to himself. He knew he didn't like that guy. Rich Green was out to make a name for himself as a member of the Junior Mafia. He was the one who had beef with Qua's young bucks.

"She fucks with Rich Green too?"

"Yeah, but that's supposed to be on the DL."

"I know Rich Green. Does Black know about them?"

"I don't know. Tell him."

Qua and Gena kicked names around for a long time. It seemed that for every brother Quadir named, Gena had one of her girlfriends to match with them.

"Do you know who Black's woman is?" said Qua.

"Bridgette," said Gena, looking at him.

"No. Her name is Pam," Quadir retorted. "And she is set for the rest of her life. If you ask me, Black is running game on your girlfriend. She's so busy thinking she's being sneaky and getting over when in reality she's getting played." He paused.

"The sad part about it is that if Bridgette isn't careful, she will probably wind up like your girlfriend, Sahirah. That's why you're on probation."

"Why am I on probation? I haven't done anything."

"I know you, Gena. I have been watching you for a long time. I heard your name before. I saw your face and trust me, baby, the two go together well."

"Well, what did you hear about me?"

"I got the dirt on you. I had to dig deep. And you're not so trustworthy, are you?"

"Yes, I am."

"No, you're not."

"You just don't know what you're talking about." Gena hated when people talked about her.

"I know at least two brothers you messed with while you were supposed to be with Jamal," Quadir laughed.

"What are you talking about?"

"You said your conscience was bothering you and you couldn't see them anymore because of Jamal. You came off like a saint. That's why you're on probation."

"Who?"

"I'm not saying,"

"That's because you're lying. It's not true." She was so fucking convincing she should have been on television. Until he said a name.

"Dion. Remember Dion?"

Gena just couldn't believe the boy was coming at her with the dumb-ass shit. *Damn,* she thought, *no one knew about that one.* "That's different. I didn't care about him and I didn't do anything with him. I never cheat," said Gena.

"If you didn't care about him, then why'd you take his money?"

"He was throwing it at me."

"Damn, I wish a motherfucker would just throw money at me," said Qua, making a funny face.

"How do you know about him?"

"Aha! Don't *choo* wanna know. I don't think so, baby doll."

Gena, headstrong, refused to be caught and continued sticking to a story she thought she had sewn up. "Well, at the time Jamal wasn't spending any time with me, but I never cheated on him," she said, as if there was absolutely nothing wrong with that.

"How could the man spend time with you if he was busy making money to keep you happy, meanwhile, you're out foolin' around?" Qua said. "You should be ashamed of yourself. That's why you're on probation."

This one was different, Gena thought. He had inquired into her past, knew shit he wasn't supposed to, and then threatened her with probation. *What exactly is probation? Does it mean no money or something? What part of the game is this?* Gena just couldn't figure him out. Most male creatures were simple as fuck. Quadir, however, was in a class all by himself. He didn't just want to play. He wanted to win.

During the following months, she stayed on probation. Qua played a lot of mind games. He even paid a friend of his to push up on her. The guy pulled along Gena in a candy apple red convertible Saab in the Starling Mall parking lot. He offered her dinner, then gave her some roses he already had in the backseat, which she gave right back. He talked real nice, giving her all kinds of compliments, but to no avail; Gena wouldn't give him

the time of day. Quadir really gave her a hard way at first, then
he started to ease up. Things just happened like they were meant
to. Gena stayed right up underneath Qua. She was even with
him when he would be taking care of business. She knew it was
no place for her, and so did he. They did everything together.
By the time Christmas came, she was staying at the apartment
where he usually entertained his women. Gena felt so at home,
particularly after she burned all the evidence that indicated he
had a life before she came along. Gena cooked, cleaned, even
did laundry all between trips to Bloomingdales and Ann Taylor.
She had a ball hurting the feelings of every female who called for
him. "Bitch please, I'm his woman; you're a fuck. He doesn't care
about you. Quadir, tell her you don't want to fuck with her."
She would always pass him the phone, demanding her position
be exposed. He would do it too. Gena had put her thing down,
real hard. Her power and wiles were so strong that Quadir for
once was keeping his interest. He liked coming home to her at
night, and he loved her jealousy. She made such a fuss over every
little thing that Qua soon realized that he would have to be a
man about his extracurricular activities and keep them hidden
from Gena. Quadir, being Muslim, didn't celebrate Christmas.
But, he promised that every other year they could celebrate with
gifts. One day before the holiday, he hid a box in the house and
made her look for it. Finally, she found in the kitchen closet—a
big box with gold wrapping paper and a red bow.

"Not my to-the-floor fur, Qua?" She kissed him before she
even opened it.

"How'd you know?" he asked.

Gena paid him no mind, too busy now ripping at the paper.
"How'd I know," she muttered, looking as if that was the stupid-
est question ever asked. Gena thought she would die. It was the

coat she had been requesting for months. A mink, to the floor, the most beautiful thing she had ever seen in her life.

Everything was going so good. The past six months had brought them close, real close. The best part of the whole relationship was that they were on the same level with each other. Though they were both the biggest flirts in the world, it was clearly understood that there was no messing around. Quadir already knew that it would be stupid of him to think that there wouldn't be guys trying to see Gena; she looked too good. The brothers would always try their luck. Gena handled it though; she was never loose. She always maintained her composure and represented Quadir, which was a lot of representing. Qua had always been a flirt, except his flirting was different from hers.

Three days after Christmas a baby girl was born at 4:30 PM. She weighed six pounds, and fifteen ounces. She was a beautiful baby, with locks of black hair and beautiful brown skin. Cherelle, the baby's mother, was in the Germantown Hospital alone. She couldn't believe that she had given birth all by herself. She had paged Quadir and told him she was in labor. He didn't call back. Even though she wasn't absolutely sure it was his, she played the entire nine months as if it were. She was so glad she finally knew who the father was once she saw her daughter. She hadn't been too sure, but when she came out, Cherelle took one look at her and knew she would be called Quanda.

Qua knew his flirting was going to get him into trouble. That was even his New Year's resolution. No ho's in 1989.

Gena's resolution was much simpler: to save money. Something she'd never been able to do. Gena spent money as if it were falling out of the sky like rain. She didn't save one dime. It was

1989. She would be turning nineteen in March, and she didn't even have a bank account. Jewelry, clothes, shoes, even a fur. And no bank account.

If Qua left her today or tomorrow, if he went to jail, or if anything happened to him, she would have nothing.

1989

SURPRISE

The months passed quickly. Ever since Sahirah's funeral, Quadir and Gena stayed together and everyone knew it. He let her drive the Range Rover while he drove the BMW.

He bought her a house in Montgomery County. It had four bedrooms, a pool in the backyard, and a huge front lawn that required landscaping. There were a total of eight chandeliers throughout the house. The vestibule, bathrooms, and kitchen were all complete with coordinating marble. The basement was Quadir's. No women allowed, just his boys. It had a pool table, a bar, and sixty-inch-screen TV. He had a sound system throughout that could shake the entire neighborhood. The living room had eggshell carpet, off-white furniture, and contemporary marble. A large curio sat cornered against the wall where Gena had placed thousands of dollars worth of crystal. Where the furniture came from Qua didn't care. He did care that she spent $32,000 on the room.

The family room had butter soft navy blue leather furniture and a custom-made light-blue carpet with dark blue trim. In the middle of the far wall was a fireplace. Another big-screen TV sat catty-cornered in the family room next to a stereo system twice the size of the one in the basement. There were sliding glass doors that led out to the backyard and the pool. The kitchen had been remodeled and had everything from a dishwasher to a food processor. The dining room floor was black marble with a black mirrored dining room table that seated twelve in its center. A matching breakfront sat against beveled mirrors adjacent to a gray stone wall.

Their bedroom had rich, dark green carpet. A huge king-size bed connected to an elaborate wall unit, which stretched across the entire wall and sat facing the door.

The closets were filled with shoes and clothes. Gena and Quadir had so many clothes, neither rarely wore the same thing twice.

There were two extra rooms. One Gena made into an office, complete with a maple desk, computer, and fireproof file cabinets. In front of the desk sat two bone colored leather chairs. She had a bookshelf the size of the wall built for the room and went out to bookstores and purchased hundreds of books to occupy the shelves.

The other bedroom was really like a storage area, even though it was actually a guest room. Though the family rarely visited, Gah Git called every day.

Quadir stayed gone, as if he was lost and just couldn't find the house. Gena didn't understand it. He would stay out all night, usually not returning home until the wee hours of the morning.

Even though he was never there, he wasn't going anywhere either. She felt secure, and she felt happy. But Gena unknowingly had allowed herself to be isolated. Quadir had conveniently and successfully excused it as a safety precaution. None of her girl-friends was allowed in the house. That was first and foremost. Only a few family members had visited. Not only did Gena believe this was right, but also she protected her home and protected Quadir by all means. She never took anyone there. No one except family was to have their home number. She could only be paged. Traveling in certain parts of the city, even talking to certain individuals was a no-no. And, for the love of money, it was a small price to pay. It was nothing. She had no worries, but she was left alone.

One rainy day, Quadir stayed in. It was a treat to have him home. The two cuddled on the sofa with a blanket and popcorn and watched daytime TV. That's when a commercial came on. The "make each day count" speech, and "why waste another moment?" grabbed her. She turned to Quadir and asked if she could go to college, really wanting to.

"What do you want to study?" he asked.

"You know, I hadn't thought about it. But I like the idea of business management, and it would give me something to do, Quadir. You're not here a lot, and there's nothing left in the malls. I have everything," she said throwing her hands out in the air, really wondering what he expected her to do. Quadir was excited for her. He wished he had it in him to go to college with her.

"Maybe I'll go too."

"For real, I can go? You're going to come, Quadir," she said moving over to him, hugging his neck, and giving him kisses in a circle motion over his face.

"Well, I can't do it now. But, when things lighten up, I'm going back. I always wanted to be a dentist," he said trying to get her off his neck.

"I want you to be a dentist, Quadir. I think you would be a

great dentist. I really do." She said it meaning every word, and he knew she knew what she was talking about.

"I love you, Gena."

"I love you back, Quadir."

With that Gena started college two months later, and was doing quite well. She occupied most of her days in classes and her nights studying.

Hearing the BMW in the driveway, she peered out the bedroom window to see Quadir pull into the double door garage. She flew down the stairs and met him as he walked in the door.

"Hey, baby. You all right?" he said as she walked away from him into the kitchen.

"I'm fine," her voice kind of cold.

"What are you going to do today?"

"I want to go shopping and pay my credit card bill," she said following behind him.

Quadir knew that meant money.

"What are you doing?" she asked.

"Nothing. I got to be somewhere in an hour." He took off his clothes and left them in the middle of the floor for her to pick up.

"It's ten thirty in the morning. Where have you been?" All she needed to complete the picture was a little steam coming out of her ears.

"I been in the street."

"What the fuck is the street? What kind of answer is that? You're always in the street. You never have any time to spend with me. You're never here anymore because you're always in the street," she stared him down, waiting for an answer.

"Gena, you know what I'm in the street doing? Hustling. Making money. You know, that green-colored paper you love to spend so much of? Look at it, Gena, ten thousand for a dining room. Where's the chairs, Gena?"

"You know they will be delivered next week."

"Yeah, for an additional eight thousand. Ten thousand and no chairs, and the bedroom, fifteen thousand dollars, Gena. Not to mention a living room no one can go into because it's white. That was thirty thousand right there. Our living room is someone's house. Your fucking wardrobe and jewelry is twenty working motherfuckers' salaries per year, and you got a problem with me 'cause I'm in the streets. Don't you think I want to come home? But what the fuck! When I do, I got to hear a bunch of bullshit. I can't even get my dick sucked because you're too busy using your mouth to ask me stupid questions like, where have I been all night." He stopped to catch his breath and she just stood there looking at him. *He definitely needs some pussy,* she thought to herself. He acted as if she were the one with the problem and not him. Finally, he calmed down and gave in a little.

"I got a surprise for you. Meet me here at six." He handed her a piece of paper with an address on it. From there nothing more was said about the hours he was keeping. Gena went downstairs and Quadir went into the kitchen. As usual, Gena had made his breakfast and sat his plate in the microwave. When he was done eating she followed him back upstairs to ask him for some money. She felt bad after hearing his speech about all the money she had spent. If he started hollering again, she was going to tell him to forget it and just walk away.

As she walked into the room he was on the phone, saying, "You what?" When he looked up and saw her, he just hung up the phone.

"Who was that?"

"Nobody," he said with a stupid looking smile on his face.

"Quadir, please."

"It was Ra." She knew he was lying. She could tell. His beeper went off, and he picked it up immediately and turned it to the vibrate mode but he didn't call back the number. It vibrated again, but Gena couldn't hear it.

"I need some money."

"What's new?"

"Quadir, is there someone else?"

"No, Gena. Why would you ask me a question like that? Do you got someone else?"

"Of course not. It's just that you don't spend any time with me. I come into rooms and you hang up on people. What's that?"

"Gena, that is not true. We go to Atlantic City almost every week and we go out to dinner at least four or five times a week. Hell, you'd starve a nigga to death so we got to go."

"Sometimes I really think you don't love me."

"Come here."

Gena's fingers busily removed his clothes. Qua kissed her mouth and kissed nipples that reached for his lips in the promise of deep pleasure. He touched her with his wonderful, knowing fingers, becoming more excited with every moan that escaped her lips. She made him hold still while she worked her knees to the floor. She took him into her mouth and sucked, up and down, on the fleshy instrument God had provided him. Clenching his teeth to prevent himself from exploding too soon, Quadir picked her up with great strength and pinned her up against a wall. She was so wet and so hot. He hadn't seen her this passionate in months, and he was taking every advantage he could of her. He knew she was an undercover freak and would do the mailman if he wasn't on his job. He turned her around so her back was to him and she faced the wall and in a standing position put his thing down. As she felt herself climaxing, she told him to come with her and he did. Releasing, as she basked in the heady state of shimmering pleasure, he whispered, "I love you."

Following her in to the bathroom, he stood above her as she was sitting on the toilet. She looked up, seeing his dick pointed straight at her ear. "I've missed you too," she said, as he lifted her onto the bathroom counter. Wanting every inch of him inside her, she spread her legs open and let him in. He held her thighs so tight as he attempted to push his body and soul into her, all the while whispering in her ear, "It's all about you, Gena. All about you." Holding onto the counter's edge, she felt his body shudder, giving up the demon, releasing what seemed like all of his life force.

How could she doubt him after a shot like that? *He is in the street. He'll never cheat. He loves me,* Gena thought.

Finally able to move, Qua helped her off the counter, re-entered the bedroom, and turned on the CD player.

After they showered and dressed, Quadir went downstairs. She knew he was going to the safe. She didn't know the combination; he wouldn't tell her. In a few minutes, he returned and placed three stacks of money on the bed.

"You gonna meet me at six, right?"

"Yeah. How much is there?"

She couldn't take her eyes of the piles of bills in front of her. What bag would she use to carry all that cash?

"Seven or eight thousand."

Quadir was ready to go. "I'm taking the jeep. I'll see you later." She was holding out a piece of paper, which he pocketed then kissed her good-bye. He got as far as the jeep before curiosity got him.

Lying Still

I'm lying still and I sense you're there
Your fingers all over, touching everywhere.
I feel your strength, I feel you inside
You're taking me someplace insanities hide.
On top of me now, you feel big and strong
You're making me open, and you're taking control
The deeper you're able, the deeper you'll go
'cause you have the power, and I can't say no.
Giving me all and everything that you've got
I feel you inside me, so warm and so hot.
I'm lying still now, I'm sweating and wet
It's four thirty a.m. And you're not home yet.

Where are you, what are you doing, and who
    are you doing it with?

Qua turned the key in the ignition and went to work. Happy.

Gena called Tracey to see if she wanted to go with her to the mall. She and Tracey had become good friends since Sahirah's passing. The girls talked for a few minutes before Gena left to pick her up.

They went to the Gallery Mall in Center City, something Gena did every day and never got bored with. The established department stores were connected under the ground. It was many shops in a spacious wonderland. It was like a shopping amusement park, and it felt real good to be able to buy whatever she wanted. She picked out a lounging robe for Gah Git and paid for a belt Tracey was admiring. Quadir now had a dozen more pair of polo boxers, and Gena got a couple bottles of perfume for herself and her cousin Brianna. Her only choice was to buy a fragrance she didn't already have.

After leaving the mall, Gena went to Gah Git's house. She was so happy to see her grandmother and fell right into her arms. Of course, Gah Git was always glad to see Gena.

"How's my baby? Come on in here and sit down. Where's Qua? How's he doing?" Gah Git was asking questions so fast, Gena hardly had a chance to answer.

"Quadir is fine. He's at his store."

"How are you, Tracey?" Gah Git said, finally acknowledging her.

"I'm fine. How are you?"

"Oh, I'm pretty good. My leg hasn't been bothering me, praise the Lord."

"Gah Git!" Gena hollered her name so loud, she scared her grandmother half to death. Gena remembered the packages and headed for the door. "I got you something from the mall. It's in the car."

"What's the matter with her? Child scared me half to death." Pausing she waited a few seconds and then asked, "Gena know about the party?"

"No, she's worried Quadir has forgotten her birthday," Tracey said.

Gena came running back in. "Here you go, Gah Git."

Gah Git's face lit up at the contents in the bag. "Oh, Gena, baby, thank you! It's so nice. I can't wait to wear it tonight. You hungry?"

"No."

"What about you, Tracey?"

"No, thanks."

They both turned their heads to the clatter on the porch and the opening screen door.

Bria and Brianna, Gena's twin cousins, came bursting into the house. They were drop-dead gorgeous, wore their long hair in wraps just like Gena, and were identical except for a mole on Bria's right ear lobe, plus she had larger feet. Gena couldn't stand Bria and Bria couldn't stand Gena.

"Brianna, I got you something."

Taking the bag Gena handed her, Brianna exclaimed. "I been wanting this for so long. Thanks, Gena. Do you think you can loan me twenty dollars?"

"What you trying to do?" asked Gena.

"Nothing. I just need twenty dollars. Come on, please?"

"Here," said Gena, handing her a twenty-dollar bill.

Bria was mumbling something under her breath. She could not stand it when Gena came around. Everybody acted like she was some goddess. With the presence of her archenemy now full faced, Gena decided to leave. She dropped Tracey at home then found Quadir engaged in a craps game on the corner of the Av. After Quadir lost a couple thousand right quick, Gena followed him to his new store. It was a nice corner storefront property. Quadir sat and told her his plan of opening up a beauty salon. Gena worried for a minute but soon realized that her man was all about her. "This is for us. This beauty salon is for you. I want you to decorate it and run things for me. Run the business, our business. So, you down, or what?"

"You know I am, baby. I love you, Quadir," she said kissing her man.

"Come on, let's go celebrate our new beauty salon. It's your birthday, right?"

"Where will we go?" she asked, happy he hadn't forgot her.

"I don't know. Let's go get dressed and go to dinner."

Once they got home, Quadir just stood there looking at Gena. She was as beautiful as the night he met her on 125th Street in Harlem.

"Something the matter?"

"I don't know if I should give you your birthday gift now, or if I should wait until tomorrow."

"You know, I was beginning to think you had forgotten."

"Me forget and have to hear that shit forever? Besides, I know how nice you perform when I remember holidays, birthdays, the day we met, the day we first did it. You know, all your reasons to get a gift."

"Qua, please, you're exaggerating. Now, where is it?" She looked a little possessed as he stood there picking the dirt from under his fingernails. "Quadir, don't mess with me."

"Just pretend you're coming through the front door." She went into the vestibule that connected to the hallway, which spread throughout the rooms of the first floor. On the marble table, placed on the marbled floor near the doorway sat a 5 by 10 professional picture of them, a candy dish, and a crystal vase with red and white roses in it. Quadir would buy her two dozen roses every week, which she placed in the same crystal vase week after week. Gracing the upper corner of the 5 by 10 picture was a twenty-four-karat gold and diamond bracelet designed with carat diamond charms, giving it a total weight of twelve karats.

Gena delicately removed the charm bracelet from the picture, adoring it like it was the Holy Grail. "It's the most beautiful thing I've ever seen. I love it. It's so blue," she said, trying to get the bracelet on.

"Here, let me help you," he said, fastening the clasp for her.

"So blue," she said, marvelling at the radiant colors that were bouncing off the chandelier.

"I got you something else upstairs."

"Kiss me." Letting him go was so hard to do. Pulling from her, he held her hand and walked her upstairs.

It didn't take her any time to open the boxes and find a black Versace pantsuit, a pair of gator boots, and a black Chanel bag with thick gold Cs on the side.

Both of them dressed in black Versace and black gator boots, then arrived at the Malibu Dining Room. Quadir informed the hostess that their reservation was for Richards. She grabbed two menus and escorted them away from the dining room downstairs to the lower level.

The entire lower floor was quiet. As the hostess opened two large double doors, everyone stood simultaneously and yelled, "Surprise!" They'd only been waiting about forty-five minutes. For the first five minutes, Gena was inundated with people in her face wishing her: "Happy birthday! Happy birthday!" All of her girlfriends were there, as if they would really miss a free meal. All she could do was stand beside her man and take it all in.

"How much did this cost?" she whispered in his ear.

"I don't know. I haven't gotten the bill yet."

She spotted Gah Git, her cousins Bria and Brianna, and Gary all ready to eat, too. All of Qua's friends were there, which meant all the players were in the house. Everybody was determined to make this a good one. As Gena's girlfriends began standing around her, Quadir drifted off to find Rik.

"Come look at the bracelet this bitch got on!" said Andrea, dragging Bridgette over to see it, who after a glimpse, was as astonished as Andrea.

Looking across the room, Gena spotted Quadir and Forty

surrounded by some girls, but didn't pay it any mind. Rik and his wife Lita walked over to where Gena and her girlfriends were standing.

"What's up, Rik?" said Veronica. The hair on Lita's back stood straight up.

Lord, thought Gena, *they gonna tear this motherfucker up tonight on my birthday!*

"How you doing, Veronica?" he said.

Lita spoke up. "Why are you talking to her? Do you know her?"

Lord, here it comes, thought Gena.

Rik tried damage control. "Lita, all the girl said was hi."

"Whatever. Happy birthday, Gena." She leaned forward, kissed Gena on both her cheeks and said, "I hope you like it." Then Lita walked away. Gena would have never walked away. Rik looked better than he ever looked in his entire life. Or, maybe it was the diamonds blinding everyone, since Rik wasn't the most handsome man in the world. Yeah, it must have been the rays of light emanating from his body.

They all stared unbelieving as Veronica turned her venom on him and whispered in his ear, "What happened? I still want my abortion money, or your bitch is gonna find out how her man spends his spare time."

"See, that's why I got nothing for you. And even if you did tell Lita, she'd just kick your ass and still stay with me." Rik stood his ground with Veronica, leaving everyone else standing still trying to figure out what the hell she whispered in his ear. Unfazed, he turned to Gena.

"Happy birthday, G." He kissed her cheek and handed her a small ribboned box.

"Thank you."

"No problem," he told her, rolling his eyes at Veronica before returning to Lita's side.

Everyone near was eager to see what was in the box, reaching their hands out as she opened it. She glowed as she felt the envy.

"It's so nice. A diamond initial pin. G. For Gena."

"That is nice," said Andrea.

"It sure is," added Bridgette.

"Let me go thank Lita and show Gah Git," Gena said, playing the perfect hostess. "Excuse me."

Gah Git was overwhelmed. "Oh, Gena! Look at you. Look at that!" Her eyes roamed all over her fine granddaughter, taking in the bracelet, the pin, and Gena's beauty. "That Quadir is a good man. You take care of him, you hear me, girl?"

"Gah Git, I am taking care of that man. Until the day I die, I'm gonna take care of him." Hugging her grandmother, she asked, "Where are the twins?"

Looking about for the girls, Gah Git noticed a bit of commotion across the room. "What's going on?"

"I don't know. I can't see."

Across the floor, Rik and Quadir were wrestling with the girl Quadir and Forty had been talking to earlier. Before Gena could get a glimpse of the whole picture, the girl had been ushered out of the dining area by the staff.

"What's happening?"

Gena touched her grandmother's shoulder and told her, "I don't know, but I'll find out."

Approaching Quadir, she asked, "What's going on?"

"Nothing."

Why the hell does he always say nothing, when it's perfectly clear something is going on. "Q, aren't you gonna tell me what happened?" Rik jumped in, asking her how she liked the pin.

"I love it, Rik. Look, Quadir, did you see the pin Rik and Lita got for me?"

"Let me see."

She showed him the pin and let him kiss her, waited a moment longer, then asked, "So, are you gonna tell me who that girl was?"

"That bitch followed me here and was questioning Quadir about me. Qua told her that I didn't want to fuck with her like that and she got mad."

Quadir broke in, glad that Rik had lied for him. "She's a stalker." He added, laughing weakly, "Rik, I don't know how you do it."

Rik finished the lie. "You're not gonna tell Lita, are you?"

As the men lied to Gena, others were watching the girl through the window.

"Look, that girl is staring at Quadir," said Tina.

Gina noticed, "Look, Bev. Look out the window."

Beverly took a good look. "Damn, she looks like she's about to cry. Don't she?"

Once the girl realized she'd been recognized, she hurried away.

"Bitches are so desperate," said Bev.

"She straight played herself," said Tina.

"I know. Did you see them haul her ass out of here?" asked Gina.

"So embarrassing," said Tina, shaking her head.

Bev was savoring the gossip. "Wait til I get back in the hair salon. You know, she the one who is supposed to have the baby by Quadir, but don't say nothing."

"We won't." Tina and Gina gave each other a knowing glance.

Gena was across the room greeting everyone. She finally saw her cousins, Bria and Brianna. Quadir was busy introducing his friends to Gena's friends, trying to hook everybody up. Gena couldn't believe the number of people surrounding her.

"Tonight's the night," whispered Rik.

"Rich Green?" asked Qua.

"Yes."

Quadir was thoughtful. "You know Jerrell isn't gonna like this."

"I know, let him bring the noise. He started this shit. He's been fucking up my pockets for the longest. Enough is enough. He pushing every motherfucker I know not to buy coke from me. You know how many bricks I can't get rid of because of him?"

"You, what about me?"

Quinny Day showed up at their table. "Yo, this was really nice, man. I can't stay for dessert, but I just wanted to let you know this was real smooth, Ock."

"Where you got to go, Quinny?" asked Rik feeling a heavy weight of frustration just seeing Quinny's happy face.

"Nowhere. I just got to meet this girl. She's going back to Connecticut and, you know, I'm just saying good-bye to her tonight, if you catch my drift."

"I hear you, player," said Quadir.

Rik spoke up. "When you gonna have my money, Quint?" He'd given Quinny two keys three weeks ago and was starting to wonder when he was going to get paid.

"Nigga, I got you. Don't sweat that shit, baby. Be cool. I got you." Tyrik just shook his head, watching Quinny mingle himself away in the crowd. Wasn't nothing he could do with the boy. Quinny Day never had his money. If he weren't Lita's cousin, he'd have had him knocked off.

"Why do I continue to even ask that motherfucker for my money? Do you know what he owes me? Them motherfuckers Lita's related to are a trip."

"Rik, I want to get out of this shit," Quadir said.

"Out of what?" Rik had no idea what his mentor could be talking about.

"The game. This shit is too much for me. I want to sit at home instead of hustling out here in these streets."

"I know that's right. The motherfuckers is passing out time like it's government cheese."

Qua turned to face him. "I don't know what I'm going to do. Cherelle calls the house and she follows me around. The bitch is a fatal attraction."

"You played it real cool, though. You didn't even blink when you seen her walking over to you."

"Shit, I wanted to run my ass the fuck out of this motherfucker, but Gena's nosey-ass girlfriends would've had something to say."

"Those bitch-ass girlfriends she got. How do you take it? I done fucked almost all of them." Qua's eyebrows went up at the revelation and Rik warmed to his subject. "The only one I was really fucking with though was that Veronica bitch, and she tried to baby trap me, man."

"Yeah, right. I heard."

"I admit I was sweating the girl back in the day, but sis wouldn't give me no play, then I got a little paper. You know, became the man, and who do you suppose was on my dick?"

"Veronica."

"I been playin' that bitch ever since." The brothers clinked their glasses and drank. On the table sat two bottles of Dom and one bottle of Remy XO.

Gena took advantage of a lull in her own conversations to look around. The Malibu Dining Room was fabulous. The only thing missing was Sahirah. Her pretty face, her small frame, and her warm smile. If only she was there with her. She's the one that pulled over Rasun that day in Harlem. If it hadn't been for her Gena wouldn't be standing there, portraying the perfect queen of the crack stars. "Sahirah," she mouthed. *I miss you so much,* she thought. Not a day would pass without Sahirah being in her thoughts. She held her glass up, and there was Sahirah with her. *A toast for old times,* thought Gena. She toasted to the memory of her best friend.

"Hey, Gena. Happy birthday," Black said, trying to figure what she was staring at.

"Hi. Where's Pam?"

"Home with the kids. Where's Q?"

"See him? He's over there, at that table in the corner," she said, pointing as Black brought Rik and Quadir into view. As soon as he had left, she heard someone singing, "It's your birthday, happy birthday, it's your birthday."

"Charlie tuna, you're so crazy."

"Yo, Gena. You think you can hook me up?"

"Hook you up how?"

"I'm trying to see your girlfriend."

"Who?"

He suddenly noticed her wrist. "Goddamn! That motherfucker is all that."

"Isn't it?"

"You playin' with this piece right here. This is some real high-powered shit. Damn, let me step the fuck back!" She stood there laughing and smiling as Charlie gassed her head up. Finally getting back to the point of why he stepped to Gena, he asked, "Are you gonna hook me up or not?"

"Hook you up with who?"

"Baby, it don't matter. Give me a quiet one. Y'all women got too much mouth these days, always yappin'. Give me one that don't talk."

"What? We're not supposed to talk?"

"Yeah. When somebody says something to you."

Charlie spotted a girl who attracted him. "Hook me up with her?"

Gena smiled. Charlie had chosen Bev from LeChevue and she never shut up. "Beverly." Gena took her girlfriend's hand and made a complete introduction. She left them there to talk as she walked over to Quadir. Coming up behind him, Gena put her arms around him, bent down and started licking his ear. "I'm ready to go home," she whispered.

They began to say good-bye to everybody who'd come out to get a free lobster and champagne meal. Qua told her, "I'll be back. I'm going to take care of the bill so we can go home." Gena turned to see Andrea watching her slink into her to-the-floor mink.

"You leaving?"

"Yeah, we're going on home."

"I know you've had a happy birthday, and the shit ain't until tomorrow."

"Yes, this is true." She jingled her bracelet for Andrea. "Qua really surprised me. First the bracelet, the outfit, and to top it off, dinner with all our friends. This was enough."

"You're so lucky."

"I'm blessed."

Rik was just hanging up the pay phone outside the dining room. "Yo, check it out." He pulled Quadir over to him. "Rich Green is no longer a member of the life force as it exists on this earth."

"Dead?"

"Through the heart and through the head. Nigga said since he fucked his baby mom, he shot him in the dick too."

"Damn."

"Quadir, don't look so sad, 'cause the nigga was plotting. Always riding around the same corners, all damn day and night. Trust me, the boy Rich had a list. Junie was locked up with my brother and told him everybody was on the list. Shit, the nigga's list was so long, by the time the Junior Mafia finished, it wouldn't be nobody left."

Quadir said good-bye to Rik and shook hands with a few other brothers before finding Gena. Getting into the car Gena looked at her man. "I can't believe you did all of this for me."

"Gena, tonight was nothing compared with what I have in store for us. This is just the beginning."

THE CHEDDAR WILL BE BETTER

Qua sat in the living room of his secret hideout, and placed the counting machine on the table. Pulling a chair, he organized all the money in the safe. He plugged the counting machine into a socket, sat back, and watched it do its job. Two hours later the total was looking him in the face. *Got to be a mistake,* he thought. But, there was no mistake. He was speechless. The machine totaled his money at 17.2 million dollars. "I'm a millionaire," he said to the fish in the tank. He had an idea but had never counted the money that was in the safe. He wanted to jump, shout, knock himself out!

Then he sat down and began counting it again. The total was the same. He ran his hands through the bills, stuffing them into his pockets, his shirt, his baseball cap, in his jeans, all hundred-dollar bills.

In front of the mirror, seeing all these green pieces of paper falling out of his clothing, he thought to himself, *All that money. Drug money! There's a lot of paper in the ghetto.*

Quadir sat back and looked at all the stacks of money surrounding him. The years of hustling had paid off. People spend their entire lives working to retire and still don't have shit. Quadir, on the other hand, had hustled for five years, and could retire at the age of twenty-five a millionaire, never working an honest day in his life. He sat down on the sofa in the sea of money scattered around him. It made him nervous. For the first time, he saw his wealth and for the first time, he saw what he really was: a drug dealer. He knew it was wrong. All that he did for the hustle was a constant reminder of his own greed. Down to his last 200 kilos of cocaine, he didn't want to purchase any more. For $3,800 a kilo, who wouldn't? But with seventeen million staring down your throat, why? He was not thinking of finances. He was thinking about the Junior Mafia. He knew that it was a matter of time before he was a direct target. Things were getting real complicated in the streets. The police were downright dirty. They would stick you up, set you up, and give you a case.

The brothers were just as bad. Everybody had guns. Everybody. Even little kids had guns. Your life meant nothing. It was all about money, who had it and who didn't. Not only had Quadir beat the odds, but also lived to tell about it, not owing any debts and not owing any favors. That in itself was a task, as most of Quadir's friends were dead or in jail.

He thought of Tony Santero and the Cartel. He thought of Barranquilla, Colombia and Carlos Escobar. He met Tony's uncle, Carlos Escobar, only once. Carlos was so captivating, even with his intense dislike for the United States. Quadir totally enjoyed his conversation. The man had everything he wanted and desired at his fingertips. Tony's mother was an Escobar. She married a Santero and had three sons. Two of the sons and her husband were killed in a boating accident on the Panama Canal in 1968, when Tony was a little boy. She and her only son then moved with her brother, Carlos. Carlos raised Tony like his own son. He turned over some of the family affairs to Tony, who took on the responsibility of serving the United States. Through governmental and diplomatic contacts, Tony was free to serve countries. Carlos had two brothers and three sons all of whom controlled and shared the Colombian drug profits.

After Quadir understood the trade game, he understood who had the power. It definitely was not the brothers. The brothers got caught up too, but not just them. It seemed like everyone was getting high. The upper class, not just the poor, contributed and depended on it. He thought of the sisters who were out there using and selling their bodies for a gusto, the brothers and sisters who were robbing their own mothers and grandmothers. He thought of his financial destiny: matches torn in two. He thought of the seventeen million dollars. Shit was too good to be true.

How could he stop? How could he tell Tony? What would he say? What would he do? For three weeks, Quadir continued business as usual. Dropping his price down to ten thousand dollars a kilo. Everybody and their mother was trying to see Rasun and Reds, who had basically taken over the Av. Quadir couldn't figure it out. Seemed like out of nowhere, not only were they selling his shit, but also buying shit from him and doing their own thing. Rik and Forty were tearing up the drug game down Richard Allen. After the death of Rock, Rik and Quadir paid out two hundred thousand dollars to have five members of the Junior Mafia assassinated. Within the past three weeks in the city there had been twelve drug-related murders, all of which directly involved the Junior Mafia.

Quadir was tired of the small circuit. He was tired of the drug game. He wanted to not have to walk or drive so fast. He didn't want to look over his shoulder or peek around corners. He was ready to take his money and sit back, enjoy life.

Finally, Qua paged Tony and sat back and waited. An hour later, Tony Santero was telling him that he would be there in three more weeks.

"That's what I was calling to speak to you about."

"Is there something wrong, Quadir?"

"It's like this. I'm not going to re-up."

"What? What the hell do you mean, retire?"

"What I said, Tony. I'm done, man. I'm finished. I can't take it anymore. This shit is really starting to get to me. It's like, every day and every night, I got people chasing me down. Gimme this and gimme that. And then there's the Junior Mafia. They been knocking off my family."

"Well, kill them back," Tony said, not understanding.

"Everyone is going for self. Things are changing. They are losing honor. Everybody's snitching now, and then there's Gena. I'm not spending any time with her. I want to retire alive."

"Yeah. Yeah, I know. That's one nice-looking girl you got there. She's real nice, man. You know I would love to fuck her."

"Yeah, but you can't, so why feel it?"

"See, that's the problem with you black guys. You don't like to share, do you?"

"I'll share some pussy with you, Tony. Just not that pussy."

"Well, are you sure that's what you want to do?"

"Yeah, I'm positive."

"Well, how can I say this? Um, you can't do nothing, man; you can't lie to me. But, if you're really stopping and you want out, then fine, okay. Give me five million dollars and you are free to go." Five million rolled out of his tongue behind the Colombian accent, as his voice grew stern. "And, remember, you're retired. I find out that you're lying to me, you know you'd be betraying me and my family. You know I'll know what you're doing?"

"Tony, on my life, you took care of me and you helped me. I would never cross you. Why not two?"

"No, for you, four million, Quadir, and no less."

"Three."

"Four."

"Three and a quarter."

"Three and a half and that's it."

"Okay, three and a half it is."

"Take it to the Princess docked at the harbor. Give it to my cousin Sancho; take his number."

Breathing easier, Qua thanked him.

"Keep in touch, Q, and remember what I said. You're retired."

Quadir separated three and a half million dollars, and put the rest back in the bags and locked it in the safe.

Gena was glad to be out of chemistry class and drove straight home. She marveled at the sight of Qua's keys on the vestibule table. "Quadir, are you here?"

"Yeah!"

"Where are you?"

"Down here!"

"What's up?"

"Come here, baby, we got to talk."

She joined him in the playroom, wondering what was up, and walked into his arms.

"I've been thinking lately, Gena. You know, I haven't been home a lot lately. I've been so busy taking care of business that I haven't been taking care of you."

True enough, thought Gena, taking a seat. *So, he's finally fessin' up about the bitch Cherelle.*

"I talked with Tony today. I told him I was done. Finished. Out of the game. The coke I got, I'm going to get rid of, and then that's it."

Gena couldn't speak, her mind racing to compute the implications of his retirement from the game. *Did I push him too far? Did I demand too much? Will they let him retire? Where will all that shopping money come from, if he stops?* She kept her cool and listened to him.

He slipped a small baby-blue box out of his pocket. He opened it and showed her the contents. "Will you marry me, Gena?" He took the ring out of the holder and slipped it on her finger.

"I have never seen a diamond this big before!"

"It's ten karats."

Gena was in shock. She couldn't believe he was coming at her with marriage.

"Gena, you haven't answered my question. Do you want me to get on one knee?"

"Qua, please," she smirked. "You would get on one knee?"

He bent his knee to the floor before her, and said, "Janel Louise Scott, will you marry me?"

"Quadir, please get up. You're going to make me cry."

"Not until you answer me, not until you say you'll marry me. You're all that matters to me, and I want you to be my wife."

His face told her this was not fun and games; he was serious.

"Yes, Quadir Montell Richards, I will marry you." She got down on her knees with him and put her arms about him.

The ringing phone broke the reverie. He smiled, watching her run upstairs as he picked up the phone.

"Hello?"

"I need some money for your daughter, Quadir," said a female voice.

"Look, don't ever call my home again," he said as he slammed the phone down. It immediately rang again.

"Hello."

"Don't fucking tell me not to call there, motherfucker. You got a child that you don't do shit for," said the girl.

"Look, Cherelle, if you need something for the baby, I will send it to you. I will call Rasun and he can bring you whatever you need."

"No bitch, you bring it. Rasun didn't fuck for this baby, you did."

"Who you think you're playing with?"

"Who am I talking to? Ain't nobody else on the goddamn phone."

"I told you if you need something, then page me. I'll see to it that you get it." He hung up as the phone rang.

"Bitch, stop calling my motherfucking house."

"Yo, Qua. Man, it's me, Rik."

"Oh. What up?"

"Damn, my brother havin' problems today?"

"Yeah, Cherelle. She is fucking with me again. She got the phone number somehow."

"How did she get the number?"

"I don't know. I don't know what to do."

"Now, you just calm down, partner. You'll be all right."

"What am I gonna do, Rik?"

"Get a motherfucking blood test. You the only one who thinks the baby is yours."

Qua hadn't heard Gena return. "Quadir, I'm gonna take a shower, want to come?"

"No, baby, I'm on the phone."

"Who's that? Gena?" Rik asked.

"Who else is going to be up in my house?" asked Qua.

Rik started laughing at him. "All these ho's runnin' around talking about it's Qua's baby, shit, you might got Virgin Mary up in that motherfucker. How the fuck am I supposed to know?"

Gena was still trying to entice Qua. "Okay, if you don't wanna shower with me, you're gonna miss out," she said, dropping her robe in front of him on the way to the bathroom.

When she was gone, he turned back to the phone. "Rik, I asked Gena to marry me."

"What, Qua? You getting married, man?"

"Yeah. I'm gonna have a big wedding."

"Well, what's up? I'm waiting."

"Oh, yeah, and I want you to be my best man."

"That's because you know I am the best nigga out here."

"You gonna be my best man or what?"

"Oh, nigga, stop bitchin'. You know I got your back. However, there is a problem."

"What?"

"You selling keys for five thousand is the motherfucking problem, man."

"I'm not selling them for no five. I'm selling them for 10."

"What's the fucking difference. How is you playin' with this ten shit."

"Look, me and Gena are about to go to Atlantic City. When

I get back I'm gonna come and see you. I got something for you."

"When are you coming back?"

"I'll be back later on tonight and then we'll talk."

"Pick me and Lita up some Gucci sneakers while you down there."

They gave each other the salaams and hung up the phone.

While Quadir and Gena were walking on the Atlantic City boardwalk waiting for their dinner reservation, the Junior Mafia was having a meeting in the southwest part of the city. Jerrell was pacing a trail in his peach carpet, talking on the phone.

"I don't understand why no one is buying weight! And no one knows why?" he asked as he stared around the room using his eyes to demand an explanation.

Finally, someone spoke up. "No one is buying. For the past three days, no one has called or needed anything, or nothing."

"Khyree, I figured that out since none of ya'll motherfuckers got my money."

Jordan looked at Jerrell. "No one is buying weight."

Jerrell looked at all of them as if they were thieves. "Well," he finally asked, "who owes us money?"

"No one from this end owes anything," said Khyree.

"The caps are moving, but the bricks are just sitting there," said Mont.

"Well, do something about it!" Jerrell shouted.

"What do we do?" said Khyree.

"Figure it the fuck out. Somebody got it. They're getting coke from somewhere. It's not like motherfuckers stopped getting high," said Jerrell.

Ran arrived, gave and received acknowledgment of his presence as Jerrell continued.

"Ran, where the fuck is Reece and Derrick?" Jerrell did not like anyone to miss his shareholders meetings. He felt it was important. It brought everyone in the Junior Mafia together. The meetings were short but informative, or at least Jerrell thought so. After everyone left, Jerrell paged Reece, then Derrick. He was really starting to worry, not so much about them, but about the five bricks and three million dollars they were carrying. A few minutes of pacing, with Ran right behind him, Jerrell spoke again. "You know, I really don't like this shit. Somebody that gets rid of ten kilos every day ain't moved a motherfucking thing all week."

"Who?"

"Khyree," he said, walking out of the room.

Ran, following, asked, "Well, why not?"

"I don't know."

Mark picked up the ringing phone. "Yo, man, where you at?"

It was Skip. "I'm at the hospital. You not gonna believe this shit. The cops just brought Reece and Derrick here. I saw them pull them from the back of a fucking paddy wagon. The cops are everywhere. I got to get out of this lobby and get back in the room with my girl."

"Yo, Skip, hold up. Jerrell wants you."

Taking the phone, Jerrell inquired of Skip, "What the fuck is going on?"

"The cops just brought Derrick and Reece in here. Man, get somebody down here. My girl just went into delivery. I'm saying, it fucked me up, Ock. I don't think Reece is gonna make it. Call Reece's girl and get her ass down here. I got to go."

The news spread through the city like wildfire. Jerrell's right-hand man, Reece, was dead. Derrick was listed in critical condition, however, and would be arrested upon his recovery. Reece and Derrick led a high-speed chase through the city, fatally shot a police officer, and wounded another. They got away, then crashed into a wall on Lincoln Drive. The police did not call for an ambulance; they just threw the bodies in the back of a paddy wagon, hoping they would die. The Volvo they were driving was taken into custody. The police reportedly found two guns, five kilos of cocaine, and one million dollars.

TONIGHT'S THE NIGHT

Things changed, and they changed real fast. Quadir met with Rik and decided to hand him the rest of his cocaine supply in exchange for a quarter of a million dollars. He arranged for Reds and Rasun to do business directly with Rik. Amar and the other brothers he dealt with were free to do as they pleased; but Rik's price was better than Quadir's, so the money stayed in the family.

Then there was Gena, who was becoming unbearable to deal with. She knew something was going on, but she didn't know what it was. Quadir wondered if the gossip about Cherelle having his daughter was in the street. He figured it was—that was why she asked him. She came right out one night after dinner and asked whether he had a daughter by the girl, and he told her no. That was all she wanted to hear and left it alone. Why hadn't he said yes? He wished he could have freed his conscience. Instead he went out and bought her a baby-blue Mercedes-Benz 300 CE with a license plate tag that read "MY CE."

Cherelle, on the other hand, continued to dare him. Fuck me, suck me, and give me loot or if you don't I'm gonna tell. Quadir was tired of dealing with her. He knew he could not take much more. He was gonna tell Gena. The only problem was what Gena would do.

The worst thing he did was get Gena the car. She didn't know how to act now, gone all the time. He had to get her a pager shortly thereafter, just to keep up. Every time he paged her, she was at the mall or on her car phone—never home.

"Hey, baby. What are you doing?"

"Oh, nothing, shopping. Meet me at the party 'cause I'm not coming home to get dressed. Got to go. Quadir, I need another cellular battery."

And with that Gena was out spending drug money, keeping the economy alive. Nine thousand here, another eight thousand there. She just shopped. Anything that was more than ten thousand had to have Quadir's approval and his credit card, but don't think it could not be obtained. Gena picked up both Lita and Tracey and headed to Black's party. She had already told Quadir to catch a ride with Rik so she could hang with the girls.

Lita couldn't get over the ten-karat diamond engagement ring. Quadir had really outdone himself. Tyrik told her it was ten but hearing about it and actually seeing it was two different things. She herself had a four-karat diamond, and once Rik told her about Gena's ring, Lita told him to upgrade her shit and make it snappy.

"Do you see all this attention we are getting just from this car?" asked Tracey.

"No, do you see these motherfuckers staring with no understanding?" asked Lita.

"Mmm, hmm." Gena already knew and understood the attention her man got in the street. What she didn't understand was why he lied about it and kept her in the dark.

"Quadir is so good to you. I hope I find a man that buys me shit like this," whined Tracey.

"This is Quadir's conscience. He feels sorry. He knows he's fucked up and that it's only a matter of time. He buys me shit to make himself feel better. That's why he went out and got this car, to try to make up for some shit he can't even confess."

"Make what up?" asked Tracey.

"Cherelle and her baby."

"When did you find out?" asked Lita,

"I found out four days ago. Why didn't you tell me?"

"Bitch, Rik was gonna kill me. I got a home too. Don't think I didn't want to tell you, and I was going to. It's just that if you and Quadir broke up because of something I said, Tyrik and Quadir would blame me. Besides Gena, did that motherfucker get you ten karats, or what? Did he ask you to marry him? Please. Fuck Cherelle and her baby. That nigga don't want that broke bitch. Rik said the bitch ain't nothin' but a whore and Quadir can't stand her. Rik fucked her too. Don't feel bad. Mmm, hmm, Rik said they both fucked her. I think they did the jawn together."

Gena just looked at Lita. She hated the way she knew everything and could just hold it inside. Gena's motto was "Tell me, 'cause I'm telling it all." In Gena's mind, the fact that Quadir would not tell her could only mean that he was still fucking with Cherelle. Gena was scared of losing him, the house, ring, Mercedes-Benz, and all. A baby was a bond, and Gena didn't have that with him. She was jealous. What ifs popped through her mind. Quadir telling her he was leaving her. Gena couldn't take that. She would probably faint or beg him not to leave. She didn't want him to be with Cherelle, and she didn't want Cherelle to have any money either, but she knew Cherelle existed before her. And Cherelle had a baby.

The other side said fuck it. He wants the bitch, then he can have the bitch. That was tough because not only would she give up her man, but also her lifestyle. Gena wasn't about to lose Quadir. She would fight for him to the end. Wasn't no way she was gonna give up all the shit that made her life happy. He was hers. He'd asked her to marry him.

"Quadir had a baby with someone else?" asked Tracey.

"Who do you think we are talking about?" asked Gena.

"Quadir got a baby by Cherelle?"

For some reason, Tracey kept asking the question over and over.

"That little tramp had the nerve to name it Quanda," Gena seethed. "Quadir must be out of his mind or just stupid if he thinks I don't know what the fuck is going on."

"I seen her too, the other day. She did have a baby with her," said Tracey.

"Did you see it?" asked Gena.

"No, I didn't see the baby. I wonder do it look like him," said Tracey, passing the spliff to Lita.

"Shit, it ought to look like him as much money as he gives the bitch."

"Damn, look at all those people waiting to get in!" They had reached the club and smoothly pulled up to the entrance to take a look.

"Well, you know everybody was going to come out to Black's party. You know how it is."

"I hope we can get in," said Tracey.

"We will," said Gena parking the car.

The girls turned the corner and walked down the street. People were everywhere. "Is this the club Sahirah was at?" asked Gena.

"No, she was at Chances," responded Lita.

"Rasun," Gena called out his name, spotting him walking down the street with Reds. "What's up?"

"Nothing, baby. Just came to do my thang, you know what I'm saying? I'm trying to meet one of your girlfriends. What's up with that?"

"Here, meet Tracey."

"Damn baby, you looking mighty good tonight."

"Where's Quadir?" asked Gena, seeing that Tracey didn't seem interested.

"I don't know. I haven't seen him."

"Him and Rik are probably inside," said Lita.

"Come on," he said as he ushered everyone to the door. He told the bouncer, "They wit me, boss," who stood aside, admitting them without hesitation. Once inside, Rasun asked the women, "You all right now?"

"Yeah, where you going?"

"I'm gonna mingle and jingle," he said, looking at Tracey as if she didn't know what she was missing.

Gena and Lita went looking for Quadir and Rik while Tracey talked to some guy she knew from junior high.

Gena led the way through the crowd, bumping into someone who she knew every step of the way. "Damn, everybody in here or what?"

"Yeah. It looks like the crew is in the house," said Lita.

"Hey, Gena baby," said Quinny Day, giving her a hug. "Hey, Lita baby," he said, doing the same thing to her. "Goodness gracious, the Lord has truly blessed us all when he put y'all on the face of the earth. God bless America!"

"Quinny Day, what's up?" asked Lita.

"Nothing, baby. Just kicking it."

"You seen Quadir and Rik?"

"Yeah, they're downstairs all the way in the back at a table. Gena, do Qua know you're dressed like that?"

"Like what?" she said, looking down at herself.

"You're gonna hurt something, baby. You're definitely out to hurt something up in this motherfucker, and I got to get away from you, 'cause it's not gonna be me."

"Quinny Day, shut up!" she told him as she moved toward the stairs to go find Qua.

Everybody was in the house. Amin was sitting in a corner with a couple of bottles of champagne on his table, surrounded by at least five girls.

"Damn," said Lita, "You see how he's playing?"

"I see how Quadir's playing," said Gena, noting that Qua was talking to some girl. "Who's that?" she asked Lita.

"I don't know, but whoever it is, don't you start nothing in here tonight, you hear?"

Qua looked up, sensing Gena, and noticed that she didn't look too happy.

"Rik," he said nudging his friend. Rik spotted the girls and he turned to Black and started talking. Qua was getting frustrated with Cherelle. It was the same old thing.

"I'm your baby's mother and you don't do shit for me or your baby. I need some money."

"Look, I'll call you," Quadir said, walking away from her and heading for Gena.

"Who's that?" she asked, looking at Cherelle standing behind Quadir. Quadir had no idea the girl was right behind him. *Where is Tyrik? Why doesn't someone usher her away? Why does Gena look like that?"* thought Quadir feeling extremely uncomfortable as Gena stared at him and Cherelle.

"Gena, this is Cherelle. Cherelle, this is my wife."

"I'm his daughter's mother," said Cherelle, correcting Quadir.

"Oh, shit," said Lita. "Rik, go break it up before something gets started."

"Bitch, everywhere I am, you want to be. I know who you are. Quadir told me all about you."

"Whatever," said Cherelle, throwing her hand like Gena didn't know what she was talking about.

"So, what you want? He don't got nothing for you. How many times the motherfucker told you to stop calling our house?" Then Gena punched Cherelle in the face, grabbing her hair with her left and throwing nothing but rights. By the time Quadir and Rik stepped in, Gena had handled her business. Even after they had separated the shit and the music had stopped, you could still hear Gena, "Bitch, please. You one of them motherfuckers that need their ass whooped every day. Fuck with Quadir if you want to, bitch, and see what the fuck happens." All said in one breath ready to throw down again over the bullshit.

As the music returned and Cherelle was escorted away as usual, Quadir went to explain. The problem was that Gena didn't care. She would beat up Cherelle every day if she had to. Quadir knew he should have told her. Not only did he not tell her; he lied about the girl and the baby.

Quadir led her to the table and fixed her hair, poured her some champagne while attempting to explain. "I send the paper to her through Rasun. Don't think I deal with her, Gena. I can't stand the girl," he said shaking his head trying to figure out why Gena had to bring her Richard Allen bullshit to Black's party. He knew that shit was gonna happen sooner or later, though, and he was so glad Gena beat her up, he didn't know what to do. Cherelle made him sick, always taxing him. And wouldn't even let him see the little baby half the time.

"Quadir, I don't care. I can handle the truth. I can't handle lies. You put me on the spot. I should be able to handle a situation because you hipped me to it, not because I heard the shit through the grapevine. Ask you, and don't know what to believe. I can't believe you left me in the dark like that. I'm really mad at you. You should have gotten me a Rolls Royce for this shit. It would've gotten you out of the dog house a lot sooner than a CE."

"Gena," said Bridgette, walking over to the scene, "I'm so glad you didn't tear this motherfucker up."

"I don't know what ya'll gonna do with her simple ass," said Rik shaking his head.

"Put the bitch in the river," said Black.

"I tried to tell him," said Rik.

"Well, I'll be at Saks tomorrow getting over all this," Gena said, kissing him so that everybody would see that they were happy and nothing had changed.

Black wanted Rik and Quadir to come with him to the bar. It was too many girls crowding Lita and Gena. The guys understood. Everyone would be talking about that ass whoopin' for days to come.

Before he got up to go with his friends, Gena leaned over and whispered in Quadir's ear, "Is there anything else I should know about?" she asked calmly.

There's so much stuff you should know about, I wouldn't know where to begin, he thought to himself.

"No, and if there was, I would tell you," he said, ever so sincere. He got up to leave and Gena watched him as he walked across the floor.

"Damn, I love that motherfucker."

"We know, there's no doubt." Lita's sarcastic charm couldn't let that pass by.

"Well, I know everybody thought the house was coming down," said Bridgette.

"Shit, Gena did tear it down," Lita chimed in. "I'm glad Gena beat that bitch up, 'cause if she hadn't, it would have been a whole different story."

"Yeah. She dealt with the situation rather well, didn't she?" said Bridgette.

"Better than me, 'cause I would have killed the bitch," said Lita looking at Bridgette as if to say, Now try your luck with Rik. Gena left the table and followed Quadir.

Qua poured her a glass of Dom and walked her to a table, with Rik and Black opposite them ordering another bottle of champagne.

"It's crowded in here, Qua."

"I know. Too crowded for me."

"So, that is Cherelle," she said.

"Yeah, that's her."

"Well, she's better-looking than I thought."

"She don't look good to me, and I don't want to talk about her no more."

She wanted to have a good time and decided that, as the saying goes, there's no need crying over spilled milk. She kissed her man gently on the lips and went back to the table with Lita and Tracey.

A hush rustled through the club a minute or so later when Pam came in. Her entrance was definitely remarkable. Pam was sharp. She knew exactly what to do with Black's money. She wore it well. "Where's Bridgette, 'cause she could get her ass kicked next up in this motherfucker," whispered Lita, nodding Pam's way so Gena could see what she was talking about. "Mmm, hmm. That's another one that's gonna end up getting hurt for fucking with somebody's man. Shit, Bridgette gots to be crazy. Ain't no dick worth having to deal with Pam. I don't know how Black even find bitches crazy enough to fuck with him, 'cause Pam don't be bullshitting."

"Oh yeah, Pam rolls on motherfuckers about her man," agreed Gena.

"Shit, the motherfuckers been together since eighth grade."

"Where's Tracey?" Gena asked.

"She's over there talking to Muhammad," pointed Lita.

"Oh," said Gena. "Maybe I found her a friend."

"She looks like she needs one," said Lita, glad she didn't seem to have to worry about her fucking with Rik.

The guys had come back to the table with bottles of champagne. Black pulled out a spliff and started smoking it. Pam looked at him. "Black," she said, "you're not supposed to do that."

"Who paid here, Pam? Huh? Who?"

"You did, Black."

"Okay then," he said, passing it to Qua.

"Sit your Happy Birthday ass down, nigga," said Rik. "Didn't nobody ask you who paid."

Everybody was having a good time when Blair walked over to the table. He greeted everyone and gave his best wishes to Black.

"This is my wife, Blair. This is Gena."

"Oh! It's nice to meet you. Do you like your car?"

"I love my car. How do you know about my car?"

"He sold it to me," Qua told her.

"I suggested that he get that particular car. Do you like it?"

"Definitely," she cooed. "It's so blue."

"I know, I like that color." He didn't get it, but it didn't matter. Just then Andrea walked up to the table, as if she belonged.

"Girl, what are you wearing?" asked Gena.

"Looks like nothing to me," whispered Qua.

"Nigga, you better stop looking," said Gena with an evil glow.

"Do you like?" asked Andrea.

"Do you?" Gena hissed, nudging Lita under the table. Gena wanted Andrea and her see-through dress away from her man, far the fuck away. You could see, but you couldn't see. It was one of those dresses that would make you stare until you did see something. "Thank God it's dim in here," said Andrea.

"How could a person come out lookin' like that?" said Lita, challenging the girl.

Oh, shit, Gena thought. *Here goes Lita.* Qua was looking, everybody was looking, and Andrea just played it off all the while, deeply knowing that they were all jealous of her. She was body, and those bitches, especially Lita, were just jealous. Of course, Rik's slobbering on himself didn't help.

Kim, from out of nowhere, walked up to the table. "Andrea," she said, hugging her.

"Oh, no. They got to go away from here," said Lita with her eyes on Rik the whole time.

"So, Gena, what's up? How you been?" said Kim.

"Oh, I'm fine," she said, expressing just how fine she was with her left hand.

"I heard about you, Quadir. You naughty, naughty boy," she said, hitting his hand as if that was just punishment.

"I'm glad. I'm glad you know now, Gena."

This bitch is crazy, thought Lita, looking at Gena, silently asking her if she wanted to roll on 'em. To ease the tension Rik was feeling from these unwelcomed travelers of the night, he decided to add relevance. "Does anyone have the time?"

Everyone especially looked at him as if he were crazy. "Oh, I have a Rolex. I forgot."

"Damn Black, where's the food at?" asked Kim.

"It's over there," said Black, glad they'd gone over there before something was said and Pam came out her shit.

"That's Forty, right?" whispered Tracey, star bound.

"Yeah, that's Forty in the blue," said Lita. Pausing, she added, "I heard he got Richard Allen locked."

"I heard he got a nice shot," whispered Gena as she sipped her champagne.

"Mmm, hmm, I heard that shit too," said Lita looking at him, wondering if his dick was as big as everyone made it out to be.

"I heard Forty eats the shit out of some pussy, too," whispered Gena, knowing the rumors had to be true.

"Would you fuck him?" asked Lita as the girls looked Forty up and down.

"No," snickered Gena as Quadir wrapped his arm around her.

I would, thought Tracey to herself.

Oh, shit. There goes Jamal, Gena noted to herself. It had been such a long time since she had last seen him. Sahirah's funeral. That was the last time, as a matter of fact, with bitch-ass Kim on his hip. Gena just turned away and pretended she hadn't even noticed him. She didn't fool Qua, though. He saw everything.

Just then, Brother Ramier came by with greetings. "As-Salaamu Alaikum," said Brother Ramier.

"Alaikum As-Salaam," said Quadir, as the brother greeted Rik and Black. "How you doing, Bridgette?"

"Hi, how you doing, Ramier?"

Gena could tell something was up; Bridgette had too many skeletons in her closet for there not to be something going on. Rich Green, Charlie, Kevin, Coleone, Winston, Amar, Rock, Black, all the big boys, their brothers and cousins, the list went on and on.

Rasun and Reds came downstairs.

"Black, where did you get the girl in the see-through dress to do your party?" asked Rasun.

"I want her at my party," said Reds.

"I didn't get no naked lady," said Black, as if the young boys were bugging.

"They talking about that whore, Andrea," said Lita.

Gena started laughing. "She came like that, Rasun."

"Well, damn! I thought she was getting paid to wear that."

"My bucks, they've grown up, haven't they, y'all?" said Qua. Everybody toasted to Qua's squad of young boys.

"Damn, I really thought you paid a motherfucker to dress up like that," said Rasun.

"Maybe soon all of them will dress like that," said Reds.

"I hope so," said Ra.

"If you pay 'em enough, they'll do anything you want," said Ramier, looking at Bridgette, remembering the night he and two of his boys did her in a hotel room. Sis was a serious gun. He couldn't take his eyes off of her.

"Qua, come on. Let's go upstairs." Black and Rik got up from the table. "Q, you coming or what?" asked Black.

"Gena, stay here. I'll be right back," said Qua.

"Why do they always say stay here?" Gena asked Lita.

"They don't want you to follow them 'cause they don't want to get caught."

"I'm tired. What time is it?" Gena looked at her Rolex, answering her own question.

"What time is it?" asked Pam.

"It's four o'clock," she said, looking at her cousins standing over by the bar. "I'll be right back." She left the table and walked straight over to Bria and Brianna.

"What are you two doing here? How did you get in? You're only sixteen."

"We came with this guy," said Brianna.

"Bria, I don't know why you're standing there with an attitude. You should be at home. I can tell on you, you know," said Gena.

"You gonna tell anyway, 'cause that's how you roll. So what difference does it make?" she said, staring Gena eye to eye.

"Have you been drinking, Bria? Oh my God. Both of you have been drinking. You need to go home now," said Gena.

"Why? You go home," Bria said, as she walked away looking for her ride home.

"She got so much to say for someone who never says anything to me at all. She lucky I don't hurt her in here," said Gena.

"Gena, don't pay Bria no mind."

"Brianna, what are you doing in here? You're not supposed to be in no club. If Gah Git knew . . ." Gena didn't even want to think of what would happen to them. "I bet she knows you're not in the house and is worried half to death."

Suddenly, Gena thought she was in a western film in the middle of a cattle stampede. Her heart stopped as the sound of gunfire unleashed itself above. People were scrambling trying to find safety. *Bap, bap, bap, bap, bap, bap, bap, bap, bap.* Screaming could be heard above and below, and a mad rush for the lower level caused people to trample over one another and fall down the stairs. Gena grabbed Brianna's arm and took her behind the bar.

"Stay down!" she said as the girls huddled about for safety. The gunfire was ongoing, and Gena could distinguish the sounds of several different guns. It was true blue pandemonium. The music had suddenly stopped, and Gena realized that the quiet before the storm was the result of the DJ's panic in separating the plug from its outlet while scrabbling under his turntables in a move focused completely toward survival.

The lower level was now filled with all those who had been upstairs. A last shot was fired and silence reigned. Slowly, almost as one, the members of Black's birthday party began lifting their heads and looking about, but none moved as if to do so would violate the certainty the silence inspired. And through the silence, Gena heard her own certainty calling to her.

"Gena! Gena! Gena!" It was her man. He was covered with blood, but he was alive, and that was all that mattered.

"Quadir!" Gena popped up from behind the counter.

"Baby, come on! We got to get out of here!"

"I'm so glad you're okay, baby. I was worried. I was so scared! Qua, look at you. You didn't get shot, did you?" Qua seen that she was shaking as if a seizure was imminent.

"Gena, calm down." He suddenly noticed something wrong with the picture, as though anything could be wronger. "What are you doing here, Brianna?"

"I don't know, but this is not where I am trying to be," she said with a personable attitude.

"Qua, what happened?" Gena was still rooted to the spot as Pam and Lita ran over to them.

Lita's expression changed rapidly from hope to loss and back to hope again.

"Q, where's Rik?"

Quadir stopped, turned around to her, and took Lita by the shoulders. "Lita, Rik got hit. He's upstairs. Lita, I can't stay. You got to help Rik, baby. You got to stay with Rik and don't tell the police shit. Black got hit, too."

"What?" said Pam as she pushed her way to get to the stairs.

"Oh, my God! Qua, what is going on?"

"Gena, baby, I don't know."

"Is it safe to go outside?"

"Baby, I don't know. Where's the Benz?" asked Qua.

"On Market Street, two blocks down, right on the corner of Fifty-eighth."

"This is what I want you to do. Wait for me upstairs. Wait for me!" he said as they reached the top of the stairs. She handed him the keys. "Gena, stay inside."

"I will. Qua, please be careful, baby." Pam and Lita were frantically searching for Black and Rik among the bodies, lying under tables, or slumped in booths. Gena, surveying the carnage, couldn't believe what her eyes told her was the truth: there were five to ten people lying dead in pools of blood, others were hit and injured. Gena, unable to move, looked from one face to another, hoping to see Black or Rik.

Pam stopped dead, seeing the suit, knowing the shoes, recognizing the jewelry as her mind was telling her she'd found the one she searched for, her breath frozen in her throat. Finally, she screamed. "Omigod! No! No! Baby, please, no! Not Black!" Brianna was nauseous as Pam stood there looking at flesh parts covered in blood. But through the blood, the parts of his body that no one ever saw, the organs whose job it was to keep Black walking, talking, smiling, reproducing, thinking, and functioning under the covering of skin that protected them, were now outside his body. The skin blown apart by the force of the infrared glock .45 covered the walls. It looked as if the protective covering keeping everything together had been shredded off of him. He was gone, Black was gone. Gena heard another voice call out, "Omigod, Rik!" Lita was shouting, "Please! Where you at, man! Come on, Rik! Answer me!" at the top of her lungs.

Gena saw a chair moving, hope filling her and replacing the horror. "Lita! Over there!" She pointed toward the corner. It was him. It was Rik, under a table.

"Lita, don't move him. Wait for the ambulance. Don't move him."

Lita found her way to him. "Okay. Okay. Rik, baby, can you hear me?" She gently covered his hand with hers, continuing to murmur gently.

Pam was in shock, unaware of anything going on around her. People were trying to get out of there, giving thanks to God it wasn't them on the floor. As they glanced at the bodies and the blood, no one stopped to acknowledge the others who were looking for loved ones, friends, and grieving over what they found.

"Here's Qua," Brianna said, hanging out the doorway.

Gena looked at her friend, "Lita, I got to go." But Lita didn't respond, she took a deep breath, ordering herself to function. "Okay, Gena."

"Can you help Pam?" asked Gena.

"Pam? Pam who? My man might die, Gena. Shit, can she help me, 'cause Black is gone and I don't want to lose mines! Please don't leave me, Tyrik!" She held his hand and started crying. "Where the fuck is the paramedics?" she hollered.

Gena grabbed her friend's shoulder trying to calm her down before she left. "We'll page you." Brianna and Gena ran over to the Benz, where Quadir had the doors opened, ready to speed them away.

"Black is dead." At that moment, Quadir went cold. He couldn't think.

Dead? Black? He couldn't believe it. He didn't want to believe it.

"What happened, Qua?"

"I don't know. It happened so fast. They just started shooting at us! Damn, why Black and Rik?" he hollered as he pounded his fist on the steering wheel.

Together, Rik and he were standing on the wall directly across the bar where Black was. The mirrors on both sides of the wall bounced a red light. Rik watched the light as he told Quadir to look at it. The mirror told the ending before it even began. The light ended at Black. As soon as they called out to him, the bullets rang. Within seconds a bullet pierced Rik in the chest causing him to spin and take a hit in the back before falling down on top of Quadir. Quadir reached on the side of Rik for his gun. Tyrik used all his strength to grab his friends arm.

"Don't go up, Qua. If both of us die, who's gonna make it?" he asked, as they stared each other in the eye.

"You ain't gonna die. Stop fuckin' with me, baby." Quadir looked at his friend who was half on the floor, half on him. "Don't die on me, Rik."

Quadir wondered whether or not his friend was gonna make it. He was shot real bad. Checking the rearview mirror, his train of thought was completely interrupted. "What is Brianna doing here? Brianna, what do you call yourself doing? You're sixteen! You're not supposed to be out in no place like that! See what could have happened to you?" Gena had never heard Quadir use such force in his voice.

"I know," she sniffed. "I came with this guy, that's all."

"Who's the guy?" said Qua, ready to wring someone's neck.

"His name is Charlie."

Please don't let it be Quick Pockets Charlie, he thought to himself. "Brianna, you stay out of those kind of places until you're old enough to be in those kind of places, you understand? When you turn twenty-one, then you can go where you want. Until then, you need to keep yourself in the house where it's safe so you can get to be the age twenty-one."

"Don't worry. I will."

Just then a car pulled up along the opposite side of the street, and stopped in front of Gah Git's house. A few seconds later Bria hopped and ran up the door.

"What are you doing, Bria?" hollered Quadir, glad it wasn't Quick Pockets Charlie she was with.

"Shhh," she said turning around to see Quadir, Gena, and Brianna.

"Gena, I'ma kill 'em. Let me catch you out again, Bria," Qua fussed waiting for them to get in the door. He pulled the Benz off of Gah Git's block and went to a gas station. He drove on the sidewalk right up to the pay phone so that he wouldn't have to get out of the car. He dialed Rik's pager and within a few minutes Lita returned the call. She was frantic and Qua soothed her and told her he would be right there. He slid back into the driver's seat and sped away.

Lita was waiting for them in the hospital lobby. "Come on," she said. "They got him back here." She led them to a waiting room.

"Where's Black?"

"Black died, Qua. They was putting him in a body bag when the paramedics took Rik out."

"Where's Pam?"

"I don't know, but she . . . she was just standing there until the paramedics took her."

"They took Pam?"

"Yeah, they took her, too," said Lita. "I haven't seen Pam since we left the club. They let me ride in the truck with Rik while they brought him here. Qua, they was sticking him with all kinds of shit," Lita said, as she started crying. Quadir held her as Gena looked on, feeling horrible because they could do nothing.

"Lita, come on," said Gena putting her arms around her friend. "It's gonna be okay. Rik is gonna be fine. Rik is real strong and big. He'll pull through this."

"I know, Gena, but he was bleeding so bad, you know. What if he don't?" said Lita.

"You can't think like that. You gotta be strong, baby. You got to be strong for him."

"You call his mother?" asked Quadir.

"No. Not yet."

"Well, somebody has to call his family," said Qua.

"You can call them," said Lita, knowing once they got there they would take over. Qua left to find a phone and called Rik's mom. Within forty-five minutes his entire family had arrived. Gena curled up on a couch and fell asleep. Quadir consoled Rik's mother while she spoke to the Lord and told the hospital staff at the same time about her precious baby, how good he was, how the Lord couldn't take him, and begging the doctor to save her baby. Seven hours later, a doctor walked into the waiting room and called out, "Mrs. Smith?" expectantly.

Tyrik's mom was up like a shot. "Yes, doctor?"

"He's gonna be fine. We removed two bullets, and we moved him into ICU. He lost a lot of blood, but he's stable."

"So, he's okay?" said Mrs. Smith.

"Yes. In several weeks he'll be as good as new. I see no sign of any complications with surgery. The bullets were easy to remove and there was no damage to any of his organs, so he should be just fine. We'll be keeping a close eye on him for the next couple of days, but I'm sure he'll be just fine."

"When can I see him, doctor?" said Lita.

"Well, I think we should let his mother see him and then I think we should let him rest. He's heavily sedated. But tomorrow you can see him."

"Okay, okay," Lita said, upset she couldn't see her man.

"Oh, thank you. Thank you God, for saving my baby," said Rik's mother as she grabbed the doctor's arm.

"You're welcome," he said, liking this woman for recognizing him.

"Lita, come on," Qua said. "We're gonna take you home."

Quadir said nothing, just drove thinking about him and Rik laying on the floor in the club together. He was so greatful Tyrik was still alive. But thoughts of Black cut deep. He grew up with the man. It seemed like everybody he came up with was dying or in jail. He pulled up along side of Lita's Cadillac.

"Thanks," she said.

"We'll follow you home," said Qua.

After leaving Lita's mother's house, Quadir and Gena drove home. The ride seemed longer than before. Quadir's mind was racing over and over the minutes and seconds before the gunfire began. People who had looked at him real weird or the guy who bumped him. He was the guy shooting, too. The whole night was a setup. The entire night. The guys standing on the wall, with gators on, no women around, not partying or getting down. He saw all of their faces when the infrared light went on.

Gena knew the shit was out of control. She knew her man was not safe and neither was she. Both were touchable, both were accessible, and both could have anything waiting for them when they reached home.

She looked over at Qua; her man was in the zone. Her presence did not surround him, as it usually did. So she just let him sit. Sometimes it's better to just let a person be. No conversation, no radio.

As they pulled into the driveway of their lovely home, he finally asked, "Gena, what's it all for?"

"I don't know. I just don't ever want to lose you. Nothing is worth losing you for. Nothing."

"You'd give all of this up?"

"To be with you? Please. In a wink of an eye."

THE WAY PLAYERS PLAY

Jerrell Jackson was riding through Mt. Airy in his brand-new black Jaguar. Mafi-65, read the license plate. He had blown up, and in such a short period of time. He knew he was making enemies, but for some reason he didn't fear them or care.

He checked the time. *Forty-five minutes late,* he thought, thanks to some girl he ran across at the bus stop needing a ride. He gave her a ride, too. Went inside the house, talked to the girl for a few minutes, had his way with her, then stepped off into the sunlight. It didn't matter, though. Girls would sit around and wait for him all day if they knew he wanted to see them. And they did want to see him. Be it for the money, be it for his car, be it for who he really was: for whatever reason, they was trying hard to see the boy. Jerrell had a magnificent home up in Monticello County, complete with marble floors and waterfalls.

Jerrell pulled into the long, narrow driveway of perfectly landscaped grounds. Everybody was there. He could tell by all the foreign vehicles sitting in his driveway.

"Yo, I'm here," he said, coming through the door.

"What's up?" Khyree said. They were surrounding a pizza, which had just been delivered. Everybody shook hands, as usual, and Jerrell sat himself down and grabbed his slice.

"What's up?" Ran asked.

"Man, I don't know. You tell me."

"Everything is rolling smooth."

"Money's right," Sam added.

"People are buying weight," Ran informed.

"Everything is fine," said Khyree, taking a bite of pizza.

Jerrell finished the mouthful he had and told them about Quadir's retirement. "He was just trying to get rid of the last little bit of stuff he had. That's why wasn't no coke moving, remember? The motherfucker was selling keys for ten geez."

"Quadir ain't quitting, is he?" asked Ran.

"That's what the word is on the street." Jerrell took another bite.

"Now," he said standing up, "If Qua has stopped, that means you-know-who is going to take his place," he said, pointing at Ran.

"Rik!" Ran shouted, as if he scored points for the right answer.

"Exactly, which means Rik now has his, plus Quadir's piece of the pie."

"Rik supposed to be real upset about Black. He told Lita that we was behind it, so now she talkin' 'bout, don't call for awhile. She'll just bring Khyree to my mom's house. Man, I don't know what Rik is calling himself doing with my son, you know?"

"Wait a minute. What did he tell Lita?" Ran asked.

"He told her that we was behind Black's party and Black gettin' killed," said Khyree.

"Like he know something don't nobody else do," Ran laughed. "What else he say?"

"That's it. I doubt if he would tell Lita anything he was gonna do, with her having my son, you know," Khyree said.

"Man, he would tell her. The question is would she tell you?" Jerrell interrupted. Khyree just looked at him. Jerrell looked around the room like a general commanding an invasion. "Let's kidnap Forty." Jerrell waited for the repercussion.

"Kidnap! Why do you want to kidnap him?" Khyree asked.

"Who is running this shit?' Jerrell just looked at him. He hated the way Khyree always had something to say behind him.

Khyree, as well as the others, sat around in silence trying to figure out what Jerrell was talking about. There was no need in asking, 'cause if he wanted you to know he would let you know.

It was Christmas Eve. Club Phoenix was packed. Everyone was dressed to impress and the champagne was flowing. The night was going well. Rik was out with Lita, of course. Rik didn't travel far. Lita didn't let him. Amin and Zafa were there; Charlie and Forty were standing in a corner talking to Jamal and some girls. Rik couldn't help himself; he had to walk over. There were girls there. The Muslim brothers arrived like the mob in long coats and brim hats, surrounding Amin as if they were his bodyguards. Brother Ramzidin, Brother Ramier, and Brother Muhammad were all there. Winston and Blair were over at the bar. Tracey had called Gena to see if she was coming to the Christmas Eve party, but she and Qua had decided to spend the evening at home. Tracey, being as single as she was, couldn't have stayed away from that party if she wanted to. Everybody was there, even the city's football and basketball players. The radio personalities were transmitting live from the party. Andrea, Veronica, Bridgette, and Kim were standing together at the open champagne bar, trying to get with somebody else's man. Tracey knew Lita couldn't stand none of them, especially Veronica.

As the evening went on, everybody danced and had a good time. Lita mingled while keeping a real close eye on Rik, never losing sight of him for more than a few seconds. Amin and Zafa sat at their table. Occasionally, Amin would talk to a girl, but it must have not been anything 'cause his wife was sitting right next to him.

Kim was dancing with Jamal. *Lord,* thought Tracey, *Gena really needs to be here.* Jamal was all over Kim, and vice versa. Some girls acted like they didn't care if guys felt all over their bodies when they danced, but Tracey didn't think it was right. When she was dancing she wouldn't let no stranger touch her like that. When she was slow dragging and felt their dick getting hard, she would just walk off the dance floor. She hated that, especially when it was some broke-ass nigga trying to get his groove on, on a dance floor. *Men, they're so desperate.*

"Guess who?" a man said from behind her, covering her eyes.

"I don't know."

"Who do you want it to be?"

"Dr. Dre."

"Oh, you just straight played yourself with that one, sis," Quinny Day said, uncovering her eyes.

"No, baby. You know I was just joking," she said, really wishing it was Dr. Dre.

"No, you wasn't, but it's cool." Quinny Day was standing there in front of her, looking too good.

"I'm joking, Quinny Day. You know who I'm trying to see," said Tracey. "You, boy. You, you, you."

"Don't be playing games, Tracey."

"Quinny, please. You know I take you personal."

"Hi, Quinny Day."

Tracey heard a girl's voice and turned to see Bridgette. She looked horrible. Her outfit was cheap. Her makeup looked worn and she had bags under her eyes. After Quinny brushed her off, he and Tracey looked at each other.

"Damn, she needs to find another fool, like Black had to be to fuck with her trick ass, 'cause sis is going down," Quinny said, looking at Tracey real serious.

"I heard the money ain't been right since Black got killed," Tracey said.

"Her simple, retarded ass should have something," he said.

"Like he had a will? He didn't bequeath nothing to her."

"Huh?" said Quinny Day.

"I said, he didn't leave her anything."

"So, why did he have to leave her anything? She should have saved something for a rainy day. Come on. You females aren't slow, just stupid. Yo, would Gena be messed up?" Quinny Day asked.

"No, of course not."

"Okay, then. Besides, even if Black didn't leave her nothing, she got herself. If I was a woman, there wouldn't be no way my black ass would ever be broke."

Rik was on the dance floor with some girl. He was getting

drunk, but he hadn't lost his mind yet. Of course, Lita was walking around looking for him. Veronica, a true blue slut with a capital *S* on her chest, danced with another guy over to the right of him. She always thought that she was playing somebody, but the truth of the matter was, she wasn't playing nobody but herself. Rik took a closer look, and damn if it wasn't Forty dancing with her.

"Hey, Forty!" he called out. Veronica didn't look 'cause she had already spotted Rik and knew how he was. They were straight up playin' on the dance floor. Rik couldn't help but watch them. Most people couldn't do nothing but watch them. Veronica and Forty was doing some serious grinding out there and the thing about it was that, while she was dancing with him, another guy on the dance floor came and danced behind her, even pushed up next to her while she was already pressed up onto Forty. Girls couldn't stand Veronica, and guys were always in her face but talked about her behind her back like she was nothing. Trying to tell Veronica about herself was a waste of energy. She liked getting attention so much that you could tell that's really what she was after: someone to look at her, and that's exactly what guys did. Look at her, play mind games on her, and always give her attention, the kind of attention that she really didn't need.

Forty was all over her. Rasun thought he was getting ready to pull her skirt up and start fucking her. He'd already flashed her tit to everybody on the dance floor. The girl was drunk and she needed somebody to get her ass home. Andrea and Bridgette, the "friends" she came with, knew that she was drunk 'cause she was at the bar drinking up Forty's champagne like she never had it before.

"Forty, I got to go outside. I need some air." Veronica was flashing hot and felt like she was going to faint.

"Well, come on." He helped her fix herself and got her outside. "Come on, here. My jeep is parked right over there. Come on." Veronica tried to get herself together, but she felt so light, so out of touch, that she just couldn't walk without holding on to him. Forty's jeep was parked way in the back of the club.

"Damn, Forty, I thought you said it was right outside."

He took her to his jeep. Once he helped her inside he rolled the window down. "If you start to feel sick, just open the door," he said, not wanting her to throw up in his jeep.

"Here, let me move this seat back for you," he said, playing with the control panel on the far side of her seat. Suddenly, Veronica was prone, but she hadn't felt a thing. She just thought it was part of the headspin she wished would go away. Everything felt dizzy and when she closed her eyes, it was worse.

She didn't feel Forty's fingers, running along her inner thigh, and by the time she noticed anything, he was already pushing her legs apart, getting her skirt out of the way, moving into place, with a big fat juicy dick sticking into the air. It was too late. Forty had his shit out, her panties down, his condom on and was ready to go to work. Veronica was too far gone to put up a fight. Just to raise her arm and mutter "no" took too much effort. Forty kept his head up to make sure he didn't get caught doing what he was doing. Veronica wasn't really moving, but she was breathing, eyelids opening and closing in slow motion, only the whites showing.

Forty couldn't believe how easy it was. He was used to having to buy a big ass pair of gold earrings or something, but this was just too fucking easy. Veronica was too weak to hold her arm up, couldn't tell him to stop, couldn't hold him off of her. He was pounding her little ass half to death.

When he was done, he took a rag from the backseat and wiped himself. He tried to get Veronica to get up, but she just moaned. He checked his Rolex. Wasn't much time left. He pulled her underwear up off the floor and pulled her dress down enough to cover her panties, and went back to the party. Nobody seemed to really miss him.

"Where's Veronica, Forty?" said Andrea.

"She's out in the car. She didn't feel good. Hey, I can't take the girl home, so don't leave her."

"Forty, you ain't shit!" Andrea said, as she headed for the lobby.

"Mmm, hmm, whatever. Your girlfriend gonna be assed out if you leave her. Think I'm playin'?" he hollered back.

Jerrell walked out into the lobby where Ran was talking to some girl.

"Yo, what up? You ready or what?"

"Man, chill. I got this shit under control. There's a car waiting outside."

"All right, I'm out."

"What's the matter?" Andrea asked, sensing something was going on.

"Nothing, he's just ready to go, that's all," Ran answered. "So, we gonna get together or what?"

"Yeah," said Andrea.

"Well, write down your number so I can call you."

"Can't we go get some breakfast? This is almost over." Everybody was pairing off for the night, but it looked like Andrea would have to seek a meal somewhere else.

"I can't, baby. I got shit to do. I wish I could, but I can't. I'll make it up to you. We'll go get a nice lobster dinner, okay?' he said, slipping her number into his pocket. "I'll see you later. Don't give nobody none, either."

"Who?" she said, looking confused.

"You know, that nigga you gonna get to take you to get breakfast." Wasn't nothing slow about Ran. "Damn," he said, thinking about the pussy he could have gotten instead of having to take care of shit for Jerrell.

Forty caught up with Andrea and Bridgette and walked them over to his jeep to get Veronica. She was out cold. Her skirt was on the floor of the jeep and from the waist down she was completely exposed.

"What you do to her?" Bridgette asked.

"I didn't do that! That was not how I left her," he said.

"This don't make no sense." Andrea got her friend up and out of the drunken sleep she was in. Veronica didn't know what the fuck was going on. Andrea pulled her skirt up and put her panties in her pocketbook. Bridgette came around with the car and Andrea helped Veronica get into the backseat. Forty stood a few feet away talking with some girl as if nothing had happened.

Quadir and Gena were lying together in the living room with the fireplace glowing, listening to Sade, sipping on some Alizé, languid from their lovemaking, appreciating the fireplace for more than its glow.

Much to Gena's surprise, Quadir had a gift for her. Over in the corner sat a lidded box, covered in shiny red paper with a silver bow on top. "What is that?"

"Look and see." He placed the box on the floor next to her and she removed the lid and looked inside.

"Qua! She's adorable!"

"It's a he."

"Oh, he's so adorable."

She gently gathered up the tiny furball, cuddling it.

"I saw him and I thought he was cute." Gena inspected the diamond and gold tag. "Gucci?"

"I named him Gucci," he said, grinning. "You know, he's a Persian. He's gonna have a lot of hair."

"Qua, I figured that," she said with a hint of sarcasm. "I don't believe you. This is so sweet."

"I got something for you, too."

"Really, is that so?"

"It is," she said, standing up completely in the raw. "But you have to catch it," she said, running up the stairwell butt naked as he ran after her.

The black Pathfinder pulled into the back of the parking lot of the West Point Motel, under a tree and out of the light, where it sat and waited.

"Man, what the fuck is the bitch doing?" said Ran.

"Don't ask me. She your peoples. I don't know nothing, don't even know why I'm here. All I know is that sis would want to bring her ass on," Sam said, picking some dirt from under his fingernail. Ran grabbed his pager out of his pocket. No number. He already knew that. He checked it for sound and sat it on the seat.

"Give her some time," Ran said.

"I'll give her some time, all right."

"Who knows? They might be up there getting their freak on," said Ran.

"Man, I don't give a fuck if he up there eatin' her ass, I want the bitch to come on." The scream of the beeper violated their contrived composure, scaring them half to death, causing them to be thrown against each other in an effort to shut it off.

"Anticipation is a motherfucker, ain't it?" said Ran.

"Man, is it her?" said Sam.

"No!" hollered Ran.

"Damn, I'm tired. Jerrell got me out here kidnapping motherfuckers in the middle of the night. And what's up with your peoples?"

"I don't know! I'm gonna wring her neck if she fucks up." His pager went off again. "Why do girls got to keep calling my pager over and over again? I'm saying, when you can get to a phone, you'll call a bitch back, right? Why must they do that?" Ran was irritated.

"Who is it?" Sam asked.

"Jennifer. I swear she calls me over and over and over again all motherfucking night. I went to sleep, the girl was paging me. I woke up, she was paging me. You would think the girl would have figured the shit out by now."

Sam just sat there listening to another one of Ran's stories, as usual.

"Man," Ran continued, "don't you know she dialed the pager so much I had to buy batteries every other day. I swear to God, the bitch has to be the fuck possessed to page me like that." Ran's pager went off again. "Damn, I been trying to see this girl right here," said Ran, showing the number to Sam. "She all that."

"Is she?" said Sam, memorizing the number for himself. "What's her name?"

"Tia. She got a beauty salon, Rippin' It, up in Germantown.

Now this girl is bad with her pretty ass. You gots to see it to believe it," said Ran.

I plan to, thought Sam.

Ran's pager went off again. "If this ain't her, I'm gonna smack her silly," he said.

"Yeah, I'm gonna slap her ass around some too, for making me sit out here like this."

"Yo, this is it," Ran said. "Look at the time. Three twelve. She said she would need twenty minutes, and then she would be ready."

KIDNAPPED

Inside the hotel room, Simone and Forty was going at it. Simone had no problem making herself at ease with Forty. He was real nice-looking, and Ran was right. He played right into her hands. Ran had come to her with that ol, "I need you baby, you got to help a brother out" talk. Time after time, Simone was always doing something morally wrong for Ran. But the twenty thousand he offered her for her trouble was worth it, and she jumped at it like she was an Olympic contender. Now here she was in a hotel room with some stranger she had met at a nightclub.

Slowly Simone eased herself from the double bed and tiptoed over to the door. Carefully, she unlocked it. Then she picked up the phone. Just as she placed the hook on the receiver, Forty opened the door to the bathroom.

"Damn, you're big. You look deformed." Looking, she didn't want him fucking her.

"Think you can handle it?"

"Do you think *you* can handle it?" she asked him back.

"Talk now, cry later." Forty stood at the foot of the bed. Meticulously, he picked up his pants and carefully laid them on the back of a chair. He then placed a gun and a condom on the table. He laid on the bed, picked up the remote, turned on the television then clicked off the light. Not watching the television, he concentrated on Simone. Within a matter of minutes he had Simone's mouth wrapped around his private part. He had a thing about his penis in a woman's mouth. He had to have it, and within minutes he was giving it to her. While he concentrated on neutralizing his high, Simone was surreptitiously reaching for the gun he'd so cavalierly placed nearby on the nightstand. Finally making contact with the cold piece of steel, she was able to slip the gun from the table and nudge it neath the pillow, while still simulating enjoyment of Forty's superior anatomy. Not that she could, but he was high and she was on a mission. Forty was definitely the man you would want to get snowed in with on a cold winter's day. It just would never be in this lifetime, and particularly not tonight.

"Roll over," he whispered in her ear, thinking of some sexual innovation, but was interrupted by an out-of-place sound, which disconcerted him. "Can I join in?" asked a voice that was neither his nor Simone's. He reached for his piece, which was also out of place. He felt a setup as a hand reached around his throat and pulled him off the bed.

"What the fuck is going on?"

"Nigga, shut the fuck up," said the voice, emphasizing his instructions with a gun against Forty's jawbone. "You want to live, don't you? I know you do, especially since you're laying up here in all this pussy."

Forty didn't say anything, and he wasn't going to. They duct-taped his hands behind his back then tied him to a chair naked and blindfolded him, while Simone got dressed in the bathroom. Ran looked in Forty's pants and in his jacket pockets. When he was done, Ran had the car keys, money, pager, and cell phone.

"The gun is under the pillow," Simone whispered to Ran as she came out the bathroom. Ran grabbed the gun, and the two of them left in Forty's jeep while Sam stayed with Forty.

"Damn, I wish this nigga had tinted windows."

"I know, right."

"Yeah. Here's your money," he said, handing her a bag.

"Thanks, Ran. Mmm, twenty thousand. I don't know what I'm gonna do with all this money."

"Simone, so help me God if you say anything, I swear, if you say one little word, if I even have a reason to think you told someone where you got this money from, I will kill you. You hear me?"

"Ran, I'm not sayin' nothin', straight up. You not gonna have to worry about me, okay?"

"I hope so." Ran parked the jeep on a deserted side street. "Damn, we need something to wipe the jeep down."

"Here," she said, pulling a pair of panties out of her pocketbook.

Ran just looked at her. "Man, don't give me your drawers."

"They cool. I haven't worn them or nothing, see?" she said putting them up to his face.

"Yo, Simone! Is you out your mind? You need to get some motherfucking help," said Ran.

"Yeah, don't we all?" she said getting out the car. Ran took the panties and wiped Forty's jeep down. Then he got out and locked the doors.

"Remember what I said," he told her as he led her up the block.

"I swear, Ran, you don't have to worry about me."

"I just hope you didn't catch no feelings for the nigga or nothing, while he was runnin' up in you."

"Ran, come on, it takes more than a fuck, you know what I mean?" she said, looking up at him.

"Yo, just keep your mouth shut and everything will be cool."

"Ran, I don't know shit. I don't know a damn thing."

"All right, baby." Ran whistled at a cab but it kept going. Another cab was turning the corner.

"Here, wait a minute." Simone stepped out in the street and hailed the cab down. Ran got the next cab back to the hotel where Sam and Forty were and he let himself in. Sam had put Forty in the corner facing a wall.

"Why you put him like that?" Ran asked.

"I don't know. Seem like he not here, right?"

"Man, come on. Why you didn't get him dressed?"

"What, and untie him?"

"No," Ran said, "dress his ass tied up."

"Man, he's butt naked, man. I don't want to dress him."

Ran looked at Sam, with his one and only look he gave to people when they were getting on his nerves. "Dress him, I said."

"How I'm supposed to dress him all tied up, man? Huh?"

"Never mind, okay? Never mind. Hand me his clothes." Ran pulled the ski mask over his face and ordered Sam to do the same. He uncovered Forty's eyes.

The swirling blackness and specks of light faded into one, and finally there was vision. Forty looked around. He couldn't believe this was happening. After Ran untied him, he threw his clothes at Forty and told him to get dressed while Sam had the gun pointed at him in case he tried anything.

Forty picked his clothes off the floor and put them on. He

couldn't see his assailants' faces because of the ski masks. He didn't say anything; he just stayed real calm and played along with what was going on. He just wanted to go home, home to his wife Sharon and their three sons, Christopher Jr., Brandon, and Andrew. She told him to stay in with her, cried about it 'cause it was Christmas Eve, but he had to be out there. Christmas didn't matter. He had to be out there. And now look what was happening to him. He wasn't even sure what was happening. He thought about asking but decided not to. He thought about how, in a few more hours, his sons would wake up and run downstairs to the living room and start opening their presents with or without mom and dad, and then how they'd then run into Mommy and Daddy's room to wake them up. Only, this Daddy wouldn't be there.

When Forty finished dressing, Sam retied him to the chair and blindfolded him. There was some movement about the room, and Forty could tell things were being shifted. Suddenly, his arm stung, like a bee got him, and in less than seconds, he was slumped over in the chair.

"Let's clean this place up."

"Why? We got gloves on."

"Well, just wipe everything off anyway," said Ran. "No fingerprints, no body, no weapons, no case."

"Yeah, except that Simone. I think we should have killed the bitch."

"Why? She been helping out for years."

"Man, I would take her out. She know too much."

"Yeah, yeah, I know. But we don't have to worry about her right now. All we got to worry about is taking care of this."

They carried Forty downstairs and put him in the back of the truck, then Ran went back upstairs and took another fifteen minutes to rub down the room one last time. Placing the room key on the table, he closed the door behind him. He drove out to West Philly, where they put Forty in the basement of a house that had been abandoned. They tied him to a chair, went home, and spent Christmas with their families.

Gena took her time, as she opened the little tiny box wrapped in gold paper with a blue velvet bow. "Quadir!" she gasped. "They're beautiful! You don't think they're too big?"

"No, not at all," Quadir said.

"They're beautiful, baby. I love them, I really do."

"They're pear-shaped."

"I don't care if they were shaped like kumquats. I love them. I wanted a pair of diamond earrings. I was tired of these little dots. Quadir, I'm gonna get robbed with all this jewelry."

"No, you're not. When you're this large, you don't get robbed. People just stare."

"Here," she said as she turned the tree lights on. "I have something for you." Quadir didn't know what he was doing, but it felt good. He knew that it was wrong to have the tree and have the gifts, but it still felt good. Gena was a mad woman when it came to money and a mall. She had spent thousands shopping for all the gifts under the tree. She handed Quadir a big box.

"What is it?" Qua said as he opened the box. His eyes glowed when he pulled out the black leather jacket customized by Dapper Dan. "I'm scared to ask how much it cost."

"Then don't. Here," she said, handing him another box. Inside was a Cartier watch. Qua put his watch on, his eyes sparkling like the diamonds surrounding the bezel.

"I like it."

"I knew you would. Here." She had more. One box contained

more than twenty different colognes. "I didn't know which one you would like so I got them all." He just looked at her. She'd gone mad. In another box, there was a week's worth of Armani ensembles. Quadir was really getting into it, opening up his gifts and throwing the paper to the side. Gena just stood there, watching, knowing he had never celebrated nobody's Christmas.

"No. Open that one." Gena knew what was in each box. This one had Genesis cartridges for his Sega.

"Did you get me boxing?"

"Yeah, I got it." Gena got him records, tapes, and CDs. Gena lingered over a little box she'd spotted earlier.

Quadir saw her looking at it. "Here," he said.

"What is it?" she smiled.

"I love you. Open your box."

It was a diamond ring, a cluster of twenty-five point diamonds totaling seven karats in weight.

"Good Lord, but it can't top this. Here, I got you one more thing." She felt under the torn paper next to the tree trying to find the tiny box for him. "Here it is." She handed Qua the box and watched as he tore at the wrapping paper. He opened the box and picked out a key chain sporting a diamond "Q."

"Check you out," he said. "Real diamonds. I like this."

"It's a key chain," she said, like he wouldn't know.

"Baby, it's the best key chain I ever had."

"You like it?"

"I love it."

For twenty-five thousand, you ought to, she thought to herself.

"I'm really scared to ask you how much this cost. So, I'm gonna skip that."

Has he been saying that a lot tonight or is it just me? Gena asked herself, as she sat there organizing the stuff under the tree like

Gah Git always did. She never had this much stuff under a tree. It was like someone else's life, someone else's man.

Life had never been easy, and most the time it was hard. No matter how hard it got, there was always a lot of love. Gena remembered Christmas with her family. One gift, two if you were lucky. Today, she had everything she wanted. Gah Git always said to have everything and no love is to have nothing at all. But, to have love, is to have everything. For the first time Gena understood that, when she looked up and saw her man staring at her. It wasn't the gifts that meant anything. It was only the love she had for him and all the love he gave her.

Gena leaned over and on her knees she wrapped her arms around him, gave him a real strong hug, kissed him, and told him she loved him. Then, she went back to organizing the gifts.

He looked at her and thought of how much he loved her, how much he needed her and how for the first time he was happy. If he didn't have anything, just having her would be okay. "Do you know what I want from you?"

"No. What?"

"I want a son. I want you to give me a son."

"That's all you want?" she asked with a sexy grin on her face.

"That's all I want," he said, laying on top of her as he held her in his arms.

"Then a son you shall have," she whispered. Then he kissed her.

A MILLION'S WORTH

Forty was dazed and had lost track of how many hours had passed. But, he was still aware that he had been kidnapped while fucking a girl he could barely remember in a hotel. *Where was some help? There should be a goddamn superhero saving the day by now,* he thought. But, Forty knew he wasn't getting no help. *That bitch, fucking trick-ass bitch got me set the fuck up.* Forty swore on his life that her ass would see no more sunshine if he got the fuck out on the streets. He would hunt her down to the ends of the earth if necessary.

As he sat in the dark, listening to his stomach growling, wondering what the fuck was going on, Forty thought about what was going to happen next. His mind scrambled as he tried to remember specific details. His heart raced as he thought of his girl, Sharon. Any other time she would call the police on him. Now was the time. Where was Rik? Where was his peoples with the army brigade, ready to battle and get him out of there? It was like that when you hustled for a nigga like Rik.

The door opened and a tall skinny guy wearing a ski mask

walked down the stairs and threw Forty a bag with a sandwich and soda in it. When Forty was finished Sam tied him back up and left the basement.

Forty was hurting. He couldn't believe that he had been kidnapped. Deep down inside he had a feeling he wasn't going to make it.

Forty's girlfriend was crying. She had been crying since he left the house and her ass at home with the kids like he always did. Their three sons didn't enjoy Christmas Day at all without their daddy there. Forty's mother had called the police, but they couldn't take a missing person's report for forty-eight hours. However, the officers made an exception because of Christmas, and told his mother twenty-four hours.

"Damn, you call 911 and they tell you to call back," Forty's mom said with disgust slamming down the phone. Sharon called everybody she could think of. Everybody said the same thing—he was at a party last night, but no one she talked to knew where he was. Sharon had called the police, the Round House, and all the hospitals. It was as if Forty had dropped off the planet. All the times his black ass didn't come home and all the times he lied about where he was, there was nothing that Sharon wouldn't give to see him walk through the door. She'd be so glad he was home that she wouldn't even be mad, that's just how bad she wanted her man back.

His mother and father, on the other hand, knew something was wrong. Mom knew her son. There was no way her son wouldn't show up on Christmas Day. No way at all. The following day, the police came out to the house and took a missing person's report.

*   *   *

Forty was hurting, physically and mentally. His body was numb from sitting for such a long time. If he could just have a stretch, that's all he wanted, just to stretch. Suddenly, he had company.

"Yo, nigga, you up." A familiar voice. Forty knew that voice, but couldn't place it.

"You ready to go?" The ski mask asked, but Forty didn't answer. The blow to his midsection got his attention, giving him time to get his wind back and focus on his options.

"Let's try this shit again, motherfucker. You ready to go?"

Forty considered. Why didn't he see the shit before? How did he let it happen? He slipped up and let the motherfuckers catch his ass out there. How stupid could he be?

"I'm ready to go."

"Bitch-ass nigga, shut the fuck up. You ready to go when I say so," said the man in the mask, giving him a swift but forceful smack to his head. Forty sat there seriously trying to figure who the fuck was talking to him.

"I want a million dollars, and then I will let you go. You only get one phone call. You get that person to get the money and take it to the Springdale Mall at nine o'clock tomorrow morning. There will be a yellow school bus in the parking lot. All they got to do is put the money in the school bus. You understand? Because if they don't then it's just your time to die, nigga. You're not confused about none of this, are you?"

"No, man. I'm not confused."

"What's the number?" Still tied up with the phone held at his ear, Forty asked for Charlie when a girl answered the phone.

"Yo, man, your girl called and said you didn't come home."

"Listen, I need a million dollars put on a yellow school bus in the Springdale parking lot at nine o'clock tomorrow morning," Forty said.

"Beware of the man in the checkered suit. The iguana has landed to you too motherfucker," Charlie joked.

"I'm serious. I've been kidnapped. You got to help me," Forty said, seriously.

"What?" Charlie said, realizing his buddy wasn't playing.

"Man, you only got till nine o'clock in the morning tomorrow. Put the million dollars on the yellow school bus at the Springdale Mall," Forty said, as Jerrell hung up the phone.

"Hello? Forty!" Charlie said frantically as the dial tone rang in his ear. He hung up the phone, thought for a moment, and turned to his companion for the evening.

"Come on, you gotta go." She protested a little, so he dragged her by the arm. "Get dressed, you got to go. Come on."

"Fuck you, Charlie! Where's my money?"

"Bitch, you gets nothing. I'm having a crisis, and I need you to get away from me so I can solve it." He spoke with sincerity in every word.

He gave her fifty dollars, and she was pissed. "No, you didn't. No, you didn't play me for no paper and be so small about it, with your little dick self," she hollered, expecting to get her usual three fifty.

"Bitch, you is a flea. Here, here you go: another fifty. Didn't you here me say I'm having a crisis?" he asked angrily, pushing her out the door before slamming it in her face.

Charlie got on the phone and immediately called Rik. Rik could not believe it. He knew who had his peoples, and he knew why. Ever since Quadir stopped serving the city, Jerrell had been coming at him instead of Quadir. Quadir never took care of no serious business. Quadir let Jerrell push him out of the game by killing all the people who bought hundreds of kilos a month from him. But Rik wasn't giving up nothing. He was coming the fuck up in a major way and had just started to come into some serious paper, like Quadir. He wasn't going out like no sucker.

He sat back and listened carefully as Charlie told him about the phone call from Forty. Rik already knew something was going on when Sharon paged him, talking 'bout, "Where is my man? I know he fucking some bitch with you, Rik." Rik did everything but hang up on her. He sent Charlie over to Sharon's to explain what was happening. Then Rik hung up the phone. There was no problem putting together a million. Forty was worth a million, so paying the money wasn't a problem. Within minutes, a dozen phones were ringing off the hook and the city's ghetto gazette flashed the news headline that Forty had been kidnapped by the Junior Mafia. Rik called Quadir and told him what was happening.

"How much?" asked Quadir.

"A million."

"You got it," asked Quadir ready to put up the paper.

"Yeah, of course. It's just that there's no guarantee in a situation like this."

Rik and Charlie drove toward the Springdale Mall with a duffle bag placed on the backseat containing the million requested for Forty. All the while Rik warned Charlie that if it was a set-up, to take no prisoners. Entering the Springdale Mall parking lot, Rik could see the yellow school bus parked in a corner off in the distance. He sped in its direction. Reaching the bus he circled the entire area. There were a few cars parked in the lot off in a distance, but the bus stood alone.

Rik pulled up on the side of the bus. Charlie emerged from the car with the duffle bag of money in one hand, and his hammer in the other. The double doors of the bus were slightly open. There was enough space for Charlie to push open the doors. Taking his first step up onto the bus he pointed his hammer in the direction of the bus seats. He was ready to lay anybody down that popped out at him. He placed the duffle bag on the floor of the bus. Then he carefully pushed it with his foot down the aisle past the first row of seats. Then he exited the bus pulling the doors back to how he had found them.

With the task complete, everyone sat back and waited for the phone to ring with the news Forty was home.

The following morning, a yellow school bus pulled up on the 1300 block of Conestoga Street, and parked down the block. Ran stepped from the bus with a million dollars in a duffle bag. He went inside.

"The nice thing about this is that everyone got what they wanted. I got the money and you get to go home. I say it's time to celebrate, don't you?"

Forty couldn't see him 'cause he was still wearing that ski mask. Jerrell directed Sam to untie Forty from the chair, but to leave his hands tied. Forty was barely able to stand, he'd been tied up so long. It sure felt good to get out of that chair. Once he felt a little bit of strength coming back into his body, he knew he would be all right. Then he welcomed his anger. Looking like an old man with arthritis, Forty turned on Sam and with all his strength threw his tied hands around Sam's head and yanked the ski mask off.

"Sam?" he said as he watched Jerrell remove his ski mask, then Ran did the same.

Forty was livid. "You fucked up when you kidnapped me. You

know you not getting away with kidnapping me and taking my million dollars."

"Nigga, I already did."

"You think you did. This shit ain't never gonna be over, so go ahead. Kill me motherfucker," Forty said already knowing they were going to do that.

"Pussy, take that!" said Jerrell, shooting him in the right leg. "I already did get away with taking your million dollars. I got it right here."

The bullet ripped through his flesh, as his body dropped to the floor.

"I wish I'd known you were the one behind this one, 'cause you woulda never seen no paper from me!"

"Man, fuck you!"

"Nigga, fuck you, too," said Forty, as another explosion tore into his other leg. The pain was agonizing, leaving him screaming, and reaching for his other leg.

Jerrell shot him again, getting his arm. "You would'na paid if you knew it was me."

Pow! went the gun as Jerrell shot him again in the arm.

"See, baby, I'm running this shit and you or nobody else can stop me," said Jerrell as he circled Forty's body.

"Fuck you" Forty rasped, as he layed on the basement floor.

Insane with anger now, Jerrell shot again, getting him in the chest, *Pow! Pow!* Then he stood over Forty. "Say your prayers, nigga," he said, and put the gun right between his eyes and squeezed the trigger just as Forty tried to duck. The bullet fired and grazed the side of his head, taking him out.

Realizing Forty was dead, Jerrell jumped back into the reality of having a million dollars. "Let's get the fuck out of here. We'll come back tonight and take care of the body," said Ran.

"Yeah, we can dump that nigga right in the Schuylkill River," Jerrell sneered. "Come on. Let's go."

After going about their regular business for a few hours, that is, hitting their regular customers, Ran and Sam pulled on Conestoga Street at two o'clock in the morning. Yellow police tape was everywhere. "Stay here," said Ran. He got out of the truck and went up on the porch. Blood was everywhere. He pushed open the unlocked door and went inside and there was more. It looked like a paint roller had made a trail from the basement.

"I don't fucking believe this," he panted, running out and pulling the door shut behind him. "I don't fucking believe it. Get Jerrell on the phone."

They would find out later that a neighbor had looked out his window, thinking he'd heard shots, but didn't call the police. When Forty dragged himself onto the porch and the man saw his bloody body, he then called the police. Forty laid alone on the porch until they arrived. No one came to his assistance, even to lay a blanket over him. Forty laid there, dying in the winter cold, all alone until the ambulance arrived to take him to a nearby hospital.

The police had searched the house, dusted it for fingerprints, and left about forty minutes before Ran and Sam arrived to take Forty's body away.

"Shit. Jerrell gonna be mad as shit. We got to call him," said Ran. "We got to call him."

Sam found a pay phone and pulled the Cherokee over so Ran could call Jerrell. The phone rang. A few seconds later a girl answered. "Yo," said Ran.

"Hello," said the girl.

"Who dis?" Ran asked.

"This is Val, Jerrell's sister."

"This is Ran. Where he at?"

"They got him."

"Who?"

"The police. They came and arrested him."

"What for?"

"Attempted murder and kidnapping."

"Oh, shit."

"They said he tried to kill some guy, Christopher Cole. Who's Christopher Cole?"

"That's the boy, Forty," said Ran. "I got to go," he said and hung up the phone. He knew that he and Sam would now have to find someplace to stay, since the police were probably looking for them, too. Ran went straight across the bridge and into New Jersey. He did not pass go and he did not collect two hundred dollars; he went straight to New Jersey.

1990

ALL OVER

Happy New Year! It was 1990. Fireworks exploded through the night sky as people of all races and ages joined in the New Year's celebration in the middle of Penns Landing.

"Happy New Year!" Rik found himself being patted on the back by a white man.

"Yo! Has he lost his mind?" said Rik.

"Come on, Rik. Be happy. It's New Year's," Qua told his friend.

"Fuck the New Year," Rik said, jerking his shoulders as if to shrug off the encounter.

"You see him, Lita?" Qua asked.

"Yeah," she said laughing. Ready to party, they ended up at Amin and Zafa's New Year's Eve party. Qua and Rik talked all night while Gena and Lita floated around, mingling through the crowds greeting all their friends. Qua finally got them some nice seats at the bar and the bartender replenished every bottle of champagne they went through. Both Quadir and Rik bought lots of champagne for everybody. Rik poured a glass and passed it out to all the sisters who had given him a shot in the past year.

"Damn," said Rik, "You know her?"

"Talia?" Quadir asked.

"The bitch is all that."

"Been there, did that?"

"You better watch what you say before Gena creep up behind your ass," joked Rik, as both of them laughed.

Qua looked over his shoulder. "It's cool."

But there was a face missing from the proceedings. Rik observed, "The shit is fucked up about the boy Forty."

"I know they say if he make it, he not gonna walk again," Qua said.

"Man, fuck that! They better know their days are numbered, dig me?"

"So, Ran and Sam is still on the run?"

"Yeah, they're on the run from me and the police, and Jerrell is in jail."

"Good."

"I tell you this much. Ran not gonna make it, and if Jerrell sets foot back out on the street, he's not gonna make it either, and neither is that pussy-ass Sam. Their future has already been planned by me, and they don't have one."

Qua knew he meant it. Rik was no joke. The boy would take you out if necessary. Quadir had already known about the half a million that was up for grabs for whoever killed Ran and Sam. The word was in the street.

"Look, there goes Veronica," Qua said, directing Rik to look her way.

"So, you fuck with Forty now?"

"What are you talking about?" she asked with a serious attitude.

"I'm talking about you and Forty. Remember last week in the parking lot, or was you that fucked up?" Rik asked, laughing at her.

"Why you worried about me? You the one that wanted that homely bitch, so mind your homely ass business and leave me alone," she said walking away.

"She's a Reebok ho," Rik said, flagging his hand at her.

"You liked it!" she spat back at him.

"Hated it!" he shouted back. Qua sat there falling out laughing, 'cause he had heard the parking lot story, especially the part about her clothes not arranged quite the same way as when Forty left her. Of course, it wasn't right, but who was to say what was wrong?

The night went on, and the party came to an end. Quadir pulled Gena over to the side and kissed her gently.

"Happy New Year, baby," he said, letting her go.

As everyone made their exit, the cold winter air sent a chill right through Gena's sable. As usual, Quadir looked around the entire set. Girls were hopping into rides and cars were riding back and forth as people scattered about the sidewalks pairing off for the night.

"Shit," Rik said, as he pulled up behind his back. "Yo, Quadir baby," he hollered, seeing Ran's face in the crowd.

"Yo! Go this way," he said, pushing Lita trying to move them out of Ran's range. Quadir saw Rik had his gun pulled. Panic struck him and he grabbed Gena.

"Quadir!" she screamed, as she saw a guy pull a gun and aim straight at them. For one brief second, her mind returned to the fast-food parking lot and the gun that jammed. The face behind it was his. He pointed the gun at her and fired as the seconds lapsed between one another, Gena's heart pounded like waves against the seashore as Quadir threw her body to the ground like a protective shield. The party people out celebrating New Year's Eve were caught in the middle of a drug war as hundreds scattered, screaming and ducking down on the ground.

Quinny Day saw Quadir go down and began firing aimlessly into the air. The sound of the gunfire left Gena alone to a point no one could touch her as she huddled in Quadir's strong arms.

Rasun spotted Sam and Khyree and began firing at both of them. He watched Khyree tumble to the ground as bullets pierced his lower abdomen. Reds took a shot in the arm and fell behind a car parked on the street. Jamal saw everything in front of him. He stopped his car dead in the middle of traffic. He reached under his seat, jumped out of his brand new Mercedes-Benz, and aimed for anybody he knew Rik wanted dead.

Rik took his time, as he aimed carefully. From nowhere, the bullets hit him, crippling him to the ground. His back burned like fire as the metal ripped through his flesh. With all his weight, Rik turned around and fired the infrared glock, dropping one of Ran's rookies. Rik ducked behind a car as red lasers flickered through the air. His bullets met the enemy as the laser fired directly on its target. His pain was unbearable, but Rik held steady until Ran fell dead to the ground.

The deafening silence that followed allowed the remaining Junior Mafia assasins to hear a familiar motor, as a black four-door Cherokee slowed down long enough for everyone to hop in before it sped away, leaving a trail of smoke and bodies sprawled in the middle of street.

The silence of gunfire was like an alarm, alerting everyone that they could come from out of their hiding places. People peeked out from under cars, buildings, and windows to see if it was over.

"Quadir come on. They're gone," said Gena realizing something was very wrong. Freeing her body from his, she realized he had been shot in the chest as she rolled him off of her. She looked at his lifeless body and began to cry. She picked up his head and layed it in her lap hovering over him to keep him warm. Unknowingly realizing that the nightmare of her girlfriends was becoming her own reality. "Quadir, please get up." She tried to lift him. "Get up, baby. Quadir! Oh, no! Please baby, get up! Somebody help me! Somebody help me, please! I need someone to help me. Please!" Covered in his blood, she continued to plead, "Qua, please, please . . . baby, don't leave me. Don't leave me now! Boo, talk to me!"

"Gee," he rasped, scaring her silly.

"Quadir, I love you, baby. Please don't die. You're gonna be all right."

"It hurts, Gena. It's burning!" Gena's head spun about, looking for help, only to see Lita sprawled on the sidewalk in a pool of blood and Rik lying next to a car. She was all alone; there was no one left. They were all dead.

"No! No! Qua, hold my hand please." The bleeding was so bad, and she could feel his body tightening in her arms. Gena heard the sirens, but saw no ambulance.

A police officer hunkered down next to her, speaking softly, "Miss, is he alive?"

"Yes! Yes, but he needs an ambulance!"

He touched her shoulder and told her, "There's one on the way. It will be right here." He stood and started counting bodies.

"Take . . . take . . ." Quadir whispered.

"What, baby? What?"

"Take it, take . . ." He closed his eyes again and she began to remove his jewelry. "Key chain . . . take it." He was able to slip the key chain to her, the diamond Q key chain she'd given him a week ago.

"Qua, please hold on. The paramedics are on their way." She stayed as close to him as possible without smothering him. Finally, the ambulance arrived and the paramedics gently helped her stand before placing Qua on the stretcher. She watched as they went to work on him, never letting go of his hand. The moist drops made their silent way down her cheek, unnoticed. "Quadir, I love you. Please don't leave me. God, don't take my baby from me."

Quadir looked up at her, squeezed her hand tight, and winked at her the same way he always did.

"Qua, it's gonna be okay," Gena told him; her face awash with tears. "You're gonna be all right, baby. Everything is gonna be fine." She said looked down at his blood-drenched body. She knew the paramedics were still working, trying to save him, but she didn't know that Qua was already on his way to everlasting peace, the journey that would take him to paradise, and that he had to leave Gena. He didn't want to. He wanted to stay with her. She loved him and made him happy. She was the only woman who loved him: without the paper he knew she was with him. But he just . . . just couldn't. He wanted to fight. He was fighting for every breath, but he was too tired. *It looks nice there.* His energy waned. *But what about Gena?* He wanted the pain to stop. He was hurting so bad. He looked up at his beautiful Gena one last time and knew they would be together one day. Then he closed his eyes and exhaled his last breath.

Gena heard a funny sound, something she recognized, *You only hear that on TV, don't you?* The beep of the heart monitor stopped like a never-ending pause, like an unending scream, and she was confused.

"I'm sorry, ma'am. Ma'am? He didn't make it."

She sat there, holding his hand, looking into his beautiful face as the ambulance continued its route to the hospital. She held onto his hand but he wasn't holding onto hers anymore. The vehicle stopped, and Gena heard someone speaking.

"Ma'am? I'm sorry, ma'am. You're gonna have to let us take him. Ma'am?"

Someone was helping her take a step down, guiding her through a door. She was entering a building. She couldn't feel the floor, but this looked like a place where you get help. Yes, help. Help for Quadir.

Gena sat in a place they put her, and wondered, *What is it I have to remember? Something happened, I think. Why am I on this table? Where is Quadir?* She noticed a man in green scrubs, *Oh, okay, a doctor. I'll ask him. He'll know what . . . what will he know?* "Doctor," she said, "Where is . . . where is Quadir Richards?"

The doctor flagged down a staff member who escorted Gena to a gray hospital bed and pulled back the sheet. She moved closer. "Qua?" she said. "I'm here, honey. I'm right here. You know I wouldn't leave you, didn't you?" she said, her voice cracking. *I bet if I kiss him.* She leaned into him and kissed his lips. What her soul knew as fact would not make its way to her conscious mind.

Qua's body was cold where she kissed him. There was moisture tracking his still cheek that she slowly realized was falling from her own eyes. She felt a vacuum suck the strength from her midsection. She began to shake him as she kissed him, letting all her tears flow onto his ashen skin.

"Oh, God! Please, Qua! Wake up! Don't leave me! You said

you would never leave me! What am I gonna do?" A big hole was opening up beneath her and she tried not to fall in. "Why, baby, why?" Her man, her only man, the only man who loved her in this cruel, angry, vicious world lay lifeless in a gray hospital bed.

"You took care of me. You loved me so much. Don't do it, Qua." *These words should bring him back. He should listen to me.* And yet, he heard every word.

"Qua, I can't live without you. I don't want to live without you. God, please take me, too. Please take me with him." She started crying, loud, startling an orderly. People came in, looked, and then left. She was holding him, kissing him, trying to bring him back to life.

"Miss," someone said. "Miss, you have to leave."

'Who's touching me?' Her arms flew out. "Get your hands off of me!"

"Miss, please. He's gone. There was nothing we could do."

Gena shot him a look that could kill. "You motherfuckers can save every goddamn body else. Don't touch me! Don't fucking touch me!"

She was reciting, over and over again, like a mantra, "Please don't take him. Please don't take him. Please don't take him. God take me. Oh my Lord, why?"

The orderly couldn't deal with it and called the nurses' station, glad that Quadir's parents had arrived. He asked for their assistance. "Sir, his wife is distraught. It's just a mess in there. She's lying on top of him, she refuses to leave the room, I don't know what to do."

"Let me talk to her." The man's heart broke seeing the lovely girl, desperately clinging to his son's dead body. "Gena? Gena,

I'm here." She heard him, but said nothing. "Gena, baby, he's gone. Come on. His mama wants to say good-bye. Come on."

The crooning sounds comforted her and she let herself be lifted from the cold shell that had been her lover, into Montell's arms, and she let him surround her with consolation. "He's all I had," Gena told him. "All I had. He was my life. Without him, there's no me. I can't live without that man. I don't want to."

"Yes, you can, Gena. You have to live. You have to be strong. Why you think my Quadir loved you so much? 'Cause you're so strong. He loved you. Gena, you meant the world to that boy. It was just his time," Montell added, as tears filled up his eyes and slowly melted down his cheeks.

"No, no, no. It wasn't."

"Yes, it was, baby girl. And you will pull through this."

"I can't leave him here. They might not treat him right."

"They gonna do their job, Gena. Quadir is in good hands. Nothing can ever hurt him again. Do you know if he could look down and see you right now, and see how you're acting, he'd be hurt to see you like this."

"Dad, please let me stay with him tonight. Please, I can't leave him. I got to stay with him. He's so cold. He needs a blanket. Can't they get him a blanket?"

"Gena, the boy don't need no blanket. Girl, you scaring me. Now, you got to pull yourself together."

"Dad, why they take him from me?" she sobbed. "Why did God take my baby from me? Oh, God, why?" Montell tightened his hold on Gena so she wouldn't fall to the floor. She leaned over on the bed and hugged Quadir's lifeless body and kissed his cheek one last time. "I'll always be with you," she whispered in his ear. Then and only then did she let Quadir's father lead her from the room.

He passed his eyes one last time over his dead son and continued walking, holding the grieving woman, remembering that there was another waiting; Quadir's mother.

Montell took Gena home and stayed with her. When she awoke, Gah Git was sitting in a chair by the bed and Gucci was laying on Quadir's pillow. "You okay, baby?"

"Where am I?" The scene was like Dorothy and Toto and it was all a bad dream.

"You're home. We brought you home last night."

"Who are you?"

"I'm your grandmother, child. What, you done lost your rabid-ass mind?"

Gena's mind had to rewind itself. She wasn't in the projects, she was at her house and that wasn't Gah Git sitting there.

"Who are you?" Gena asked the girl, not having a clue as to who this stranger was sitting before her.

"I'm Nitah, Jalil's second wife." The girl spoke as if being someone's second wife was some normal shit. Nitah was so peaceful, though, and so soft-spoken. She was humble even in her jewels and looked like a queen. She was fully garbed, with a beautiful kemar covering her head.

"Where's dad?" she asked.

"He's probably at the hospital, with the funeral director and members of the Masjid. They are making the funeral arrangements for Quadir."

"I got to go there," Gena said, trying to get out of bed.

"You can't go. There is no one who can go there. Here, honey, just try to relax. I made some tea. Here, drink some. It'll make you feel better."

There isn't a goddamn thing that will make me feel better, thought

Gena. She swallowed the prescribed sedative Nitah handed her, which happened to be the first of many.

Nitah was a wise woman; only sleep could fix some things. She knew Gena was only nineteen and this kind of trauma could damage her if it wasn't handled right. *Poor thing,* Nitah thought as she stroked Gena's forehead. She stayed by Gena's side until the funeral.

It was the hardest day of Gena's life. She hadn't been outside or seen anyone other than Nitah since Qua had been killed. The funeral was packed. Rik called Gena from the hospital room he laid in. He cried for her and for Quadir, but most of all for Lita. Gena had never heard a man cry, not even Quadir. She didn't know what to say; she didn't know what to do. She felt his pain, and she began crying with him, especially when he talked of Lita. She died that night. She got shot in the neck and Rik never saw her go down or nothing. He wasn't by her side and he never told her good-bye.

Gena could not see the splendor that the funeral director had arranged for the people who loved Quadir Richards. She only knew her legs wouldn't hold her up. She felt her belly sink some more and an aching pain twist at her insides as thoughts of him darted through her mind.

"He looks so fine," someone remarked.

No, she thought. *He looks dead.*

"The flowers are so beautiful," someone else replied.

The flowers smell like death, she thought. Someone was pulling at her, murmuring to her, "Gena, Gena, come on, baby. Sit down. You gonna hurt yourself. Please, come on."

She heard the person pulling at her tell people: "Please, please, she can't handle it. Never mind the condolences, she can't hear you." All Gena could hear was someone crying. So loud, and it hurt so bad. Her body could no longer hold her up, and she dropped in front of his casket to the floor.

Something's holding me. I can't feel nothin', but I'm standin'. How'd they do that? Then she forgot a lot for a time, and then she was outside, still standing, but not alone. It was pretty outside. *We in the park. Look, there's birds. What's that noise?*

The whirring sound of the casket being lowered into the ground registered and brought Gena out of her mental closet for a moment. Into that black hole went all of Gena's hopes, her babies, her life, her one true love. The only man who really loved her. And as his casket sunk deeper and deeper into the ground, her body sank into her grandmother's arms. Gah Git knew her baby would never be the same.

The weeks passed, and Gena never once went outside. The day Rik was released from the hospital, he went to see her and stayed in the guestroom. Together, they took care of each other and listened to one another's stories about the good old days. Rik knew Gena was not the same. He wished she would come out her darkness. He tried everything from jokes to reminiscing about his own memories with Quadir, but nothing seemed to work.

And then, someone knocked at the back door. "You expecting somebody, Gena?"

"No."

Rik opened the back door to find Quadir's mother standing in the freezing cold.

"Hi," she said.

"Hi," said Denise.

"How you feeling, Gena?" asked Viola, walking through the house into the living room no one was allowed in.

"I'm feeling better," said Gena. "Can I get you something?"

"I'm not on a social call."

"Oh. Well, um, what's up?" asked Gena, wondering what the fuck she was there for.

Viola didn't beat around the bush with idle talk about the weather. She got right to the point and she broke that shit down without blinking an eye.

"Listen, Quadir was my son, and I loved him dearly. However, he is gone now, and life must go on." She reached in her pocketbook and pulled out a sheaf of paperwork, which she shoved in Gena's face. "As you can see, this house is in my name. I own this house, dear, and I have plans for this property."

Gena couldn't believe what she was seeing. Not just the deed to the house, she had paperwork on the Range Rover and the BMW. "Everything," said Viola Richards, "Not Montell. Not Montell and Viola, just Viola." The only thing that wasn't in the bitch's name was Gena's furniture, the jewelry, and the Benz. That was it. Gena just sat there looking at the bitch.

Rik stepped in. "I think you should leave, now. I really think it's time for you to go."

"Well, I will give you a week. I hope you understand." She stood up and shook it off as if she had said nothing out of the ordinary. "This has all been so difficult for me to deal with."

No one had noticed Gena coming alive. "Difficult for you? It hasn't been that difficult for you to sink your claws into all of Quadir's shit!"

"These assets are in my name. Therefore, that makes them mine."

"And what exactly, now that Qua is dead, is yours?"

"The house, the furnishings, the cars, and the jewelry. I want it all back."

"Oh, no, bitch. That's where you fucked up. The Mercedes-Benz is in my name. Would you like to see my paperwork? And the furnishings I bought." By now she was towering over the woman. "Would you like to see my receipts? And the jewelry is mine, too. Everything in this house is mine. All you're gonna get is the walls!" The teenaged widow stood there waiting, wondering why grownups could be so mean.

Denise came to her mother's aid. "Who you think you talking to?"

Gena slipped into superior gear. "Whom . . . do you think? Let me tell you something. When your son came into this house and needed something, the motherfucker came to me. When he had a problem, he told it to me. I am the one who gave Quadir what he needed. Anything he needed, he came to me!" She was into it now; her eyes were boring into the cold-hearted woman and her violin string, tight-ass, chicken hawk daughter.

"That man, my man, has only been in the ground two weeks and you're already here to claim his shit."

"My brother would have wanted us to have his things, that's why he put it in our mom's name."

"Bitch, please. He put it in your mother's name, Denise, because he was a drug dealer. Shit don't mean he wanted her to have a motherfucking thing. Did the motherfucker ever invite you over? Hell no. What's this, your third visit? I know it, and you know it, and you know who your son bought this house for. He bought it for me. You remember that when you turn the key and unlock the door, you miserable bitch. And you never liked me, so I'm not surprised you got the fucking audacity to come in my house and tell me some bullshit like this."

"Who you calling a bitch?" asked Denise.

"You heard me. I didn't stutter. Your mother is a miserable

bitch that goes around trying to make everyone else miserable. Shit, she can't even hold her man. You want me out? Fuck you, both ya'll can kiss my ass. I hope you burn in hell!"

Rik was up. He'd been letting Gena get everything off her chest, proud as a peacock and just as happy to see her again among the living, but enough was enough. "I think you two should go. You really have no place here. Neither of you do, and what you're doing is wrong. Qua wouldn't have wanted nothing like this. He wouldn't have wanted this to go on." He stood his ground against the chicken hawks.

"They don't care about Quadir. How could they? How could she? That bitch didn't even raise him, Rik. His grandmother did, and his sister never knew him. Come in here telling me about my goddamn man. Motherfuck you and this motherfucking house!"

"You curse all you want. You can say whatever you want, you just get your low-life ass out my house."

"Fuck you, bitch," said Gena, as she spit at Viola missing her by a blow of the wind as Viola opened the door.

"Hey, Gena, don't let me see you in the street, bitch, 'cause your ass is mines," said Denise.

"Bitch, we can go round for round right here and right now. Let me go, Rik," said Gena, ready to fuck both they asses up. Gee was hyped. She was ready to be world champion.

"Gena, chill the fuck out!" Rik yelled. He ushered the chicken hawks out the door and closed it behind them. They must have caught a cab to the house or had someone drop them off 'cause they damn sure were taking the Rover and the BMW with them. Gena wanted to stop them, but what the fuck for? She wanted to kill the bitches, but it wasn't worth it.

"The bitch can have it, Rik. She can have it all. Shit, the

insurance is up on the BMW. I should blow it up." Looking around, she felt her belly sinking again. But only for a second. "What am I gonna do, Rik?"

"Call a storage company, pay them to come and pack your shit up and store it for you. Then you're gonna figure out where you're gonna stay and you're gonna move. If you want a house, I'll get you one, or you can come and stay with me."

"No, Rik. I'm okay." She finally sat down. "I want to go home." For the first time in her life, she wanted to go home to Gah Git's house.

"You got money?"

"Yeah, there should be some here. Come on." She led him downstairs to the safe and unlocked it.

"Damn. There should be more. There's only two thousand here."

"Two thousand? Where the fuck is the dough at?" asked Rik.

They sat silent for a moment. Gena wondering what dough.

"There should be way more than that in the safe. Qua said he had millions."

"Millions?" Gena asked.

"Yeah, baby. True motherfucking blue millions."

"Millions?" Gena asked again.

"Gena, don't get that shit twisted. Quadir made it clear to me that he was a millionaire. Now, I don't know where, but he had millions."

"His mother must have it. She got everything else."

"Damn, that's fucked up. Gena, you don't have no money saved?"

"Yeah, a couple of thousand."

You spend thousands like it's dollars, and you have no major paper saved, thought Rik. "Gena, you holding at least a half million just in jewelry, furniture and furs, and you have no cash? Go figure. How much do you spend a week, ten?"

"No, more like fifteen maybe twenty thousand."

"See? And you have two thousand. When is the Benz coming out of the shop?"

"I don't know. It should've been ready."

"I don't know what to say. And why do you want to go to your grandmother's house? She lives down Richard Allen, right? I mean, damn, if you don't want to stay with me, then at least let me get you a house or an apartment."

"No, Rik. You act like you're my keeper. Quadir was my keeper and he's gone now. I want to go home. I haven't been home since I was seventeen. I miss home, and I'm sorry if the projects scare you, but I grew up there, remember?"

"I just can't figure out how you, Quadir's woman, is broke and going back to Richard Allen."

"And Rik, what part of that don't you understand?"

"I don't understand why you want to go back to the projects. Motherfuckers want to get out and you trying to go back."

"I want to go home, don't you understand? The projects isn't my home. My home is where my family is. They're the ones who care about me. They're the ones who will take care of me."

Rik looked at her. "Gena, you're a big girl. You can take care of yourself. You don't need to be living down in no Richard Allen. Man, those niggas down there is crazy." He knew. He ran Richard Allen.

Gena suppressed a smirk and looked at him, feeling normal again and liking it. "I want to go home for a while. I really need my family. I mean, this big old house is the best shelter from the cruel world, but without Qua, it just ain't the same. And now he's gone," she said walking over to her fireplace. "He gave me everything, Rik. He gave me a purpose and he loved me like nobody has ever loved me in my whole life. He gave me loyalty, Rik. I mean, I know he cheated on me from time to time. I could tell. But even with the bullshit, he was the most wonderful man. I don't want to really leave here, Rik."

"I know you don't. Look up in here. It's the *Lifestyles of the Rich and Famous.* Qua said he was gonna get you this house. He said his children would grow up in this house and the two of you would live in this house together for the rest of your lives."

"He really said that?"

'Yeah, he really did."

"Isn't there anything I can do to stay here?"

"Whose name is on the deed?"

"Hers."

"Then it's her house. If she wants you out, she can get you out. She can get you out through the courts."

"What kind of fucking justice is this? I lose my man, I lose my goddamn house, the bitch just straight up took the Rover. Doesn't she know the goddamn store is five miles down the road?"

"I know," said Rik. "That shit was cold. I would have never thought his mother would come as raunchy as she did today."

"I have nothing. I'm losing everything," she said sadly.

"You buy Armani underwear. Look at all this furniture. Look at it, not to mention all the goddamn diamonds you wear. You look like someone went straight to Africa. Please, you sitting up here trumped up talking like life is over. You got more than any woman I know, Gena. Shit, you got paid. Bitches don't see a portion of what you got. You better look around. All this is yours. In another apartment, or another house. What you got, five big screens up in here? Three living room sets?"

"Four," said Gena.

"Pool table, video games, and with all the cases of Dom, you could bootleg. I'm saying. I just don't want to see you back down the projects. I know goddamn well Qua wouldn't want you down there. Stay in a hotel, then, find a place. I'll pay for it."

"Rik, I have made up my mind. I'm going home for a while. When I'm ready you can get me a house."

"Shit, I really wish you would stop with that shit."

"What is it you don't understand? You don't understand where the money is? I spent all the goddamn money, Rik. You don't know why I want to go back home? 'cause I'm not scared of no Richard Allen. I don't understand what's so hard to understand. I don't want to leave here, okay?" She was crying again. "I just wish Quadir was here, that's all. If he was here, everything would be okay. Now everything is falling apart. Don't you understand?"

Rik had enough. "What the fuck do you think I been going through? Lita is gone. Lita is gone, by the hands of some nigga named Ran. Lita isn't ever coming back. Khyree is gone with his grandmom. I don't have my family. I don't have the only motherfucker out here that I could trust. So, all them tears you done shed isn't doing neither one of us no good, and don't start crying again." He really didn't understand her thinking. Gena was a hustler's wife. She was not supposed to be in no projects. It was too many other hustlers out there that would see her straight on the strength of Quadir.

"I don't know, G. What can I tell you, sister, but to find that money. Before you leave this house, you find that money, 'cause there's money here to be found. Millions, Gena. Millions. We should be looking for it now."

"Do you really think there's millions in here?" She stopped crying.

"I know there is. Qua got to have it in a safe."

"There was only a couple thousand in *the* safe."

"Then that ain't the one, baby. Trust me, there's gotta be another one. Qua had his shit stacked. Why else you think he would give up a yield of fifty, sometimes eighty thousand dollars every week? Quadir had his own thing set up, Gena, with plenty of brothers on the payroll. Quadir had all the money. That money is up in here."

"There is no money in here, Rik."

"Yes, there is. You just don't know about it."

"Rik, I live here, okay? I know every nook and cranny of this house. Trust me, there is no millions nowhere in here. If there was, I would know about it. Every week Quadir used to put money in the safe. That was it. That's where he went to get his money. I wasn't allowed to go near the safe until he told me the combination, and that wasn't until after that bitch Cherelle called my house. There is no money. Quadir did not have no millions. His father was over here the other night, and he told Quadir that he had to go on a budget."

"Then his pops didn't know about the money, Gena. Quadir was like that. I'm telling you, you can believe me or not. Quadir said he had millions, and when he said millions, he meant millions. Gena, it's like hitting Lotto. Never having to worry about making ends meet, never having to worry about how you're gonna eat, never having to worry about how you gonna get what you want. Millions. Quadir said he had saved millions and was retiring from the drug game. Now, you can believe me or you don't have to, but I'm telling you now, the boy had money coming out his ass and he didn't take it with him, baby. I think we should search the house."

"You want to search this house?"

"Yeah, I do."

"Then you go ahead, 'cause I ain't searching shit. Ain't no money in here, Rik," she said walking away from him frustrated.

He started with the walls, looking for trap doors, hollow sounds as he went around knocking. He knew he'd have had them if he had this big house. He looked behind pictures, tapped on the walls, searched all over the basement; anywhere one could store a hidden safe. After a good forty-five minutes of searching, Rik concluded that the money wasn't in the house.

"I told you." Gena went into the kitchen and poured some milk for Gucci.

"Even the cat is paid," Rik said, shaking his head. "Diamond and gold Gucci tag, and you don't have no idea where the money is."

"Rik, I don't think Qua told you the truth because there would be no need for us to go on a budget."

"Gena, where is the money? You spend twenty thousand a week. Come on, he wasn't serving the city kilos no more to be givin' you the money like that. That's why he wanted you on a budget, just you."

"Well, it looks like I'm on a budget now, since you didn't find all these millions," Gena said.

"Either that or my pockets is getting ready to hurt me."

"You gonna let me hold Lita's Cadillac?" she asked with a smile.

"Yeah, if you want it," he said, not feeling right about some one else driving Lita's car.

"Yeah, I do."

"Well, you want to go get it?"

"That would mean I would have to go outside," she said.

"Yeah, you'd be going outside to get the car."

"Okay. Let me get dressed." Gena went upstairs and threw on a pair of jeans and some riding boots, and a leather jacket.

Rik drove straight to the apartment and parked next to Lita's car and gave Gena the keys. "You know, I'll really miss Lita," Gena said.

"That girl meant the world to me, man. You don't know how bad I feel. I lost her. That girl was my friend, besides being my woman."

"I felt bad when I didn't go to her funeral."

"Hey, G, after what you went through at Quadir's funeral, I knew you was in the zone. But one thing's for sure, Viola Richards brought you back with the dumb-ass shit, didn't she?" Rik nudged her with a laugh.

"Quadir was my heart, Rik. He was the only thing that mattered to me, you know."

"Yeah, I know. Just remember that Q is up there, G. He's watching everything you do, and he expects you to move on. In time you will, but it's nice to know that there's somebody up there watching over you, somebody protecting you. And that is what Qua is doing. He's got his wings and right about now, they're shielding you. So, do the right thing, Gena, and don't sweat that house. You came out on top, baby. Fuck the money, fuck the house, fuck the cars. You still a winner. Shit, you was shootin' for the moon with the nigga and now you among the stars, baby. Just remember that." Rik handed her the keys to Lita's car. "Drive safe."

"I will." Gena kissed Rik on the cheek and got out of the car.

"Gena, don't sweat no paper out here. Call me, understand?"

"Okay. I will, Rik. I will." She drove Lita's car to Gah Git's and told her grandmother that she wanted the room upstairs and that she would pay to have all the junk that was piled in there put in storage. Gah Git understood why Gena wanted to come home, especially after she told her about Quadir's mother coming there and telling her to get her ass out in a week. Her poor baby was losing everything, and Gah Git was scared that Gena wouldn't be able to handle all of this.

Downtown in the Federal Building, Agents Fields and Burson sat with the U.S. Attorney Paul Perachetti.

"He's willing to testify sir, but we need to place him in the Witness Protection Program. Without him, we have nothing," said Agent Burson.

"If we want these assholes, we need his testimony. The death penalty is riding on his testimony, sir," said Agent Fields.

Perachetti sat back listening to everything they were outlining for him. The men waited in silence as the man considered and finally agreed.

"Our Witness Protection Program in North Dakota would serve best. Its rehabilitation facility is superior, and he'll have access to therapeutic modalities to get him back on his feet, so to speak. What about the wife and kids?"

"They'll want to be with him," said Burson.

"Fine. Well, then, we've got it all straight. The witness will be transported to North Dakota." The field agents breathed their sighs of relief as the U.S. Attorney continued. "We'll want to keep this low key, you got that? You'll bring him in by helicopter from the hospital. Collect his family now, and take them all down together." He continued to give his instructions and opinions as he made arrangements on the phone.

It wasn't difficult for Forty. The agents were glad he decided to cooperate. Actually, they were overly delighted. They had the leader of the Junior Mafia behind bars. They had a live witness. Sure, they were going to put him in protective custody, but that was their job. To them, Forty was only worth his testimony and past that was nothing but a drug dealer in a wheelchair.

Forty was distressed about the entire situation. Sharon was in tears, having to choose between her life in Philadelphia with her family and her world. She thought long and hard about it. She loved her man and now that he was paralyzed, and in a wheelchair, she couldn't turn her back on him. Besides, her sons needed their dad.

All in all, it had been a difficult call. For Forty, it was hard to walk away from the life he had lived for so long. After all, he was leaving friends and family, not to mention having to adapt to life in a wheelchair. Forty couldn't help but to sit back and ask himself, what was it all for?

MEMORIES

Gena had taken care of everything before she moved. She forwarded the mail to a post office box. She paid a company to box and store her furnishings and clothes. Rik had given her twenty thousand, and she put the majority of it away. What she didn't put up, she used to fix up Gah Git's project housing unit. She got exterminators and even painters.

Light-blue carpet was delivered the same day the handyman in the neighborhood laid down a new kitchen floor. She put the navy-blue leather furniture from her family room into Gah Git's living room, along with a big-screen TV and wall unit. She went to a furniture store and purchased a new bedroom and dining room set for her grandmother.

The nosey neighbors knew something was going on. Before it was all over Gena had a tiny chandelier in the dining room. Gah Git was overwhelmed. Everytime she opened the door, she tried to figure out whose house she was stepping into. She never thought her little project housing could look like it did.

Gena took Gucci upstairs and went in her room and closed

the door. She couldn't sleep. She hadn't been able to sleep since Quadir's passing. The entire situation was so overwhelming for her.

She laid in bed thinking about him as she cradled Gucci. There was a lot of noise outside, and she couldn't help but to peek out the window. The brothers were on the corner shooting dice. *How can they see in the dark?* Gena wondered. A huge 4 by 4 pulled up and sounded like it robbed a discotheque. The music was so loud and the bass rumbled so hard, it shook Gena's bedroom windows. Then she saw a skinny girl in a blue sweater and gray skirt with a pair of pink socks and red slippers come walking up the street. She didn't have a coat on, let alone a bra. She went over to a guy who was on the corner and Gena watched the exchange. The girl turned and proceeded to walk back down the block.

"I miss you, baby. I wish you could come back. I wish you were here." Gena felt tears well up and trickle down her face. "Why'd you leave me this way, Qua? God, you don't know what you took from me when you took him." She couldn't stop the tears or the pain. "Why is it so hard to let go?" She let her head drop to her lap and let the tears fall, hoping that each teardrop would take a drop of pain with it.

It was 3:47 AM exactly when Gena heard people hollering outside. She peeked her head above her headboard and looked out the window to see a man and a woman fighting in the middle of the street.

"Don't make no sense," Gah Git said. "Them fools is probably out there fighting over who drunk the last of the C&C. It's a damn shame. I don't know how they've stayed together. She is forever kicking his ass."

"For real, Gah Git?"

"Yeah, the police will be here by time it's over. Child, this is every weekend."

"For real?"

"Honey, this is all the time. Now, go on back to sleep," she said as she shut Gena's door and went back in her room.

The next morning a knock at the door distracted Gah Git from her tirade, and she greeted a girl who lived down the street, a smiling, skinny girl with a fat baby in her arms.

"Ms. Scott, can you help me?" she asked, looking hopeful at Gah Git. "I have a test in English class today and I was wondering, could you watch Ayonna for me?"

"Oh, Lord, child, I guess so. Where's your mama?"

The girl looked away for a split second. "She getting high again, and she said no."

"Well, you know I'll help you out."

"Ms. Scott, the house looks real nice," Brenda said, looking all around.

"Well, thank you. You know Gena?"

"No, ma'am."

"That's my oldest grandbaby. She's Bria and Brianna's first cousin."

"Hi," Brenda said. Gena acknowledged her with a look, but she didn't speak to the girl. "Well, here goes her baby bag and everything you'll need." Gena felt sorry for her. She didn't look no more than sixteen.

"Gah Git. I have to go. I'll see you around dinnertime," Gena said, kissing her grandmother on the cheek.

"Good-bye. You be careful," said Gah Git.

"I will," hollered Gena as she brushed against Brenda on her way out the door.

Brenda handed Gah Git the baby. "I'll be right back after school."

"Okay, she'll be fine."

Gena stepped and hopped in a cab to the body shop where the car was being fixed. While she sat in the lobby of the Mercedes-Benz dealership, she started scribbling to Quadir.

I Reminisce

I reminisce for you
I reminisce the days
I try to forget
But the feelings never go away.

I reminisce for you
I reminisce the nights
For the things we did
And how it was so right.

I reminisce for the love
For the love that was always there
I reminisce, I reminisce, and I know in my heart
That you really did care.

Even though my mind plays tricks on me
And I can't seem to let you go
I believe it's because you're still loving me
I reminisce, I reminisce
And the memories tell me so.

Gena got in her car and drove straight to the bank. She was seated in a room with a table where she opened her bag and carefully began to deposit her jewelry: the ten-karat diamond engagement ring, the cluster diamond ring, the charm bracelet, the diamond initial G that Rik and Lita had given her, two Rolexes, one Ebel, one Omega, one Cartier, all of which were diamond bezel, two gold Gucci watches, and one stainless steel and 18k Movado. The girl knew what time it was. She kept her plain gold Rolex. Of the five tennis bracelets she owned, she put four in the box and kept only one. She put her two-karat diamond earrings in the box and kept her quarter karats in her earlobes. Then she placed fifteen pairs of gold earrings in the box, keeping only three pairs, which she put back in her pocket.

She deposited strands of gold chains, diamond pendants, diamond pins, bird pins she never wore, and a total of seventeen gold and diamond bangles. They all went in the box except for two, which she put on her other hand, letting the smallest 6-karat tennis bracelet lay over the Rolex, instead of the twelve. Once she was done placing all her things neatly in the safety deposit box, she started on Quadir's.

Time had changed things. The fate that lay in the hands of another, altered Gena's future as well as Quadir's. Gena was ready to lock it up, taking the safety deposit key and adding it to her own key chain, Quadir's diamond Q.

By the time she got home, Bria and Brianna were fussing about homework and teachers and why Gah Git didn't go up there and defend them like the other parents did for their kids.

"What's up?" Gena said coming into the house. "Gah Git, I got the car."

"You got the car?" said Brianna.

"Let me see," Bria said, as if they both had never seen it before.

"Oh, Gena! Can we go for a tide?" Brianna asked, pushing past her to get a glimpse of Gena's 300.

"Yeah, can we?" Bria whined. Bria was just too nice these days. What a change.

"Later," said Gena.

"Good, we gonna be all that," they said, slapping high fives, not thinking about trying to get Gah Git to go curse out their teachers.

Then Gena heard a baby. "That baby still here?" said Gena.

"Yeah, Brenda not coming back for that baby no time soon, and Gah Git trying to make us take care of it," said Brianna, eating some Georgie Woods potato chips.

"Like we having that," Bria added.

"Y'all are a trip," Gena said, looking at the twins in disbelief.

"Will somebody go get that baby?" Gah Git hollered. "Ya'll see me trying to cook!"

Gena looked at the twins. They looked like they were deaf and dumb and definitely wasn't moving, so Gena went and got the baby. It was smelly and too small. Gena had no idea what to do with it. "Qua wanted me to have one of these?" she said, looking at the baby as if it were not a part of the life force here on Earth.

"Here," she said taking it to Brianna and giving it to her. "We're going for a ride later, remember?"

Brianna took the baby. "Damn, she stinks."

"What just came out your mouth, Brianna?" hollered Gah Git.

"Nothing! Darn, I said darn this baby stinks."

"That's what I thought I heard you say. You need to go to church. You want to go to the seven o'clock service?"

"No ma'am."

"Oh. Then watch your devilish tongue. Child, do get it honest," Gah Git said, mashing her potatoes. The baby was still crying. "Oh, my God, what's that child's name?"

"Ayonna," said Bria.

"No, her mother."

"Brenda," said Brianna.

"Where could she be?"

"I don't know, Gah Git. She has English class with me and she wasn't there and we didn't have no English test today," said Brianna.

"I don't know why you're always helping people," said Bria.

"You might need some help one day," Gah Git reminded her.

"Yeah, well, Brenda shouldn't have had no baby if she wasn't gonna be able to take care of her child," said Brianna.

"I know. That's Brenda's baby, not ours. She somewhere now with a boy or something, 'cause she sure wasn't in school today," said Brianna.

"I know, Gah Git, and we're the ones that suffer when you go out your way to help people," said Bria.

"Girl, hush your mouth," said Gah Git, trying to hear what was going on outside.

"You hear that?" Brianna asked.

They got up and went to the window.

"It must be those idiots next door," Bria said.

"That baby is crying," said Gena, looking at the helpless infant.

"Go get it," Bria said, nudging Brianna.

"No. Ain't my baby," Brianna answered. "Gena, you go get it."

"What I look like? I ain't never had no babies, and I never babysat no brats. You go get her." The baby was starting to cry louder.

"I wouldn't get that baby if it rolled off the couch and fell on the floor," said Bria.

"Damn, that's cold," Gena said, looking at her cousin's despicable grin.

"It sure is," said Brianna, slapping high fives with her twin. All of a sudden, Gary came running in the house with Khaleer behind him.

"Grams!" He saw his grandmother picking up a strange baby off the couch. "Aunt Gwendolyn done stabbed up Royce, y'all. The police is arrestin' her and everything."

"Khaleer, come here, baby," she said, handing Ayonna to Brianna. Brianna took the baby and sat it back down on the floor.

"You okay, son? Gah Git's grandbaby okay? Well, what happened?" she asked, holding her youngest grandson.

"I don't know. She on that shit, Grams, and she out there with her hair all wild, half naked, titties hanging out, fighting the police."

"Oh Lord," Gah Git said, shaking her head. Bria and Brianna silently went out the door to get a dose of the commotion.

"That girl is gonna have to learn the hard way. Did you call Paula?"

"No, Zorian and Avanna was out there. They seen everything."

Gena answered the ringing phone. "It's Aunt Paula, Gah Git."

Another knock at the door brought another surprise. Gary opened the door thinking it was family, but Ms. Bradley, the social worker, was standing there smiling.

"Yeah? Can I help you?" asked Gary.

"Yes. I'm here for Ms. Scott."

"Oh, Gah Git!" hollered Gary, slamming the door in her face.

"It's some white lady!" He left Ms. Bradley outside in the cold and went back in the house.

"Paula, I got to go. I'll call you right back," said Gah Git, and she went to the door. "Oh, my goodness! Come on in. You sure do come at the darndest times. Children, this is Ms. Bradley," she said, ushering her in. "Say hello. She's here about Aunt Gwendolyn's baby."

Everyone said hi to her and behaved like they had etiquette for once in their lives. You could tell that the white social worker lady had really caught Gah Git off guard.

"Come on in; have a seat," said Gah Git, sitting the lady at the dining room table. "Can I get you something to eat or drink?"

"I'm a little thirsty, if it's not too much trouble. I see you have a houseful."

"Gena, get Ms. Bradley some juice, please." She excused herself for one minute and walked over to Gary.

"Come here," said Gah Git. Calling him into the bedroom, she explained that the lady was there about the baby and how important it was that no one run in and out of the house. Especially since her child was down the street making a spectacle of herself.

"Gah Git, it's cold outside."

"Boy, don't you got no long drawers?"

"No."

"Well, you better get some. Now, go on, and don't let nobody run in here," she said, pushing him out the bedroom. "And don't go across the street with them hoodlums, either."

"They not hoodlums, Grams."

"Yes, they is. You just don't know it. Don't tell me, fool. I been here longer than you. I know a hoodlum when I see one, and I see 'em across the street. Now go on."

Gah Git returned to the dining room and explained baby Ayonna. The social worker was very impressed with the lovely redecorating that had been done, and Gah Git explained how Gena had moved in.

"But there's still plenty of room for the new arrival."

"Well, Ms. Scott, you really don't have to explain. I'm sure the baby will be fine with you, and she'll be with her family. I just wanted to tell you in person that the state has awarded you custody of Brandi Valon Scott."

"Oh, thank you, Ms. Bradley. Thank you so much. I been so worried about what would happen to that baby. You just don't know how happy I am. Thank you so much."

"Well, you're welcome. I knew you would be glad."

"Oh, I am! I'm gonna have to thank the Lord for all these blessings. I really appreciate everything you've done for me and my family," said Gah Git.

"Well, it was easy to see how much you cared, and that you can give Brandi a good home. But I must be going now."

"Thank you for coming by to tell me in person," said Gah Git.

"Bye," said all the grandkids sprawled all over the living room watching Quadir's TV. Bria had Gucci, Ayonna was asleep, and Brianna held Khaleer.

"Take care," Ms. Bradley waved to everyone in the house. Gary was standing right there by the door as she exited. He scared her half to death.

"That's my other grandson. Boy, what you standing out here in the cold for? Get your butt in the house," she said, dragging Gary inside, smiling in Ms. Bradley's face, waving good-bye.

Gah Git got back on the phone with Paula, saying "Oh, Lord," over and over again.

"She gonna have us in church tonight," said Bria.

"I hope not," said Brianna.

"Yo, you should have seen Aunt Gwendolyn beat up that lady police officer. She kicked her ass. They had cameras and everything. She prob'ly gonna be on *Cops* or something."

"Nuh-uh," Gena said.

"For real, I think I was on TV."

"Gary, you always bugging. You not gonna be on nobody's TV, okay?" said Bria.

Gena suddenly froze at the sound that meant loss: gunshots. *Bap! Bap! Bap!*

"Get down, Gah Git!" hollered Bria.

"Watch out," Gary said, running over to Gah Git. Everybody was on the floor. A bullet shattered the living room window and hit the wall, leaving a hole.

"Lord, have mercy on us all. Please, Jesus, save me. Please Lord, have mercy!" Gah Git was preaching for real. "Pray! Y'all pray!" she said.

"Praying isn't gonna do shit!" whispered Brianna.

"Sure as hell ain't," said Bria. There were no more shots, and it was over. Outside, two men were lying in the street.

Gary went running out the door. It was his boy Vic and this other kid named Freddie. Gena went running out the door too, but Gah Git wouldn't let the twins outside. Baby Ayonna was crying from all the commotion.

"Damn, he was my boy," said Gary, as he put his head down. Gena reached for her cousin, hugging him.

By now, Victor and Freddie's families were outside, losing their minds. Victor's mother just fell out in the street. "Lord, please don't take my son!" was all you could hear being said.

"Gary, come on. Let's go back in the house." Gary didn't argue because he knew if he stayed out there tonight, it was gonna be trouble.

"You kids come on in here and settle down. Gary, you okay?"

"Yeah, Grams. He was my boy, though."

"I know. I know, son. It's a shame to see these young children out here killing one another and taking away good lives that God put on this here earth. I just don't know what has happened to these young peoples out here in the world. They is crazy and they don't have no respect. Now, back when I was coming up, wasn't none of this mess going on. There was drugs and people drank, but they had sense about 'em, and not only that they had respect for one another. It's a sad shame, and what the dang-dabbit they done did to my window?"

Gena walked upstairs to her room. She moved about in the dark and sat on the bed holding her kitten. Funny how they ended up the same way, in the street, covered with blood. She remembered that night her destiny changed. He winked his eye and let go of her hand, making it happen. Gena mustered up the strength and forced the tear back inside. "Qua," she said to him with her heart, "I miss you," and she paused for a moment continuing on with her normal conversation.

Bria walked by Gena's bedroom door and heard her in there talking to Quadir. *She really needs a new man,* she thought to herself.

Gena got herself ready for bed and let Khaleer sleep with her. In the middle of the night, screeching sounds of a baby in distress woke up the whole house. Gena got up, but Gah Git told her to go back to sleep.

"I can't sleep no way," Gena said, getting a glass of milk.

"Thinking about Quadir, baby?"

"Gah Git, all the time."

"I know," she said, rocking little Yonni in her arms. "Quadir was a good man. Child, if I'd had a man like Quadir in my day, I'd have to dig deep to find a reason to go on without him too, so I know how you feel. Gena, you got to be strong, honey. You got to count your blessings and thank the Lord for being so merciful. You must keep your mind strong. Quadir would want it that way."

Flashbacks illuminated the image of the gunman aiming right at her, and Quadir pushing her out the way. She knew he would have done anything for her 'cause he did everything that he could.

"I'd give anything to be with him again."

"I know, but when God is ready, you will be. All things in time, Gena. All things in time. Be patient. I worry about you girls, I really do. But Gena, you had something special, baby. You must never forget Quadir. Keep him alive in your heart and in your soul. What you two had was pure and honest. Cherish that love. Keep it in your heart, and let it grow with you."

The next morning Gena got up to answer the bell and let Brenda in.

Gah Git took over immediately. "You know I been waiting to curse you out, but I'm not going to." She got up and went into her bedroom.

"Why did you leave your baby here all night?" Gena asked.

"I'm sorry. I went out, and I just thought I would be back before now."

Gah Git came out the bedroom and Gena left it alone. She handed Brenda her daughter. "You take your baby and you go wherever you going, but you think about one thing. That child didn't ask to come into the world and she deserve a lot better from you. You must be crazy to try some shit like this at 2432, but you will learn and you, my dear, are gonna have to learn the hard way."

"I'm sorry," she said.

"No, you not. You not sorry, 'cause if you was, you would have done what you said you was gonna do, and that was go take an English test and come back here and get your baby. You not sorry. You knew you wasn't coming back. But guess what? You won't get me to play your fool no more," said Gah Git as she gathered the baby's things and put them in the baby bag.

"It's not that. It's just that my mother was getting high, and she put me out and then I tried to stay with my boyfriend, but his mother said I couldn't stay there."

"Your mother been getting high. That don't got nothing to do with you calling. You young girls treat these babies like they something that just came out of you. Baby, they more than that. You need God. You're going down the wrong path, and I tried to help you, but you took my kindness for weakness. In life, you should never bite the hand that feeds you."

"I'm sorry, Ms. Scott. I really am. I appreciate you keeping her for me."

Gah Git handed her the baby bag and closed the door. Relief filled her. She looked at the time, noting that her babies would be home soon. She worried about them out there in the streets on their own, especially little Khaleer. "Lord, show my babies the way."

WHEN IT'S ALL
SAID AND DONE

Forty had come a long way. He had progressed quite well with the help of therapy. Despite the fact that he would never walk, he went every day for the past seven months determined to beat the odds. The FBI's Witness Protection Program had moved him to North Dakota in the mountains to keep him safe. Now it was time to bring him home. Time to testify against Jerrell Jackson.

The U.S. Attorney Paul Perachetti had an open and shut case that would defy Clarence Darrow. It was ridiculous that Jerrell Jackson, the known leader of the Junior Mafia, didn't plead guilty. No one knew why he would even want to go to trial. It was totally ludicrous. Didn't matter. Jackson was gonna get the death penalty. Perachetti knew he had him by the balls, and it felt great. Jerrell deserved to die, not just for all he did out in the street, killing and serving the city cocaine, but he deserved to die for being so damn slick and never getting caught. The

Junior Mafia was a fucking nuisance, all of them, and getting their leader, Jerrell Jackson, had made headlines in newspapers throughout the country for the past six months.

Now it was time for trial. Now it would all come to an end. Once Christopher Cole testified, it would be over. Perachetti was eating up all the publicity and taking all the credit for making the streets safer by prosecuting the criminals, especially the notorious Jerrell Jackson. For him it was a dream come true. He was finally getting what he wanted—publicity. It was time to think about running for mayor.

The courtroom was packed, the majority of the people black. They had come to sit this one in. A lot of families that had lost a life to the hands of the Junior Mafia were there watching, hoping and praying for justice, justice that hadn't been served. The prosecutor was their God. Only he could give them what they wanted. Only he could bring justice for this cruel and wanton behavior that had swept through the streets like Satan himself.

Paul Perachetti came through the double courtroom doors, his trench coat swinging as he made his entrance. He was on an all-time high. Things were looking good. He felt the power of City Hall calling him.

"All rise," said the bailiff as the Honorable Eugene Pearlstein entered the courtroom. "You may be seated," he said stiffly after sitting down.

Voir dire had taken three weeks. Perachetti had used his peremptory challenges early on, giving Jerrell's attorney, Billy DeStephano, a slight edge in the jury selection. As far as DeStephano was concerned, he wanted his client to beat the case. Hell, he knew he was defending the so-called leader of the Junior Mafia, but he didn't care. The bottom line was that the niggas and their bullshit had made him a millionaire at the age of thirty-six. Why stop now? He could not stand, nor afford, for Jerrell to be sentenced. There was no way he was gonna let his client receive capital punishment, which was exactly what the state was going for. Voir dire, one of the biggest problems with the justice system, is the method of jury selection in American jurisprudence. It was totally unfair, but DeStephano felt good about the twelve jurors who were selected.

The judge explained to the jurors exactly what their job was, which was to find guilt beyond a reasonable doubt. Court was adjourned until the following morning.

DeStephano went back to his office. He rehearsed his opening statement over and over again, preparing himself for the jurors, ready to look them dead in their eyes and tell them why they wouldn't be finding his client guilty. When he was finished not only would the jury be dazzled, but also the verdict would be not guilty. He had $175,000 so far, and another $50,000 due him for the professional services he rendered. The world had gone mad and he was making money. His dead presidents fantasy was interrupted by his secretary. "Billy, your wife is on line three," she said over the intercom.

"Thank you," he said picking up the line.

Finishing with his wife on the phone faster than his record-breaking connubial speed, he hung up and told his secretary to hold all his calls so that he could go over his opening statement one last time. It was short, simple, and to the point. It was stated as succinctly as possible, just to whet the jurors' appetites, anticipating what was to come. He had a promising future right there in the palm of his hands. The publicity alone was phenomenal, not to mention all the incoming calls for potential clients he had not yet had a chance to review. Thanks to the Junior Mafia, he was famous, and he would get Jerrell Jackson off. He had no doubts about it.

"All rise." Judge Pearlstein seemed to take his sweet time sitting his fat ass in his chair. Jerrell couldn't figure him out. Perachetti made his opening statement. Then DeStephano gave his opening performance. After opening statements were concluded, the prosecutor presented his evidence, then called his first witness, a hotel clerk who claimed he remembered two guys coming into the hotel and walking past him. When asked if either were sitting in the courtroom, he pointed at Jerrell.

"Ain't that some shit? Ran and Sam went up in the hotel," he whispered to Billy.

At least he's honest, thought Billy as he glanced over and looked at his client.

The prosecutor seemed to introduce something into evidence about every ten minutes. From pictures to diagrams, he introduced it all, except a weapon. DeStephano objected to everything, and Pearlstein was getting tired of telling his ass overruled. A great deal of investigation and preparation had been done by the DA, and it was a shame all that work he had done was a waste of time, 'cause DeStephano was going to get his client off. For $225,000, he knew he had better.

DeStephano did a good job on cross-examination. "Well, at that time of night, it's possible you were tired, and you didn't know who you saw walk into the lobby of the hotel. From fifty yards away, how could anyone know if it was my client walking in that hotel room?" He asked each question with sincerity, constantly watching the jurors.

"Objection," said the prosecutor, really wanting to say "Fuck you," as did DeStephano, but the judge overruled him anyway.

"Hah," DeStephano wanted to say, thinking about the five

hundred he spent feeding Judge Pearlstein dinner last night. "Ha ha" was more like it. DeStephano just took over the courtroom, making liars out of all Perachetti's witnesses, until Perachetti called in his last witness. "Prosecution calls Christopher Cole."

Christopher Cole, a paraplegic. Christopher Cole, aka Forty. By the time Forty got off the stand, the jurors were in tears. A mean stare was what they gave DeStephano and his client. Jerrell just wanted someone to shoot Forty's ass.

"Can't you do nothing to shut him up?" Jerrell asked.

"What do you want me to do?" Billy answered.

"I don't know, object or something," said Jerrell. "For a quarter million, do something! Damn!" Jerrell was really getting nervous.

Forty spoke directly to the jurors, telling them everything, from the girl, to the kidnapping, to the basement where he was kept until they received the million dollars. He told them how he pulled off Sam's mask, and how Randolph and Jerrell Jackson took off their masks willingly. He told them that Jerrell Jackson was the one who pulled the trigger on him, first in his legs and then in his chest. He told them that he put the gun to his head and shot him.

DeStephano cross-examined him, not able to break his story, or intimidate him into giving the wrong answer, no matter how many ways he asked his questions. That had always been DeStephano's forte, causing people to twist themselves up and make themselves sound like they weren't sure of what they were saying. But, it didn't work. Forty knew what he was doing and he knew why he was there. He wanted justice, he deserved justice, and justice would be his.

In Gena's world the months passed quickly, and with them, so did her savings. It had been six months since Quadir died and

Gena didn't know if she was coming or going. Her brooding was in direct proportion to her financial situation.

The beauty and change that comes with spring didn't come for Gena. Instead, she talked to herself and stayed in her room, which she shared with Khaleer. Gwendolyn's other baby, Brandi, stayed in Gah Git's room. Gwendolyn was still in jail because Gah Git wouldn't let Gena put up the bail money. "No need in wasting. God says it's a sin to waste and Gwendolyn ain't right. So, you just hold on to your money in case you need it."

Gena had nothing going on for herself. There were no adventures, no nights out on the town, no dinners in AC, gambling and spending frivolously, and no romance. She missed the romance of Quadir, the way he would grab her and hold onto her in a rough passion, tasting her, serving her his penis, which was one of a god, thick and fat with the perfect length. Just the thought of him sent chills down her spine. Only Qua could take Gena far beyond any fantasy ever could. Quadir. She felt him all the time. She talked to him every night. She cried for him in her sleep, twisting and turning, talking in the bunkbed above Khaleer.

Sometimes Khaleer would sleep in the bedroom with Gah Git and his baby sister. There wasn't good sleep for Khaleer with the new baby either. Normally, Khaleer would be found sleeping on the kitchen floor, in closets and in the bathtub. Gah Git couldn't figure it. Finally one night she caught him sleepwalking and called 911.

Gena couldn't believe it, not the fact that 911 woke up the neighborhood at four in the morning, but the fact that Gah Git blamed Khaleer's sleepwalking on her because she was always talking to a dead man. "You talk the boy right out of the room, Gena," Gah Git had said.

Things just seemed to be going downhill. Even Gucci, the precious Persian kitty had his share of life in the hood. One day while Gena was out, Gary and his friends were in the house rolling poor Gucci up against the wall like dice. Gena was so upset when she came in the house to see Gucci being tossed like a football, she didn't speak to Gary for two weeks. The poor cat was never the same. He had started climbing up the walls and jumping on people as they walked by. Usually, he would climb on top of the refrigerator and wait for someone to walk in the kitchen, then jump on their heads. They had worked on Gucci every time Gena left the house. He'd become a mean cat, and now he was evil. Gena couldn't stand him—he had changed so much. He wasn't cute and cuddly anymore. Now Gucci was a mean ol' tomcat with long straggly hair. Gucci blamed Gena for the bad meals and torture he was put through and usually would attack her on sight. Gah Git just wanted the cat out of her house.

Then there were the twins. Bria and Brianna weren't living in the same world with the rest of the people on the planet. They had boyfriends now. Life was Kevvy Kev, and don't tell Bria it wasn't, 'cause it would be something if you did. Brianna was blinded by the gold teeth, obviously, of some kid named Dalvin. "He's all that; he's all that. We use condoms. It's my life."

Yes, they were into sex, heavily into sex, and definitely down for experimentation. What was Gena gonna tell them? It's 1990; you can catch AIDS! Like that would lead them in the right direction. *They don't believe; they just don't believe,* Gena thought. So she kept her mouth shut and always said, "Did the condom break? 'Cause if it did, you have six months to see if you'll die."

"No, Gena, it's not like that." Brianna just stared at her as if Gena was retarded. "Dalvin was a virgin until he met me."

"He told you that?" Gena shook her head in disbelief, knowing game when she heard it.

"Of course he was a virgin. Are you crazy?" Brianna asked. This girl was out there. Gena's mental level could not deal with the minds of just-turned-seventeen-year-olds. They just knew they were grown. There was no reasoning with them, and what they wanted to do, they did.

Gah Git kept fussing, and Gena would get real tired of the whole routine inside the house, but outside it was worse. The brothers seemed so angry. People were frighteningly frustrated. The inner city streets were hard and represented hard times. Gena hated it, the way it looked, all scribbled on and wasted.

Gena had become a hermit like Gah Git. She hated going outside at night. It was always something. The brothers wasn't taking no shorts in the streets, either. They would rob you in a minute and victimize you for the smallest amount of materials or cash you may have. It was chaos and mass confusion.

She missed Quadir so much. It had been six months, going on seven, since his murder and nothing had changed. She still loved him and she still wanted him. She couldn't forget him. She talked to him every day and night.

Nightmares of Qua's death took the place of the happily ever after dreams, and Gena often woke in the middle of the night in a cold sweat, filled with a fear whose name she knew but wouldn't say: despair. When she lost Quadir, she lost it all, including her spirit.

The summer months were getting hotter, and it only added to her ennui. *Maybe an air conditioner will help,* she thought. She called Rik. It wasn't a problem.

"Two air conditioners?"

"Gena, that's not a problem."

"And five thousand dollars?"

"That's not a problem either, G."

No problem, Gena thought. *Now that's what friends are for.* "Thank you, Rik. I'm on my way," she said, hanging up the phone.

She ran into Gah Git's room. "You got some money?"

"No, baby. Not yet. I will when the mailman gets here, though. Today's the first of July," said Gah Git, playing with her false teeth.

Gena wasn't trying to hear it. She went outside and walked to the corner store. If she was lucky, she'd see someone who would loan her the money. She hated having to ask, but five dollars shouldn't be a problem since they were out there selling caps on the very corner of her block. She was wearing a pair of jean shorts with a Chanel T-shirt tucked inside and a fresh pair of Reeboks.

As she walked on the sidewalk, the kids were playing in the street. People were sitting outside anywhere they could find shade and a cool breeze. The summer heat was unbearable. Gena's Mercedes-Benz sat in the sun sparkling as if it were on a showroom floor. Gena crossed the street and walked up to the store like she was going in.

"How y'all doing?" she asked.

"Yo, Gena. What's going on, baby?" asked Rob.

"Nothing, just chillin," she said.

"Yo, Gena, think you could drop me off at my moms on Twenty-ninth and Lehigh?" he asked.

"Yeah, I could do that, but you gonna have to get some gas," she said.

"That's no problem. When you gonna take me?" he said.

"I'll take you now."

"Bet. Come on, let's go."

"No, Rob. You got to go get the gas and bring it back here before we can go."

"Girl, is you crazy? The nearest gas station is on Broad Street," said Rob looking at his boy, Shomby.

"I'll go get the gas," she said.

"Yeah, you gonna have to, 'cause it's hotter than a mother-fucker out here. Shit, I might fall out or anything," he said.

"How you rolling in a Mercedes-Benz with no gas, Gena?" Shomby asked.

"Look, times are hard, okay?"

"Here, Gena," Rob said, as he handed her a five dollar bill.

"I'll be right back."

"Mmm, hmm," he said nodding as she walked off pocketing his five dollars. "Shit, times must be hard. It wouldn't be no way. She walking to the gas station," he said shaking his head unable to believe it.

Gena walked six blocks to the nearest gas station and got a gallon of gas, which she carried in a milk container. She was tired from the walk. The hot sun blazed as she walked down the city street. She turned the corner as a black Mercedes-Benz turned the corner and pulled up along beside her. It slowed down, and Gena knew it was about to stop for her.

"Yo, Gena, you okay? You need a ride or anything?" asked the guy behind the wheel. With the sun blaring in her eyes she didn't know who it was until she bent down and saw Jamal smiling at her.

"Hi, Jamal," she said, with a smile back at him. It was good seeing him, especially since she was in true blue need of a ride. It had been a long time. So much had happened. She had changed, and one would hope that he had too. Of course he questioned the gasoline in the milk container before dropping her off in front of her car.

"I'll see you around," he said.

"Thanks, Jamal. I appreciate it."

She situated the gas problem, dropped Rob off and went straight to Rik's house. He had just moved into a nice house off the Main Line. Rik was all that. He was still hustling, of course. But he was so kind to Gena and she was truly grateful.

"Where's my kiss?" he said to her as she walked through the door. Gena and Rik sat for awhile talking about how time had changed things for the both of them. Gena, not really wanting to let him know how right he was about moving back home, sort of came out of nowhere and told him she was ready to move. Rik, just looked at her. He didn't want to say "I told you so," so he didn't question her at all. Just said they could contact a few real-tors and start looking around for her new place tomorrow. Gena was excited and content with hearing that. For the first time in a long time she thought of all her furnishings in storage.

"Can I come up here with you Rik?" she asked, knowing his house had to be a couple hundred thousand at least.

"Yeah, there's some houses around here for sale," he said, thinking of the advantages of having Gena close by.

After she left Rik, she went to an appliance shop and bought two air conditioners. A big one for downstairs, and a small one for her bedroom. Gena felt good. Rik gave up loot, like Quadir always did. There was something about walking around with a couple thousand in your pocket. Gena had forgot the feeling.

She dropped the air conditioners off at Gah Git's, and went to Le Chevue. Everyone was real happy to see her. Bev wasn't there; she and Charlie had just a baby girl, so some girl named Lisa did her hair. When she was through, she stopped by her post office box to check for mail, something she rarely did. She had gotten a post office box when Quadir's mother, Viola, put her out, with her "mine, mine, it's all mine" routine. Gena hadn't checked on the box much. There was never any mail to her, just a lot of junk mail and mail for Quadir. Unlocking the box, she found thirteen envelopes.

Getting back into the safety of the Mercedes-Benz, she opened up each letter and scanned over the mail. There were three letters from a realtor and a Notice to Vacate addressed to Quadir Richards, 234 Green Street.

"Damn, what's this?" Gena whispered to herself. She started the car and went back to the house. She called the number on the notice, but got an answering machine. It was a real estate office, but the office was closed. Gena hung up the phone. She sat on the edge of her bed and read the Notice over and over to herself. 234 Green Street. She wasn't even sure what part of the city that was.

Gah Git had the air conditioners pumping cool air into the hot and stuffy housing project unit. "Keep that door closed," she hollered to Khaleer who liked running in and out. "Child, here, drink some water," she said to him. "You gonna fall out. It's too hot out there. Sit your ass down and rest yourself some."

"I'm okay, Gah Git," he said walking toward the door.

"Boy, sit your ass down and rest a minute," she said, rocking Brandi.

Gena came running down the stairs, "Gah Git, I'll be back," she said as she flew out the door with Quadir's diamond Q key chain in her hand. Gena got in the car again and dashed through the projects, not stopping at any stop signs and turning corners like police were chasing after her. People outside just watched as her car drove by them.

Gena drove straight to Green Street and followed it down to Second. Nothing looked familiar. Gena grabbed the notice in her jean shorts and looked at it: 234 Green Street was an apartment building. Now, she remembered. She remembered all too well. One night Quadir went into the same building and left her outside. She looked at Qua's diamond Q key chain.

Parking the car, she went to the front door. After several tries, she finally found the key that fit and unlocked the front door. Gena took the elevator up to the third floor. Apartment 307 was down the hall. She stood there not knowing what to do. *Should I knock? What if it's some bitch, and she can't pay the rent since Quadir is gone?* The thoughts went through her as she desperately fumbled with the key chain. She found the key. She turned it to the left and then to the right, the lock snapped, and the door opened.

The apartment was too fly. It was living the way living used to be. Leather furniture, a pool table, and a bar in the dining room. Vertical blinds at all the windows and track lights throughout, an eighty-inch-screen in the living room, and a sixty-inch in the bedroom. On the table sat a picture of Quanda and Quadir when she was first born. She'd never seen that picture before.

Looking around the living room, she noticed the fine layer of dust covering everything. She could tell the place hadn't been occupied. The garbage in the kitchen had an unbearable odor that filled the air. She opened some windows, letting in fresh air. The bathroom light wouldn't go on since there was no Quadir to pay the electric bill. The bedroom walls and ceiling were covered with mirrors. Gena noticed a picture of Cherelle with Quanda sitting on his bureau, causing her heart to sink. There was another picture of Quadir on the dresser with some other girl Gena had never seen before. She found a photo album on a shelf, more girls. Pictures from Jones Beach in New York with every rapper and groupie on the East Coast and the Greek in Fairmount Park, the Greek in Virginia Beach, pictures at the Ruckers basketball games with the rappers, and the ballers from Kool Moe Dee to Alpo. There were pictures out in Vegas and Atlantic City at the Mike Tyson fights. Quadir was even on the West Coast in Cali with every one you could think of from Ice Tee to Ice Cube on down the line. The nigga was everywhere with everybody and had the pictures to prove it. She kept flipping the pages, scanning every pretty face and slim but voluptuous figure her man was leaning up against.

She put down the photo album and began opening up the dressers. All the drawers were filled, and neatly arranged. The walk-in closet was lined in Dapper Dan leathers and a few fur coats. On the other wall were his tailor-made clothing at one end, and down at the bottom were about fifty boxes of shoes he had never bothered to place on his shoe racks. Qua had as many clothes here as he had at the house. The different outfits, the different clothing. The constant switch, never in the same car twice. All the things she saw once but never saw again popped in and out of her mind. She went around the rest of the apartment, looking in the closets, taking her time, remembering the clothes she had seen him wear. They were staring at her. She felt good, she felt bad, she felt miserable. She went back over to the closet and fumbled through his clothes, taking items and holding them up to her as if he were in them. Quadir's scent again. How wonderful life was just to have the scent of him again.

The apartment was filled with a mysterious aura. It was as if Qua was there, as if someone was watching everything she did. Gena thought she heard something. Her poor heart started pounding, she went out to the living room, but no one was there. She looked in the kitchen and then secured the chain on the door. Gena walked past another closet door, it wouldn't open. She tried every key until she found the key that fit the lock. Suddenly she felt a hand grasp her shoulder and let her free. Her heart pounded. Startled, she dropped the keys. She turned around as a cold chill went through her body. She looked behind her to see the apartment, as it was when she had first entered. She reached down and grabbed the diamond Q key chain. Finding the key, she opened the door and staring in her face was a gray safe. A safe that sat on the floor and stood above her. It looked like something from out of a bank. Gena couldn't believe it. She could not believe what she had found. The safe. Qua's safe. Quadir's money. She dropped to the floor in disbelief.

DeStephano put forth all his evidence. There were cross-examinations, redirect examinations, over and over again. Finally, DeStephano called Sharice Harding to the stand. The prosecutor jumped up.

"I object. That name is not on the list." Counsel approached the bench. DeStephano explained the relevance of the witness' testimony and that suppressing her testimony would not be fair just because there were no prior statements made by her concerning the criminal matter. She had recently come forth with crucial information concerning the case. Finally, it was settled. Ms. Harding would be allowed to testify. Court would be adjourned for a brief recess.

Gena paced and continued pacing. Searching the apartment for anything and everything she could find. Startled by the knocking at the door, she looked out the peephole at a short, light-brown skinned man, wearing a pair of glasses that seemed to enlarge themselves through the tiny glasspeep hole in the door.

"Who is it?"

"Locksmith. You called?"

Well, it's about time, Gena thought to the door.

"You called about a safe?"

"Yeah. Hi. Thanks for coming."

"No problem."

Gena led him into the apartment.

"Is this your apartment?"

"Yes, it is. Why?" she asked leading him to the locked closet door where the safe was.

"I was just wondering. It's very nice," he said noticing that it didn't look lived in.

"You sure you can open my safe?" she asked.

"I need to see the safe."

Oh, great, thought Gena. *Just what I need.* "What do you mean, you got to see it?" she asked, unlocking the door.

"Damn, that's a big one. That cost a lot of money right there."

What cost a lot of money that wasn't worth having? thought Gena.

"You can get it open, right?" she said.

"Yeah, I can get it open."

"How?"

"Well, there's several ways to get into a safe. You can blow it open or you can use a torch," he said.

"Oh, is that what you're going to do?"

"I can. It's a lot quicker, the only thing is when you use those methods you risk damage to what's inside. You know, you can set what's inside on fire."

"Oh, no. We won't be going that route. That's not the way."
Gena could see herself now, trying to salvage burning money.
"How you gonna get it open?"

The courtroom was packed, as people swarmed among themselves finally taking their seats. All were present, waiting on Judge
Pearlstein. Finally everyone rose, then after Pearlstein's journey
to his bench, they sat. Counsel for the defendant called his witness. Sharice Wilson-Harding made an appearance of a lifetime.
The bitch wasn't bullshitting. She strutted down the aisle in a
pale blue linen suit, clutching a pale blue Chanel bag by her side.
Her hair was done and her makeup looked like something from
a beauty counter.

"Ms. Harding, do you swear to tell the truth, the whole truth,
and nothing but the truth?"

With her hand on the Bible, she answered, "I do."

"You may be seated."

And so the drama began, from, "State your full name," to,
"On the night in question . . . ?" Forty sat there and listened very
carefully to the examination conducted by the defense attorney.
Sharice Wilson-Harding was a nurse. She lived in Texas with her
husband and their four children. She had the story of life, and
sis was definitely not to be fucked with. Forty sat there intensely
staring at her. He didn't like where DeStephano was leading.

"Mrs. Harding, on December 28, 1990, where were you?"

"I was in Dallas, Texas."

"Where were you, say, between the hours of ten PM and twelve
AM on the night in question? Were you alone, Mrs. Harding?"

"No, I wasn't."

"Were you with your husband?"

"Objection, your Honor. This line of questioning is irrelevant. The crime took place in Philadelphia."

"I will allow the questioning, but please get on with it," said the judge, thinking about where to have dinner.

"I'll ask you again, Mrs. Harding, were you with your husband?"

"No, I wasn't with Charles."

"Were you alone?"

"No, I wasn't alone," she said glancing at the jurors, never once looking at Forty.

"Who were you with?"

"I was with Jerrell Jackson." The room buzzed, spectators and jurors alike. The jurors were totally confused.

Forty was not hearing this. He was not hearing this shit. The bitch was lying her ass off. He never seen no one look that convincing. "She's lying! She's lying, your Honor!" He started screaming, wanting to run over to her and wring her lying bitch-ass neck, but he could no longer use his legs. "She's lying. There's no way he was in Texas your Honor."

"Order, order!" said the judge as he banged his gavel. Once quiet reigned, he told them to proceed.

DeStephano continued. "Your Honor, I would like to present into evidence receipts for tickets purchased on Mrs. Harding's credit card, showing that she, indeed, was not alone."

"Your Honor, I object. That doesn't prove anything," argued Perachetti. And little did he know it, but that was exactly what DeStephano wanted him to do. Make a big deal over the tickets. After the battle over the tickets was settled and DeStephano had his way and the tickets were turned into an exhibit, he went back to his performance. He questioned Sharice Harding-Wilson continually, and she made a good show of breaking down, totally distraught. She was confessing to adultery and could lose her family, but at the same time she just couldn't sit back and let an innocent man go to jail. Forty couldn't believe she was sitting there.

That's when the tears came, "My whole life is ruined," she said as she took the handkerchief from DeStephano's hand. Who could deny such bullshit in the name of justice?

Christ, thought Forty, *why is this shit happening?* He could not believe it. He was paralyzed from the waist down, and counsel for the defendant had a sobbing woman on the stand explaining that she was married and she didn't want to ruin her marriage or her happy life, but she couldn't let this man go to jail knowing that he didn't commit this horrible crime. The jury seemed to like the soap opera before them and sympathized with this good woman who'd got herself mixed up with that Jerrell Jackson, who didn't really look like a criminal. Meanwhile, Jerrell was sitting there as if he was being stopped from saving the world because of this silly trial for kidnapping and attempted murder.

"No more questions, your Honor." DeStephano took his seat.

"Your witness," the judge said to the prosecutor. Perachetti knew she was lying. He went through a series of questions. The woman was a fine citizen, never had been arrested, no priors, or even a parking violation. No drug use, prescription or otherwise. She was a registered nurse and made it perfectly clear that she was cognizant of the night in question.

The drama was blinding even Forty. *Maybe Jerrell wasn't there,* he thought and thought. No, he knew it was Jerrell. He didn't regain consciousness for thirty-eight hours after he lost it, but when he came back it was Jerrell, Sam, Ran, and Sirnone, and where was Simone? He had no idea, but he knew who did. He remembered pulling off Sam's mask, he remembered that, then they pulled off theirs, then Jerrell shot him. Yes, it was definitely Jerrell who was the trigger man.

When Mrs. Harding was excused, defense counsel brought Forty back up on the stand, plunging into Forty with determination and consistency. However, Forty repeated his statements, never wavering, telling the jury again that they did, in fact, kidnap him, drug him, hold him for ransom, and then Jerrell Jackson shot him. By the time DeStephano was finished, the story read that "Christopher Cole, aka Forty, known in the street, was a drug dealer who, in fact, was kidnapped, was, in fact, shot, and yes he would be a paraplegic for the rest of his life. However, Jerrell Jackson was not guilty of these crimes."

DeStephano made his closing statements, stressing the fact that, while Christopher Cole had been starved, kidnapped, and drugged with thorazine, he probably didn't know who his captors were, he might have been hallucinating. "He doesn't know who shot him. He doesn't even know who kidnapped him, nor does he know where he collapsed. After saying he collapsed in the basement, he was, in fact, found out on the porch. This man doesn't know, and when you get up from your chairs, walk into that room, and deliberate, I ask that you merely ask yourselves, ladies and gentlemen, in light of the evidence and testimony at hand, did Mr. Perachetti prove, beyond a reasonable doubt, that this man did, indeed commit that crime? All you need is one doubt, because if you have any doubts at all, you will be sending an innocent man to jail."

Wiping his head as if he'd just saved the unfortunate in Bosnia, Iran, and Somalia, he told the judge, "That's all, your Honor."

Forty wanted to kill that bitch for lying. He wanted to take her long ass legs and wrap them around her throat and just choke the bitch. He saw the way the shit was going down. Again, the system would fail, and again the shit would fuck up what little faith a brother could have. *This is such bullshit. How could this be happening?*

After closing arguments, counsel submitted their points for charge to the court, the judge deciding what statements of law would be read to the jury and what would not. The jurors then retired to the jury deliberation room, to think real hard about the matter at hand. Forty-five minutes later, they returned. A foreman was ready to recite the verdict.

Gena couldn't believe it. She was so close, yet so far. "Is there something else we can do?" she asked, as if all hope were lost.

"Well, there's the old figure out the combination trick," he said pulling out a stethoscope.

"What's that for?" she asked.

"This is so I can hear."

"Hear what?"

The guy wasn't one for giving any lessons, but he tried to break it down to her the best he could. "Okay. See, near the combination is a chamber. Now, when you're turning this knob, you can actually hear . . . well it's like a pin drop."

"What?"

"There are seven channels set on this combination. The channels are the numbers; you don't know the numbers. So you got to listen for the numbers."

"Oh. I understand. So, you think you can do it?"

"I've done it before."

It had been an hour and a half and he was still trying to open the safe.

"Oh, my God. Maybe I should try," she said, getting frustrated.

"What's in here?"

"Why? Why do you want to know that?"

"Because I can tell whatever is in here, you want it bad."

Boy Wonder, you're a real genius to figure that one out, aren't you? Gena thought, looking at her Rolex. Gena could not believe it. He wasn't getting the job done. She didn't understand. She was ready to take her chances with the torch. This was not the way. Gena looked at him with such dismay and frustration that she wasn't quite sure what to say. Her main concern was whether or not she had to pay him for all the waste of time. Time was money, and wasted time was wasted money.

Court was in session.

"Ladies and gentlemen of the jury, have you reached a verdict?"

"We have, your Honor."

Forty sat there. He knew that the crimes charged against the defendant had been committed by the defendant, and he was guilty and whatever punishment he received would be deemed just and fair. As the foreman rose, Forty looked at him. He glanced at Forty and made eye contact for one brief moment then he did the same to Jerrell, then began to read.

"On the charge of kidnapping, not guilty. On the charge of attempted murder, not guilty."

Forty was stunned. On the charge of this and on the charge of that, not guilty. Jerrell was free as a bird. Jerrell hugged Billy DeStephano, "You the man, you know that, right?"

"Of course I am," answered DeStephano. "No gun, no witnesses, you'll always go free," he said in a low voice. The man was all that. One hundred and seventy-five thousand plus another fifty thousand, such a small price to pay for freedom. Jerrell had been down for six months with no bail. He couldn't wait to get back out on the streets and start terrorizing everybody's ass again.

For reasons understood, Forty was paralyzed, blessed to be alive. He couldn't move. His mind scrambled and "not guilty" was ringing in his ears. Jerrell strolled up to him making his exit from the courtroom.

Bending down, he whispered in Forty's ear, "See you in traffic, baby."

Once everything died down, including the reporters looking for a Pulitzer and the not guilty hype, Forty was left in the courtroom, sitting all alone. He might have been able to accept not being able to ever walk again in life if Jerrell had been punished. There was a lump in his throat too big to swallow, a tear in his eye that he couldn't hold back. Just thinking about what the rest of his life would be like as the tear rolled down his cheek, he looked up at the seal carved into the American woodwork behind the American judge's chair in the American courtroom, representing American jurisprudence. *The American eagle,* he thought. *The same eagle seal that's on all the money. The same money that got me here,* he thought as he looked down, holding some in his hand. He wiped the moisture from his face and rolled out into the hallway where the officers were waiting to take him back to North Dakota. He saw the DA approaching him. He wasn't trying to hear no more shit.

"You know, there will be another courtroom and he won't be so lucky the next time. We're gonna get him. Don't worry, we're gonna get him."

Forty just kept rolling. They would never get Jerrell. They

would never stop the Junior Mafia. The boy was too large. He was untouchable.

"It's not going to open," said Gena feeling all hope was lost. Then she heard the click. It was definitely a click, she heard it, and when his hand reached up and grabbed the handle on the safe door, Gena knew that all was not lost.

"Oh my God, where did all that money come from?" His eyes were totally focused on the inside of the safe. Gena was about to faint. *Booyah* kept flashing in front of her like a neon light. For one brief moment, Gena thought of this strange looking locksmith killing her and taking her fortune. Of course, she didn't know that the locksmith was also getting paranoid, wondering if she might kill him. It was just too much money for him not to be suspicious.

"Okay, what's your name?"

"Chris," he answered nervously.

"Chris, here, I think this should cover you for your troubles." Gena reached in the safe. Taking a large stack of fifties, she handed them to him. The guy just stood there, looking like a plucked bird unable to accept her generosity.

The guy was just staring. He couldn't believe it. Gena rushed him to the door. "Thank you for everything, Chris," she said as she closed the door behind him.

She went into Qua's bedroom and she got some pillowcases out of his closet door. She started stuffing the money in the pillowcases and sat them neatly by the door. When all the money was out of the safe, Gena had thirteen pillowcases neatly lined up by the door. It was unbelievable. She couldn't think straight. She was nervous and wanted to leave. She understood how Quadir felt having this money. Shit, how could he sleep? She looked around the apartment. And she thought of Quadir. She had loved him with all her heart, had been faithful day and night, sacrificed with patience, and even though he had cheated, it didn't matter, understanding why as if he were right there with her explaining everything. "Qua, I know you're here, 'cause your money is here. Come with me. Please come with me." Gena felt him, she felt him all around her. She knew he heard her. She knew, 'cause there was no way anyone could rest with all that money left untouched. Oh, no. Qua was there, he was definitely in the apartment. But now, he could rest. She would be okay with that paper. He had hustled for seven years. Seven years of hustling and grinding out there in the streets. Seven years of dodging jealous enemies. Seven years of dope fiends and pipers. Seven years of the streets. There was no one he wanted to take care of more than Gena. There was no one but Gena who was entitled to what was in that safe. And she finally found it. He had waited on her a long time, but she got it. She got it all.

Gena took the poster size picture of them in a platinum and gold frame off the wall. She looked at it for a moment, thinking about the times they had shared. "I don't know how I've made it this long without you, baby." She looked around for a moment as she walked to the empty safe and locked it back up. She quickly loaded the car with pillowcases, and with her pocket book strapped around her shoulder and last pillowcase of money in her hand, she blew a kiss into the air, hoping that in the breeze Quadir could feel her love. She turned and opened the door, but felt something pulling at her shoulder. She turned around, but nothing was there. "I love you, Quadir. I always did, and I always will." Gena closed and locked the door to apartment 307.

She didn't know what to do, where to go or who to call. For the first time, Gena trusted no one and on the strength of

Quadir, she never would with his paper. Not even Rik. If Qua didn't, why should she? She got in her baby-blue Mercedes-Benz and sat there trying to collect her thoughts. She wanted to go somewhere, but where? She definitely wasn't going to the projects with thirteen pillowcases filled with money. *Not,* she thought to herself.

She picked up the cellular phone and called Gah Git. "I'll be staying with Tracey," she said.

"Okay, baby. Thanks for calling me, I was starting to worry about you. You be careful, you hear me?"

"Yeah, tell Khaleer he can sleep on the top bunk."

"Knowing that fool he'll be in a closet somewhere or in the tub."

Gena could hear Brandi crying in the background. "I got to go, there goes the baby. Call me tomorrow," said Gah Git.

"I love you, Gah Git," she said, disconnecting the cellular line. Gena didn't want to tell Gah Git about the money. Gah Git didn't keep no secrets. She would be on the phone calling the ghetto gazette telling Gena's business.

"What to do?" she asked out loud, wanting guidance. Sitting in the car, Gena thanked God for his blessings. He had truly been merciful. But a reality struck her that life was about change. The funny thing about it was no matter how much you change, memories always stay the same.

Qua was gone, and the money couldn't take his place. It would never take his place. Nothing would ever take his place, and there would never be another love like Quadir's. When she sat back and thought about it all, his life and the time that they spent together, and how his life brought her more riches than the contents of those pillowcases. It was incomparable with the money she found in that closet. If she could give the money back in exchange for his life, in exchange to have him back, she would in the wink of an eye.

Gena took the diamond Q key chain and turned the car's ignition. She took a long look at the apartment building before pulling off toward the Ben Franklin Bridge and the New Jersey Turnpike. Her destination, Exit 16, the Lincoln Tunnel, New York City.

JUST A LITTLE NOTE

In a world where evil lurks on every street corner and peace within oneself is a hard thing to come by, we must travel beyond mere existence and live our lives to the fullest, the best we can.

Things have been so hard for a race of misused and rejected people that our African American families today are still suffering. The streets can make you and the streets can break you. The way you play the game is up to you.

To those caught in the trap of temporary pleasures, let me tell you this: the root of all evil, which is the love of money and the next man's pain, will surely come back to haunt you. We have a choice. I believe everyone has a heart, and within our hearts is a conscience. And I know the inner peace we are lacking in ourselves can be found. I know all the burdens we carry can be lifted. I also know our perseverance, our will to survive.

Love yourselves and love one another. Give yourself time to grow and open your minds to education because it is a key to the way out. Whatever you do, make it worth something. All your consequences in life are dependent upon your behavior. If you know what the consequences are, why do you still exhibit detrimental behavior?

Because . . . you're true to the game.

When I wake up to travel what is unknown, yet certain for me and for my life, throughout the day and night, I give thanks for all the many, many blessings embraced upon me.

Forever protect me, forever guide me, and forever love me. You are the most merciful, the most beneficent, the most gracious. I love you.

READING GROUP GUIDE

A Letter to Readers

Discussion Questions

Excerpt from True to the Game II

Dear Readers:

I think back to the beginning all the time. Before the business of publishing became my business, before it became my life. I knew back in the early nineties that I'd have to do something to get my life together. I never dreamed it would be this. I never thought I would ever write a book, let alone sell one. I was told countless times that there was no market for a book like *True to the Game*. No market? Well, I guess we made that market, didn't we?

People ask me all the time how I did it. How did I sell a million books by myself? I always tell people I've done nothing by myself. I try all the time to explain the power of my people and how they demanded this book and how they made corporate place it on those big shelves of Barnes and Noble and Borders. I love you so much for that because I could never have done that by myself. I tell people how, when I started selling *True to the Game* in Philadelphia, it was handmade with the white cover and the gold gun on the front. People bought that book from me for twenty dollars, even though it fell apart once they opened it because it was really handmade. To this day, they're holding that book in a plastic bag thinking it will be worth money one day. I love you for that.

I tell people how I came to New York and stood under the Mart 125, selling my book hand to hand in the freezing cold. The lady from the YMCA on 135th who let me, a stranger, sleep on her sofa. Amil from the Roc, who let me stay at her house, wear her clothes, and drive her BMW so I could be fly and do New York. And even Lenise (aka Queen Pen), who introduced me to Brooklyn, who let me stay in her home with her children, whenever I needed. I love you guys so much for that.

I try to tell people there were times when I had nowhere to go and so I would simply sleep in my car, but you best believe even then, I had street angels and the brothers would watch over me so that nothing happened to me. I love you for that. I try to tell people all the time I never expected others would relate to what I had written, that I had no idea my ghetto fabulous lifestyle was understood in such a way that it would transform itself into this great big business of urban fiction. I had no idea that my brothers and sisters out here would follow me and independently publish their stories and make money and have a better way of life for themselves, but you did and I love you for that. This letter is not to say thank you, but it's to let you know that I humble myself to you and I am so grateful. I want you to know that I will never take you for granted and I will always love you for all that you have done for me.

Truly,
Teri Woods

DISCUSSION QUESTIONS

1. Why do you think Gena was attracted to Quadir?

2. Do you think Gah Git should have had a stronger influence in Gena's life?

3. Do you think Gena was affected by Sahira's death?

4. Do you think Gena's attitude toward life is indicative of a certain generation?

5. What do you think was Gena's biggest mistake?

The following is a sample
chapter from
TERI WOODS'S
eagerly anticipated sequel to

TRUE TO THE GAME.

TRUE TO THE GAME II: GENA'S STORY

will be available in November 2007
wherever books are sold.

CHAPTER ONE

The second time Gena saw the black BMW in her rearview mirror, she thought it was a mere coincidence. The third time she saw the Beemer, she thought that it was just another car traveling east, amid a plethora of other vehicles. And then she saw it a fourth time, and then a fifth. It was deliberately trying to keep its distance, trying not to be noticed, trying to blend in with the other vehicles on the highway. But she noticed it. And now she suspected that she was being followed. *Who the fuck is behind me?*

She stomped on her gas, only to see the BMW increase its speed. When she slowed down, it too slowed. And now, she was about to conduct the ultimate test. She was about to exit the turnpike and turn back around toward Philly. If the BMW exited the highway and turned around with her, then she would definitely have her answer.

Being followed was a frightening thing any day of the week, but being followed when you had millions of dollars in dope money in the trunk of your car was something else entirely.

Maybe someone seen me; maybe someone else knows. Niggas had killed for less. And niggas had went hard in the paint to get paid. But this, this would be an easy come-up for anybody. She had taken the treasure out of its safe hiding place, and now someone had painted a great big fucking X on her fucking forehead. It would all be so simple for someone to rob her right now. She wondered if they even had instructions on how to do it. *Peel back cap, dump bullets inside, take money, congratulations, now go live happily ever after, motherfucker.*

Gena switched on her turn signal, slid over into the exit lane, and left the highway. Her eyes were glued to the rearview mirror. The BMW took the exit. Fear bordering on panic overtook her.

It's not supposed to be like this! Gena thought. *Who the fuck is following me? They must know I got the money.* She hadn't asked for this. She didn't deserve to get fucked off, just because she claimed what was rightfully hers. Qua *was* her man. He was going to marry her after all, and she *was* entitled to the money that he left behind. *I should have never took that key chain.* She had put up with a lot of bullshit for this money; bitches calling, bastard children, and ho's sweatin' her man all the time. *Yes, I shoulda took them keys. Quadir wanted me to have them, so he must have wanted me to have this money.* She had lost her best friend, she had lost her fiancé, she had lost Lita. She had *earned* that fucking dough. And nobody had the right to take it from her. Not jackers, not the Feds, not the Philly PD, *nobody. Fuck this.*

Gena turned onto the access road, and accelerated as hard as she could. She would head back to Philly, where she could lose this motherfucker in the tiny, narrow side streets she knew like the back of her hand. At worst, whoever it was behind her wouldn't be so stupid as to risk following her back to Gah Git's house. Niggas weren't trying to run up in Richard Allen and cause no static, especially at Gah Git's house. Gah Git was too well loved by everybody in the hood for that shit to happen. Naw, she would run back to safety, and worry about stashing the dough later.

The black BMW accelerated hard, trying to keep Gena in sight. The driver didn't want to be detected but could tell he had been spotted by the way Gena was driving.

"Fuck!"

There was no doubt he had been spotted and there was no doubt that Gena was trying to lose him. The good thing was that the mouse was heading back to the mouse hole, and that was exactly where she needed to be. She would be easier to catch that way. And so would the money.

Gena raced down the highway, trying to get away from her pursuer. She could still see the halogen lights of the BMW in her rearview mirror. And with each passing mile, she became more of a wreck. She had her whole life ahead of her, and she didn't want to die; not like this.

A yellow light blinked on, and a soft chime rang out, causing Gena to look down at her dashboard. It was her fuel light. She had millions of dollars stuffed inside pillowcases in her trunk, and no gasoline in her tank. *Damn, I ain't never got no gas when I need it. What the fuck am I going to do now? Pull over, all alone, on the side of the road, with a gank of money in the trunk of my car, be robbed or, even worse, murdered. No, that bitch ain't me,* Gena thought, while shaking her head. She was going to find a gas station. Maybe the motherfucker wouldn't risk popping her in front of so many witnesses; especially if she found a big gas station. An Exxon, Mobil, Valero, Shell, or even Luk Oil. Fuck it—we'll take Wal-Mart out this bitch! Just somewhere where there's a bunch of people around. She spotted the red, white, and blue Exxon sign just down the road, and a smile slowly spread across her face. She was going to make it.

Gena exited the turnpike riding on nothing but fumes and raced into the gas station parking lot. The black BMW exited with her, and followed her into the gas station parking lot. Gena pulled up to a pump, while the Beemer pulled into a faraway corner and sat idling. The black sedan's dark tinted windows prevented her from seeing who, or even how many, were inside of the car. She climbed out of her Benz, hit her alarm so that her trunk would lock, and raced inside of the store.

"May I help you ma'am?" the store clerk asked rudely.

Gena rubbed her sweating palms on her pants. "I . . . I . . . I . . . think that I'm . . . I don't know." Gena stuttered so bad and her mind raced so fast, that she could not form a coherent sentence. "I . . . think . . . Help me."

"What's the matter, pretty girl?" a voice asked from behind.

Gena turned in the direction from which the voice had come. She swallowed hard and shook her head.

When Jerrell saw her, he recognized her instantly. Although he didn't know her name and he couldn't place her face, he knew that she looked familiar.

"What's the matter, ma?"

Gena shook her head. "I'm just . . . having a rough day, that's all."

Jerrell smiled at her. "Well, what can I do to make it better?"

Jerrell's smile was infectious. It made Gena crack a slight smile.

"There you go, pretty girl," Jerrell told her. "That's the way I want to see you looking. You feel better already, huh?"

Gena exhaled and peered out of the glass window. "I think I had somebody following me."

Jerrell frowned, as thousands of thoughts raced through his head. *Why would someone follow this broad? She ain't even wearing no jewelry. Let me find out this bitch got a stash.* He would certainly stick around and find out. If not for some dough, then at least she would be a good fuck.

Jerrell clasped Gena's hand. "Show me who they are, ma. I'll take care of them niggas."

Gena was startled. The nigga was fine as hell, mad cute. But even beneath his good looks, a motherfucka could tell that he wasn't to be fucked with. *Thank God. I've been saved. This nigga look like he can go round for round, and he talks like he might have a little gangsta up in him. Yeah, he can handle this shit,* Gena told herself. And suddenly, she began to relax.

"It's that black car right there," she told him feeling every bit of a snitch.

Jerrell walked out of the store and peered in the direction that Gena had pointed. The black BMW was pulling out of the store parking lot and turning back toward the direction of the turnpike. Jerrell counted to ten and then walked back into the store.

"Did you see it?" Gena asked nervously.

"I took care of them, ma," Jerrell told her. "You don't have to worry about them no more."

"Are you for real?" Gena asked.

Jerrell nodded.

"Thank you so much!" Gena told him. She wrapped her arms around him and gave him a hug. "I'm sorry, I don't even know your name. What's your name?"

"Jay," he told her. "My name's Jay."

Gena shook Jerrell's hand. "I can't repay you for this."

Jerrell nodded. "Yeah you can."

"How?" Gena asked, lifting an eyebrow.

"Let me pay for your gas, and let me walk you to your car and pump it for you." Jerrell told her. "And then, let me follow you back to where you are going, so that I can make sure you make it home safely."

Tears fell from Gena's eyes and she hugged him again. "I just met you, and you're so nice. I'm telling you I was really being followed."

"Hey, don't worry about nothing anymore, ma," Jerrell told her. "You're safe with me. I got you, okay?"

Gena nodded.

"Which car is yours?" Jerrell asked.

"The blue Mercedes," Gena told him.

Hot damn, that's what I'm talking about, Jerrell thought. *Let me find out this broad is rolling. No wonder she thinks she was being followed. Niggas was probably trying to jack the bitch for her ride. Probably a bunch of youngsters trying to make a quick come-up. Jack her car, take it to a chop shop, make a few thousand. See, that's what's wrong with youngsters today; no fucking vision. Why yank the bitch from the car and risk catching a carjacking case? All you got to do is just finesse these broads out here; stroke 'em, fuck 'em, and milk 'em until they credit card bills look like a New York Lottery number. Youngsters these days have no finesse, no G. But, I'ma show 'em how it's done, baby; old-school style.*

Jerrell tossed a twenty-dollar bill onto the counter. "Put it on the blue Benz," he told the cashier.

Jerrell clasped Gena's hand and led her out to her car, where he sat her inside of the vehicle and closed the door. Then he pumped her gas.

Inside of the Benz, Gena closed her eyes and leaned her head back on the headrest. She felt a feeling that she hadn't felt in a long time. She felt that she had someone looking out for her again. She felt like she had just met a really good man, one who wanted to take care of her and keep her safe. *Wouldn't that be something?* She missed that feeling. She missed being able to wrap her arms around a man and feel safe. She missed having the *man of life* in her life.

Jerrell finished pumping Gena's gas and then walked to the driver's side window, where she had it rolled down.

"Hey, I want to call you tonight," Jerrell told her. "I want to make sure you're okay."

Gena nodded, pulled a pen from her purse, and wrote her number on the corner of an envelope. She tore the number off the paper, and handed it to Jerrell.

"I'ma follow you home to make sure you're safe, okay?" Jerrell told her.

Gena smiled. "Thank you so much, Jay. You're the nicest guy who I've met in a long time."

"No problem, pretty girl," Jerrell told her. He caressed the side of her face and then turned and headed for his vehicle, where he climbed inside and waited for Gena to pull off. Jerrell pulled off just behind her, and trailed her as she headed onto the turnpike, back to Gah Git's house, and back to safety.

His fucked-up crew had blown through all of his bread while he was locked up, and he had spent the remainder of his dough fighting that bullshit case. And now—now he had been given a beautiful, lonely, scared bitch to fuck. *Ain't life grand? And it'll be even grander if this bitch got a couple of dollars so I can come up again.*

"Woooooooeeeee!" Jerrell let out an excited scream as his imagination ran wild. He dreamed of fucking Gena on top of a pile of money, and then suffocating the bitch in that same pile of

Benjamins afterward. It was obvious that she didn't know who he was, and it was obvious that she was feeling all of the nice, concerned, protective shit that he was throwing her way. Which meant she was lonely and didn't have a man to turn to. *Maybe her man's in jail or maybe the nigga's just steppin' out on her every night. Either that or the nigga is a weak motherfucker and don't know how to protect his bitch. Either way, I got to find the story out on Ms. Gena.*

Jerrell had made up his mind and he had decided that he would get to work on that as soon as time permitted. But first, he had major important things to attend to first; like catching up with all them niggas who fucked up his dough and had nothing but excuses about why he was broke. Yeah, he would take care of them, and he would get with his baby girl, too. One thing at a time, though. One thing at a time.

"Don't worry, boo," Jerrell said to Gena's taillights. "Daddy's here! Daddy's gonna spank that monkey real good, and give you all the man that you need!"

Jerrell settled in for a long drive back to North Philly, dreaming of what he was going to do to Gena and everybody who owed him. *I can't believe them niggas fucked up my money. They must've never thought I was coming back home.* Never once did he realize that the treasure he so deeply desired was only fifty feet away from him—in the trunk of Gena's car.